New Life
- Book 1 -

A Book by B. B. Hartwich

Chapter Index.	
Prologue.	Page 3.
Chapter 1.	Page 16.
Chapter 2.	Page 29.
Chapter 3.	Page 43.
Chapter 4.	Page 57.
Chapter 5.	Page 76.
Chapter 6.	Page 90.
Chapter 7.	Page 104.
Chapter 8.	Page 118.
Chapter 9.	Page 134.
Chapter 10.	Page 152.
Chapter 11.	Page 168.
Chapter 12.	Page 182.
Chapter 13.	Page 198.
Chapter 14.	Page 212.
Chapter 15.	Page 228.
Chapter 16.	Page 247.
Chapter 17.	Page 260.
Chapter 18.	Page 276.
Chapter 19.	Page 288.
Author's Note.	Page 298.

Prologue.

The winter storm was a relentless beast, clawing at the old house with talons of ice and a howling maw of wind. Each gust rattled the windowpanes in their frames, a percussive symphony of nature's fury that seemed to echo the turbulent tempest in Jack's own soul. He sat, a solitary figure in the cavernous silence of his inherited home, the world outside a maelstrom of white. The snow, thick and suffocating, had been falling for two days, burying the familiar landscape under a shroud of glacial indifference. It was a world rendered in shades of grey and white, a perfect mirror to the bleak canvas of his life.

He thought back to the summer, a lifetime ago it seemed, when the world was a riot of color, of life. The memory, a stark and painful contrast to his present reality, bloomed in his mind with the vivid intensity of a dream. He and Julie, his then-girlfriend, were in the park, the air thick with the sweet scent of freshly cut grass and the distant, joyful shrieks of children playing. The sun, a benevolent god in a sapphire sky, had warmed his skin, a stark difference to the biting cold that now seemed to have taken permanent residence in his bones.

Julie, a vision in a sunshine-yellow bikini, had been teasing him, her laughter a melody that had once been the soundtrack to his world. She had rubbed up against him, her skin slick with a sheen of sweat and sunscreen, a tantalizing friction that had set his nerve endings alight. He could still feel the phantom sensation of her body against his, the soft curve of her hip, the firm press of her stomach. She had guided his hands, letting him explore the contours of her sun-kissed skin, a silent permission that had sent a jolt of raw desire through him. He remembered the feel of her, the surprising softness of her back, the gentle swell of her breasts beneath his palms. She had leaned in close, her breath hot on his ear, and whispered promises of a future that now lay in ruins. Then, she had taken her hand and guided it to the front of his shorts, her fingers wrapping around his erection, a bold and intoxicating gesture that had left him breathless with anticipation.

But the symphony of that perfect summer day had been abruptly silenced by the shrill ring of her phone. A call from her mother, she had said, her voice laced with a frustration that he now knew was feigned. She had to go, she'd explained, her mother was strict, a fact he had never questioned. He had been disappointed, a dull ache of unfulfilled desire, but he had let her go, a decision that would haunt him for years to come.

He had decided to take the long way home, a walk through the park to clear his head, to savor the lingering warmth of the day. And that's when he had seen her. The image was seared into his memory, a permanent scar on his psyche. She was on a bench, not far from where they had been, but she was not alone. Brian was with her, his rival, the one person in the world he truly despised. A jock from school, a mountain of muscle and arrogance who had always seemed to delight in Jack's misfortunes.

Brian's hands were up her shirt, a crude and possessive gesture that made Jack's stomach churn. He was groping her, his face a mask of smug satisfaction. And Julie, his Julie, was not resisting. Her tongue was deep in his mouth, her body pliant and eager in his arms. The sight was a physical blow, a punch to the gut that had knocked the air from his lungs. He should have said something, confronted them, but the thought of the inevitable, brutal beating at Brian's hands had been enough to paralyze him. He had just stood there, a silent and unseen witness to his own heartbreak, before turning and walking away, the vibrant colors of the summer day suddenly muted and dull.

The memory of the phone call that followed was just as vivid, a conversation that had been the final nail in the coffin of his innocence. He had dialed her mother's number, his hand shaking with a mixture of anger and hurt.

"Hi, Mrs. F.," he had said, his voice barely a whisper.

"Jack, what a surprise. I thought you were with Julie in the park," she had replied, her voice warm and friendly, a stark contrast to the storm brewing within him.

He had snorted, a bitter, humorless sound. "Oh, we were. But when I went for a soda, she told me you called and asked her to come home. Then, as I walked home, I saw her with Brian on a bench, getting very friendly." The words had tasted like ash in his mouth, a cheap shot, but he couldn't stop them from tumbling out. Julie was only seventeen, and he was just three weeks shy of turning eighteen. Brian, on the other hand, had been held back twice and was twenty.

"She did what?" Gloria Fredericksen's voice had changed, the warmth replaced by a glacial fury that had sent a chill down his spine.

"Yeah, she did what I said. I should have confronted them, but I didn't have the energy to get my ass beat up by Brian," he had said, the profanity a small and insignificant rebellion against the overwhelming sense of powerlessness he felt.

"Jack, normally I would ask you not to use that kind of language, but I think I'll let this one go," she had said, a hint of grim understanding in her voice. He had chuckled, a hollow, empty sound.

"What do you want me to do about her? Want her to call you?" she had asked.

He had actually laughed then, a genuine, albeit mirthless, laugh. "No thanks, Mrs. F. I think she made her choice."

"I understand, Jack. I hope you find someone better for you. And don't worry about Julie. I will handle that," she had said, her voice a promise of retribution. And with that, she had hung up.

That had been the last time he had kissed a girl, the last time he had allowed himself to feel anything other than the gnawing emptiness that had become his constant companion. His days had become a monotonous cycle of work and self-pity, a self-imposed exile from the world. His friends had tried to coax him out of his shell, to drag him to parties and bars, but he had rebuffed their efforts, retreating further into the solitude of his grief.

And then, a few weeks later just after he turned eighteen, the unthinkable had happened. A car accident, a drunk driver, and his parents were gone. The house, once filled with the warmth of family and the comforting sounds of everyday life, had become a mausoleum, a tomb of memories that were both a comfort and a curse. Now, it was just him, alone in the silence, the winter storm a fitting backdrop to the desolate landscape of his soul. He was a prisoner of his own past, a ghost in the house of his own making, the unrelenting grip of winter a constant reminder of the summer he had lost, and the life he had never had the chance to live.

The thought, a venomous whisper in the desolate quiet of his mind, had become a familiar companion. To just... end it. To extinguish the relentless, throbbing ache of existence that had been his constant state for six agonizing months. Three years. Three years he had given to Julie, a tapestry of shared dreams and whispered promises woven together with the threads of adolescent love. They had made a pact, a solemn vow to wait, to not cross that final threshold of intimacy until they were both eighteen. It had been his idea, a testament to a romantic ideal he now saw as laughably naive. For him, it had been a gesture of respect, a promise of a future built on more than just physical desire. For her, it seemed, it had been a mere inconvenience.

Six months. A half-year measured in sleepless nights and hollow days since he'd seen her in the park, her body entwined with Brian's. News traveled fast in their small town, a web of gossip and speculation that had been impossible to escape. He'd heard she was pregnant. The words had been a fresh wound, tearing open the barely-formed scar over his heart. And the father... Brian. Of course, it was Brian. The universe, in its infinite cruelty, seemed to delight in crafting the most exquisitely painful scenarios for him. A grim, bitter satisfaction had curled in his gut at the subsequent news: Brian was gone. Vanished. He had fled town, leaving Julie and the burgeoning life inside her behind without a backward glance, a coward unwilling to face the consequences of his fleeting conquest. A part of Jack felt a savage, vengeful glee, while another, a ghost of the boy who had once loved her, felt a pang of pity for the girl now facing it all alone.

The calls had started almost immediately after that day in the park. Her name would flash across his screen, a beacon of a past he was desperately trying to bury. He never answered. The voicemails had become a painful, one-sided conversation, a chronicle of her slow descent into desperation. At first, they were tearful pleas for forgiveness, tangled explanations that painted her as a victim of circumstance, of Brian's predatory charm. Then they had shifted, becoming desperate hopes for reconciliation, promises that it would be different, that *she* would be different. The last one had been the most difficult to ignore. Her voice, stripped of all its earlier fire, was thin and fragile, a threadbare plea. She'd asked if he still loved her, if he could find it in his heart to help her, to help raise the child. *Brian's* child. He had deleted the message, his finger jabbing at the screen with a ferocity that surprised him, his heart a cold, heavy stone in his chest.

Now, as he sat in the deepening gloom of the afternoon, the storm outside a perfect symphony for his internal chaos, the thought of ending it all felt less like a choice and more like an inevitability. The silence of the house was a physical weight, pressing in on him, suffocating him with memories of laughter and life that felt like they belonged to someone else entirely. It was in that profound, crushing silence that his phone rang, the sudden noise a violent intrusion.

He glanced at the screen, expecting to see a local number, perhaps one of his few remaining friends making another futile attempt to pull him from his self-imposed crypt. But the number was foreign, an unfamiliar string of digits with a California area code. 310. Los Angeles. A world away from his snow-entombed reality in Washington. A flicker of something... not hope, but a faint, unfamiliar curiosity...

pierced through the thick fog of his despair. For the first time in months, an action didn't feel predetermined, a step on a well-worn path to oblivion. With a hand that felt strangely disconnected from his body, he swiped to answer.

He brought the phone to his ear, the plastic cool against his skin. He cleared his throat, the sound raw and unused.

"Hello… this is Jack…" he said, his voice a hoarse murmur, the words feeling alien on his tongue, spoken into a future he hadn't, until that very second, thought he would have.

The voice that came through the line was smooth and measured, the kind of polished, professional tone that seemed utterly alien to Jack's world of silent despair. "Am I speaking with Mr. Jack Halland?"

"Yeah, that's me," Jack managed, his voice still raspy from disuse.

"Mr. Halland, my name is Arthur Westmiller. I'm a senior partner with the law firm of Westmiller and Sons in Los Angeles," the voice explained, each word carefully enunciated. "We've been attempting to locate you for the past three weeks. We are calling in regard to your uncle, Mr. William Halland."

Uncle Will. The name echoed in the vast, empty chambers of Jack's memory. It had been three years, maybe more, since he'd last seen him at a strained family barbecue. He remembered a man with a booming laugh and eyes that crinkled at the corners, eyes so much like his father's. Then came the fight, a seismic event that had cleaved the family in two. The shouting had been muffled behind his parents' closed bedroom door, but he had heard his own name mentioned, a sharp, accusatory dart in the volley of angry words. Afterward, his father, his face a grim, stony mask, had declared Uncle Will's name forbidden in their house. Jack never knew the cause of the schism, only that a door had been slammed shut, and he was on the other side of it.

A cold knot of dread tightened in Jack's stomach, a familiar sensation in a life now governed by loss. "What happened?" he asked, the question barely a whisper.

There was a pause on the other end, a professionally calibrated moment of sympathy. "I am very sorry to be the one to tell you this, Mr. Halland. Your uncle passed away four weeks ago." The words landed without impact at first, distant and unreal. "He had a very aggressive form of cancer. We're told his final wish was to see you, but he… he didn't make it in time."

The information swirled in Jack's mind, a confusing mix of sorrow for a man he barely knew and a bitter pang for a reconciliation that would never happen. "Mr. Westmiller… why are you calling me, then?"

"I am calling, Mr. Halland, because your uncle amended his last will and testament shortly before his passing. You are named as his sole heir," Mr. Westmiller stated, his tone matter-of-fact. "We require your presence in Los Angeles for the official reading of the will."

Jack let out a harsh, incredulous snort that was more a bark of pain than of humor. "Listen, Mr. Westmiller, I appreciate the call, but you're wasting your time. I can barely afford to keep the lights on here, let alone buy a plane ticket to L.A." The confession was humiliating, but it was the stark, undeniable truth of his existence.

"That will not be a concern," the lawyer replied smoothly, unphased. "My firm will cover all travel arrangements, Mr. Halland. First-class airfare, a car service from your home to the airport. We will also be glad to arrange for your accommodations at a hotel of your choosing for the duration of your stay."

Jack swallowed, his throat suddenly dry. Could he do it? Just leave this snow-draped prison behind? But what if it was for nothing? A few thousand dollars, maybe? The inheritance from a man who was practically a stranger. He knew his uncle had done well for himself in California, something in tech or real estate, but the details were hazy, lost in the fog of family estrangement. The risk of being stranded, of having this flicker of possibility extinguished, felt too great.

"Is this… is this a round-trip kind of deal?" Jack asked, the words feeling clumsy and foolish. "I mean, I don't want to be stuck in L.A. once the reading is done."

A low, gentle chuckle came through the phone, the first genuinely warm sound Jack had heard in what felt like an eternity. "Mr. Halland… after the reading of the will, should you so choose, you will be in a position to afford your own private airplane to take you home."

The world tilted on its axis. The howling wind outside, the oppressive weight of the snow, the suffocating silence of the house… it all receded into a dull, distant roar. Jack's grip on the phone slackened. "I'm sorry," he stammered, his mind struggling to process the implication. "Could you… could you repeat that?"

"Your uncle was a man of remarkable talent and foresight, Mr. Halland. He founded several successful companies and made a series of rather significant investments over the past two decades," Mr. Westmiller explained, his voice patient. "Everything he owned, every asset, every share, every property… is now yours."

Jack swallowed a thick lump of saliva, his heart hammering against his ribs like a trapped bird. He was speechless, adrift in a sudden, shocking sea of possibility. What could he even say to that?

"If you are amenable, we can have a limousine at your residence tomorrow morning to take you to the airport in Portland," the lawyer offered, pulling Jack back to reality.

Jack's gaze drifted to the window. Outside, the world was a uniform, blinding white. The snow wasn't just falling; it was a vertical blizzard, a solid wall of white that erased the street, the trees, his neighbor's house. The news had called for it to continue, relentlessly, for days. He let out a slow, shaky breath that was almost a laugh. The sheer, absurd irony of it was overwhelming. The key to his escape had been handed to him, but the lock was frozen solid.

"I'm sorry, Mr. Westmiller," Jack said, a strange sense of calm settling over him. "That's not going to be possible. We're kind of snowed in up here in Washington at the moment. The news said it's already at two feet and not stopping anytime soon. I'm afraid we'll have to postpone. A few days, maybe even a week."

"Very well, Mr. Halland," the lawyer replied with understanding. "You are the one we have been searching for; we can certainly wait a little longer. Please, you let us know the moment the weather clears, and we will arrange everything."

Jack thanked him, his hand trembling as he scribbled the lawyer's direct number onto a dusty envelope on the table. He ended the call and let his hand fall, the phone clattering softly against the wood. He stared out the window, at the impossible, impassable wall of snow, and for the first time in a very long time, he felt the stirrings of something he had thought long dead: a reason to see tomorrow.

The phone lay silent on the table, a stark black rectangle against the dusty wood, yet the conversation echoed in Jack's mind with the clarity of a bell. He leaned back, sinking deep into the worn cushions of the sofa, the springs groaning in protest. The house, which moments before had felt like a tomb he was sealing from the inside, now seemed different. The oppressive silence was still there, but it was punctuated by the phantom words of Arthur Westmiller, a ghost of a future he hadn't dared to imagine.

Just an hour ago, the thought of ending his own life had been a comforting, tangible thing… a final, quiet door he could choose to walk through. Now, a new, heavy thought settled upon him, displacing the old one with its sheer, unexpected weight: he was the last. The last Halland. As far as he knew, Uncle Will had never married, had no children of his own. The man was barely forty, a life cut short by the same indiscriminate cruelty that had stolen his parents. His grandparents, both sets, were long gone, faded photographs on the mantelpiece. The family line, a chain stretching back through generations he could only guess at, had now narrowed to a single, fragile link: him. The realization wasn't a comfort, not yet, but it was an anchor, pinning him to a world he had been ready to abandon. The desire to vanish hadn't disappeared, but it was now at war with a nascent, bewildering sense of duty.

His thoughts, like ghosts drawn to a familiar haunting ground, drifted back to Julie. The idea of leaving, of physically putting thousands of miles between his life and hers, was a powerful lure. Perhaps then the calls would finally cease. Perhaps then her name would stop being a phantom limb, an ache for something that was no longer there. It wasn't that he didn't love her. God, that was the cruelest part of it all. He did. He loved the memory of the girl who had laughed in the summer sun, the girl who had shared her secrets with him under starry skies, the girl he had planned a lifetime with. That love was precisely why the betrayal had been so catastrophic. It wasn't a clean break; she had taken a vital part of him, ripped it from his chest with her bare hands that day in the park, and he was still bleeding out. The thought of her, pregnant with Brian's child, was a fresh twist of the knife every time it surfaced. This newfound wealth, this sudden escape hatch, might be the only way to finally apply a tourniquet to the wound.

He closed his eyes, the image of the relentless snow outside replaced by the replaying conversation. He tried to wrap his head around the lawyer's words, to give them shape and meaning in the cramped confines of his reality. *"You will be in a position to afford your own private airplane."* The concept was so ludicrous, so far beyond his frame of reference, that it felt like a line from a movie. His current existence was measured in scraped-together dollars for the power bill, in stretching a can of soup over two meals. He couldn't even fathom the cost of a commercial flight, let alone owning the entire plane. The number was abstract, a string of zeroes that his mind refused to compute. It was like trying to imagine the size of the universe while trapped in a closet.

The sheer, jarring whiplash of the day... from the precipice of non-existence to the verge of unimaginable fortune... had left him utterly drained. The adrenaline that had surged through him during the call began to ebb away, leaving a profound exhaustion in its wake. The constant, gnawing anxiety that had been his fuel for months had finally sputtered out. The storm raged on outside, a relentless, howling beast, but for the first time, the storm inside Jack began to quiet. With the lawyer's impossible promises echoing in his mind, and the heavy, newfound weight of being the last Halland settling onto his shoulders, he drifted off to sleep right there on the sofa, a solitary figure in a silent house, a man whose world had irrevocably, and impossibly, changed.

Chapter 1.

The thaw was agonizingly slow, a reluctant retreat of winter in the face of a hesitant spring. For two weeks, Jack had been a prisoner in his own home, watching the mountain of snow that entombed his world shrink by excruciating inches each day. The news had become his lifeline, a constant stream of updates on road closures and plowing efforts. Finally, the day arrived. The main roads were declared clear, and a path to the outside world had been carved. True to his word, Mr. Westmiller had arranged everything.

The limousine's arrival was an event of seismic proportions on his quiet, forgotten street. It slid into view like a sleek black panther, silent and alien against the grimy, melting snowbanks. Its presence was a stark, almost vulgar, declaration of a change so profound it felt unreal. Curtains twitched in every window. He saw Mrs. Gable from next door, her face pressed against the glass, her mouth a perfect 'O' of astonishment. The Harrison kids, bundled in their winter coats, stood frozen on their porch, pointing with mittened hands. For a fleeting moment, Jack felt a hot flush of embarrassment, as if he were an impostor in a life that didn't belong to him. He slung a small, worn duffel bag over his shoulder… packed with a few pairs of jeans, some t-shirts, and the one good sweater he owned… and stepped out onto the porch, closing the door on the only home he had ever known.

As he walked the short, slushy path to the waiting car, a movement down the street caught his eye. His heart seized. It was Julie. She was a few blocks down, walking purposefully towards his house, her pregnant belly a prominent curve beneath her heavy coat. Her face was etched with a familiar, desperate determination. She saw the limo, saw him, and her step faltered. Her eyes widened, a maelstrom of confusion, hurt, and panic swirling within them. The universe, it seemed, wasn't done with its cruel sense of irony.

The driver, a stoic man in a black suit, held the door open. Jack practically threw himself inside, the scent of rich leather and polished wood a dizzying, foreign perfume. He leaned forward, his voice urgent. "Please," he said, his voice tight, "just go. Before she stops us."

The driver gave a single, understanding nod. With a silent, powerful hum, the limousine pulled away from the curb. As they glided past her, Jack saw her through the tinted glass, a figure shrinking in the rearview mirror of his old life. Her mouth opened, and though he couldn't hear it, he could perfectly form the shape of his name on her lips. She took a few running steps, one hand outstretched, a futile, desperate gesture against the inexorable pull of his new reality. And then she was gone.

A moment later, his phone buzzed in his pocket. He didn't need to look. He knew it was her. The buzzing was insistent, a final, desperate plea from a world he was rapidly leaving behind. He let it vibrate, the frantic pulse a counterpoint to the smooth, serene glide of the car. He silenced it without looking and stared out the window as the familiar, dreary landscape of his town slid by, already looking like a photograph from someone else's past.

The drive to Portland felt like a journey through a decompression chamber, a slow transition from one state of being to another. The sterile gray of the freeway, the rain-slicked pines, the distant silhouette of Mount Hood… it was all a prelude to the unknown. At Portland International Airport, the driver escorted him to the curb, handed him his duffel bag, and with a simple, "Good luck, Mr. Halland," disappeared back into the anonymous flow of traffic.

Following Mr. Westmiller's instructions, Jack found the United counter. He felt small and out of place amidst the confident, purposeful travelers. The woman behind the desk gave him a polite, professional smile. When he gave her his name, her fingers danced across the keyboard, and her expression shifted subtly, a flicker of deference in her eyes. She handed him a thick cardstock ticket. "Here you are, Mr. Halland. Your flight to Los Angeles is boarding in forty-five minutes. You're in seat 2A. Enjoy your flight."

First class. It was his first time on an airplane, his first time leaving Washington State, and he was walking past the long lines, through a dedicated lane, and into a cabin that looked like something out of a magazine. The seat was less a seat and more a personal pod, a cocoon of soft leather with more legroom than his entire childhood bedroom. A flight attendant with a warm, genuine smile offered to take his bag and then returned with a heavy glass filled with shimmering orange juice.

Now, cruising at 30,000 feet, the world he had known was just a patchwork of green and brown below a blanket of clouds. He had his feet up on the ottoman, the cold glass sweating in his hand. He was suspended between two lives… the one he had been so desperate to end, and one he couldn't begin to comprehend. The low hum of the engines was a soothing mantra, a sound of forward momentum, of escape. He was Jack Halland, a boy from a snowbound house in Washington, rocketing through the sky towards a city of angels and a fortune he couldn't imagine, leaving the ghosts of his past far, far below.

The descent into Los Angeles was a surreal spectacle. The endless, uniform blanket of clouds that had been his companion for hours suddenly gave way to a sprawling, sun-drenched tapestry of civilization. It was a concrete jungle stretching to the hazy horizon, a dizzying grid of highways, buildings, and shimmering swimming pools that seemed impossibly vast to a boy whose world had been defined by snowbanks and pine trees. As the plane touched down with a gentle bump and a roar of reversed engines, Jack felt a nervous tremor in his hands. This was it. The final destination.

He waited patiently as the other first-class passengers gathered their expensive carry-ons and exchanged pleasantries with the crew. He felt a familiar twinge of being an outsider, a stowaway in a world of casual wealth. He pulled his small duffel bag from the overhead bin, the worn strap a comforting, familiar weight on his shoulder. With no checked luggage, he bypassed the chaotic swirl of baggage claim, following the signs for Ground Transportation. The air that hit him as he stepped out of the sterile, air-conditioned terminal was a physical shock… thick, warm, and scented with a strange, intoxicating mix of exhaust fumes, sun-baked asphalt, and a faint, salty tang from an ocean he couldn't yet see.

He scanned the bustling arrivals curb, a chaotic ballet of shouting skycaps, honking cars, and anxious families. And then he saw it. A professionally dressed, burly man with a salt-and-pepper buzz cut and a stony expression, holding a crisp, black sign with white lettering: "Jack Halland." A wave of relief washed over him, a small island of certainty in this overwhelming new ocean. He navigated through the throng and approached the man.

"Hi," Jack said, his voice feeling small against the noise of the airport. "I'm Jack."

The driver's eyes, shaded by expensive-looking sunglasses, swept over him in a single, dismissive motion. He took in Jack's simple jeans, his slightly worn t-shirt, and the cheap duffel bag slung over his shoulder. A deep, contemptuous sigh escaped the man's lips.

"Piss off, kid," the driver grunted, his voice a low gravelly rumble. He didn't even bother to lower the sign. "Mr. Halland is an important client of my boss. I don't have time for games."

For a second, the old Jack… the one who would have withered under such a casual, brutal dismissal… flared up inside him. He felt a hot flush of shame, a familiar instinct to shrink away and apologize for his very existence. But then, something new and hard pushed back. It was the memory of the lawyer's voice, the image of his childhood street gawking at the limo, the feeling of ascending above the clouds. A smirk, sharp and unfamiliar, touched the corner of his lips.

"Alright," he said, the single word laced with a cool amusement he didn't know he possessed. He gave a slight shrug and turned away without another word, leaving the driver to his self-important vigil.

He walked down the curb to the nearest taxi stand, the line a chaotic jumble of tourists and business travelers. He pulled out his phone, his fingers shaky as he logged into his bank account. The balance glared back at him:

$237.54. Enough for a cab to Century City, but it would gut his entire net worth. It would leave him standing on the doorstep of a powerful law firm with empty pockets, a charity case. He sighed, the brief surge of confidence wavering. But what choice did he have? He got into the first available cab, a slightly battered Toyota Prius that smelled faintly of air freshener and old coffee.

He gave the driver the address for Westmiller and Sons, and the cab lurched into the chaotic stream of traffic on the 405 freeway. As they drove, surrounded by a river of cars under the impossibly blue California sky, Jack picked up his phone and dialed the number Mr. Westmiller had given him.

The lawyer answered on the second ring, his voice booming with a cheerful energy that was jarringly at odds with Jack's mood. "Mr. Halland! Welcome to Los Angeles! How is your limousine? A comfortable ride, I trust?"

Jack leaned his head back against the cracked vinyl seat and watched the palm trees whip past. "Actually, I have no idea," he said, his voice flat and even. "When I went up to the guy with the sign and introduced myself, he told me to fuck off."

There was a sudden, profound silence on the other end of the line, so complete that Jack thought the call might have dropped. Then, Mr. Westmiller's voice returned, stripped of all its earlier bonhomie, sharp and cold as shattered glass. "I'm sorry… he said *what*?"

"I believe his exact words were, 'Piss off, kid. Mr. Halland is an important client of my boss,'" Jack quoted, a certain grim satisfaction in repeating the insult. He could almost hear the gears turning in the older man's head... the embarrassment, the fury.

"When will you arrive at the office?" Mr. Westmiller asked, his voice now clipped and dangerously quiet.

Jack leaned forward to the driver. "Hey, what's our ETA?"

The driver glanced at his GPS. "With this traffic? Twenty minutes, sir."

"Twenty minutes," Jack repeated into the phone.

"I will have my personal assistant, Ms. Albright, meet you at the curb. She will take care of the cab fare," Mr. Westmiller said, the words coming out like rapid-fire commands. "I will handle the... other matter personally. I am so very sorry, Mr. Halland." Then, the line went dead.

Jack slid the phone back into his pocket. He had been ready to spend his last few hundred dollars, to arrive as the pauper he still felt he was. But now, he didn't have to. A slow, genuine smile spread across his face. He looked out at the sprawling, indifferent city, and for the first time, he didn't feel intimidated. He felt a flicker of power. Someone had made a mistake, and now someone else was scrambling to fix it. And he was the reason why.

The drive was a plunge into a different dimension. The freeway itself was a monstrous, living entity, a ten-lane river of steel and chrome flowing under a sun that seemed hotter and more intense than any he had ever known. Jack was glued to the window of the cab, his mind struggling to process the sheer scale of the world unfolding around him. In Washington, a five-story building was noteworthy. Here, buildings didn't just stand; they *loomed*. They were colossal monuments of glass and steel that clawed at the hazy, golden sky, their gleaming surfaces reflecting the relentless California light. They carved deep, man-made canyons that made the cab feel like a tiny insect scurrying at their base.

And the people… the people were a different species. They moved with a purpose and confidence that was entirely foreign to him. Women who looked like they'd just stepped off a magazine cover strode down the sidewalks on impossibly long legs, their faces hidden behind oversized sunglasses, radiating an effortless, intimidating beauty. Men in perfectly tailored suits, looking like they brokered million-dollar deals between sips of espresso, talked urgently into their phones, oblivious to the world around them. He saw an older man, his skin the texture of expensive leather and a gleaming gold watch on his wrist, with a girl who couldn't have been much older than Julie draped on his arm. The man looked triumphant; the girl looked beautiful and vacant. Jack let out a low chuckle, a breath of pure disbelief.

"Fucking L.A.," he whispered to himself, the words both a curse and a prayer.

As the cab turned onto a boulevard lined with towering palm trees, he saw them. Walking side-by-side, moving in a perfect, hypnotic synchrony that was both mesmerizing and unsettling, were two women. Twins. They were outrageously, ethereally gorgeous, with identical cascades of blonde hair and toned, sun-kissed bodies showcased in clothes that seemed more suggestion than substance. They laughed, and even from inside the cab, their shared joy seemed like a performance for the world to admire.

He shook his head, a cold wave of his old inadequacy washing over him. He was the boy from the snow-draped house, the kid with the worn-out duffel bag who had to check his bank balance before getting a ride. He would never, in a million years, have a chance with girls like that. They occupied a different universe, breathed a different air.

The thought, a familiar and unwelcome ghost, immediately dragged his mind back to Julie. A sharp, painful pang resonated in his chest. God, he still loved her. It was a stubborn, painful love that refused to die, a ghost haunting the ruins of what they once had. That love was what made the betrayal an open, gaping wound. The image of her pregnant belly, the ultimate, undeniable proof of what she had done with Brian, flashed in his mind. She had chosen. And now she was alone. A flicker of venomous satisfaction, which he quickly tried to suppress, went through him. Her current predicament, her desperation, wasn't his fault. It was the direct result of the loser she had chosen to sleep with, the coward who had vanished at the first sign of responsibility. It was a cold, hard fact he clung to, a shield against the pity and the lingering love that threatened to soften him. He had to believe it. It was the only way to survive.

The cab slowed to a graceful stop, its humble engine a mere whisper against the backdrop of the city's hum. It pulled into a dedicated circular driveway before a skyscraper that seemed to be made entirely of obsidian and sunlight. Before the driver could even put the car in park, a woman detached herself from the shade of the building's massive portico and moved towards them with an efficient, confident stride. She was immaculate, dressed in a sharp, slate-grey business dress that seemed molded to her athletic frame. She handed the driver a credit card through the open window, the transaction smooth and silent.

"Mr. Halland? If you would follow me, please," she said, her voice crisp and professional as she collected the receipt. Her gaze met his through the car window, and for a moment, the professional mask slipped, revealing a flicker of genuine curiosity.

Jack pushed the door open and stepped out into the full, unfiltered glare of the California sun. The heat was a physical presence, a dry, heavy blanket that settled on his skin. He squinted, his eyes, accustomed to the muted, grey light of a Pacific Northwest winter, struggling to adjust. He could feel the sun baking the dark fabric of his t-shirt. This was so far removed from the cold he'd left behind it felt like another planet. He'd checked the weather before leaving; back home in Washington, it was a miserable, drizzly Friday morning in the low thirties. Here, it had to be pushing eighty degrees already, a temperature he hadn't felt in what seemed like a lifetime.

He smiled at the woman, who he presumed was Ms. Albright. She was probably in her mid-thirties, her dark hair pulled back in a severe but stylish knot, revealing intelligent, watchful eyes. He couldn't help himself; his gaze briefly traced the confident lines of her body. It was a purely instinctual, appreciative glance, but she caught it. A small, knowing smirk played on her lips for a fraction of a second before being tucked away again behind her professional demeanor.

She said nothing, simply turned and led him toward the towering glass doors that hissed open as they approached. The lobby was a cathedral of commerce. The floors were polished marble that reflected the cavernous space like a dark mirror, and the ceiling soared three stories high, where a complex, modern chandelier hung like a captured star. The air inside was cool and smelled faintly of money and cleaning solution.

"Mr. Halland, this is Karl," she said, gesturing to a man in a perfectly pressed black suit standing behind a marble security console. He was built like a retired linebacker, with a shaved head and an earpiece that was barely visible. "He is the head of security for the building. He will just need to scan your bag before we can proceed upstairs."

Jack nodded, his eyes still trying to take in the sheer opulence of the lobby. He handed his worn duffel bag to Karl, who placed it on a conveyor belt that fed it through a small x-ray machine. "You're all clear, Mr. Halland," Karl said a moment later, his voice a polite, neutral rumble as he handed the bag back. Jack smiled his thanks and followed Ms. Albright to a gleaming bank of elevators.

As the brushed steel doors slid silently shut, encasing them in the small, quiet space, she smiled at him again, a more genuine expression this time. "This building is called the Art Tower," she began, her tone conversational. "It houses our firm, Westmiller and Sons, as well as four other prestigious law firms and three major investment companies." She paused, letting the weight of the information settle. "It also happens to be one of the primary assets of a company called Art Industries, which was owned, in its entirety, by your late uncle, William Halland."

The words didn't compute at first. They were just sounds. "Wait," Jack stammered, his brain trying to connect the dots. "My uncle... he owned this building?"

She smiled and gave a single, sharp nod. "Well," she corrected softly, her eyes holding his. "Now *you* own it."

Jack shook his head, a disbelieving laugh escaping his lips. "Fucking unbelievable. This has to be a joke. Someone is pulling a very elaborate, very cruel joke on me here."

With a deft movement, Ms. Albright pressed a small, red button on the control panel. The elevator shuddered to a smooth, silent halt between floors. The soft lighting seemed to intensify in the sudden stillness. She turned to him, her professional facade completely gone, replaced by an urgent, almost desperate intensity.

"Mr. Halland… Jack," she whispered, her voice low and hurried. "There is a great deal at stake. I am not supposed to be telling you this, but you need to understand. There are people, very powerful people, who are circling what you now have. Your uncle owned half of this town. He had his hands in everything from tech to real-all estate to private equity. You are going to be offered an obscene amount of money, a single check to just sign it all over. *Do not take it.* If you do, you will lose more than eighty percent of what it is all truly worth."

She reached out and took his hand. Her grip was surprisingly strong, her palm warm. "Do not accept their first offer," she repeated, her dark eyes boring into his. "Promise me."

Then, as quickly as she had stopped it, she restarted the elevator and released his hand, stepping back and smoothing her dress. The professional mask was back in place, but the air between them crackled with the charge of her warning. Jack was reeling, his mind a chaotic whirlwind of confusion and adrenaline. What the hell was happening?

The elevator chimed softly and the doors slid open onto a floor that was a hive of quiet, expensive activity. The reception area was vast, with plush carpets, modern art on the walls, and a panoramic view of the city. But Jack barely noticed. The moment they stepped out, a hush fell over the entire office. Every paralegal who was walking, every assistant at their desk, every junior associate emerging from an office… they all stopped what they were doing. Dozens of pairs of eyes, curious, calculating, and hungry, all turned to fixate on him. It was a bizarre, unnerving sensation, to suddenly be the absolute, silent center of attention in a world he hadn't known existed just hours before.

Chapter 2.

Ms. Albright held open a heavy, dark wood door and gestured for him to enter first. The room beyond was a cavernous conference room, dominated by a single, colossal mahogany table that gleamed under a bank of recessed lights. The far wall was a seamless pane of glass offering a god-like, panoramic view of the city sprawling below. Seated around the table or standing in small, quiet groups were at least thirty men and women, all exuding an aura of immense power and wealth. They were dressed in bespoke suits and designer dresses, their quiet confidence a palpable force in the room. The moment he stepped inside, all conversation ceased, and every head turned towards him. For a horrifying second, Jack felt like a piece of dirt that had been tracked into a pristine operating theater… a complete and utter fraud.

Then, the memory of Ms. Albright's words in the elevator… *"your uncle owned half of this town"*… surged through him. He straightened his shoulders, pulling on a mask of composure he didn't feel. He wasn't a turd on a silver platter. Right now, in this room, he was the silver platter.

A large man with a mane of silver hair and a warm, yet calculating, smile detached himself from the group and strode towards him, his hand extended. "Mr. Halland. Arthur Westmiller. It is a distinct pleasure to finally meet you face to face."

"Mr. Westmiller," Jack replied, his voice steadier than he expected. He shook the offered hand; the man's grip was firm and dry, a handshake that had sealed countless deals.

"Allow me to introduce you to a few of my partners and some of your uncle's key business associates," Mr. Westmiller said, his voice a smooth baritone that commanded the room's attention. What followed was a dizzying procession of introductions. Names and titles washed over Jack in a blur: senior partners from other firms, stern-faced financial advisors, sleek investment bankers, and hardened-looking executives who ran divisions he didn't know existed. They all shook his hand, their eyes assessing him with a mixture of practiced politeness, undisguised curiosity, and, in some cases, a predatory glint that made Ms. Albright's warning echo in his mind.

One detail pricked at his attention. The firm was 'Westmiller and Sons,' yet in the flurry of names, there was only one other Westmiller present… a young woman introduced not as a partner, but simply as Miss Constance Westmiller. She was, to put it mildly, stunning. With fiery auburn hair cut in a sharp, modern bob and intelligent green eyes, she carried herself with an aristocratic poise that made her seem both youthful and ageless. When she was introduced, she didn't offer her hand, but simply gave him a slow, deliberate nod. Her gaze was intense and unwavering, and under its scrutiny, Jack felt a hot flush creep up his neck.

"So, shall we begin?" Mr. Westmiller's voice cut through the haze. He gestured to the head chair at the table… a large, throne-like leather seat to his right. Jack sat, the leather sighing under his weight. As the others found their places, he noticed Constance Westmiller taking a seat directly across from him, her unnerving, captivating eyes still locked on his.

"Now, my boy," Mr. Westmiller began, a hint of paternalism coloring his tone, "you are going to have a great deal of paperwork to sign today. And *then*, we can begin to talk about the strategy for your businesses."

For the next two hours, the world dissolved into a surreal marathon of signatures. Stacks of thick, creamy paper were placed before him, each document representing a piece of a life he couldn't comprehend. With several cups of strong, black coffee fueling him, Jack signed his name over and over, the looping cursive of 'Jack Halland' feeling more and more like the name of a fictional character. He signed deeds, titles, ownership transfers, and shareholder proxies until his hand began to cramp.

"How many more of these are there?" he finally asked, his voice raw as he gestured to a new, formidable stack. A low chuckle rippled around the table.

"Quite a few, I'm afraid," Mr. Westmiller said with a smile, pushing the stack closer.

Jack began to actually *read* the headings on the documents he was signing. "I see four investment companies... three exclusive car dealerships... a racing track... and a casino in this stack alone," he read aloud, his voice laced with disbelief.

Mr. Westmiller's smile widened. He nodded. "Just the tip of the iceberg, Jack. The tip of the iceberg."

As if on cue, another assistant entered and placed yet another mountain of paper on the table. "These are the personal properties," Constance Westmiller said from across the table, her voice the first he'd heard... a low, melodic contralto. She slid a single summary sheet across the polished surface towards him. "The list is extensive."

He stared at the typed words, his head swimming. A palazzo in Milan. A beachfront mansion in Sydney, Australia. A townhouse on the Upper East Side and three other apartments in New York. Four separate estates across California. Penthouses in London, Tokyo, and Dubai. Then came the vehicles: a fleet of luxury cars and rare motorcycles, two helicopters, a Gulfstream G650 private jet, and a trio of yachts, one of which was described as a "superyacht" currently moored in Monaco. The list went on and on, a dizzying, suffocating inventory of impossible wealth. The room started to spin, the faces around the table blurring into a single, expectant mask. This wasn't real. It couldn't possibly be.

By the time the final document was signed, the sun had shifted in the sky, casting long, dramatic shadows across the city below. The marathon of paperwork had stretched from late morning into the mid-afternoon, and Jack felt hollowed out, his mind a numb, buzzing void. His signature, once a familiar and simple act, now felt alien, a series of loops and lines repeated into meaninglessness. He had a phantom ache in his hand, and his body was stiff from sitting in one position for what felt like an eternity. He finally placed the heavy, ornate fountain pen down on the table with a quiet click and leaned back, the soft leather of the chair groaning in protest. The air in the room was thick with the scent of old paper, expensive coffee, and unspoken anticipation.

"And with that," Mr. Westmiller announced, his voice imbued with a sense of momentous finality, "all assets, titles, and holdings that belonged to the estate of William Halland are now legally transferred into your name, Jack. Your uncle's final, most desperate request has been fulfilled."

As he spoke, Mr. Westmiller reached into his leather briefcase and retrieved a single, heavy envelope. It was made of thick, cream-colored parchment, a stark, analogue object in a world of digital transactions. The flap was sealed with a disc of dark red wax, impressed with a complex, ornate 'H'. It was a relic from another time, imbued with a gravity that silenced the room. The lawyer slid it across the polished mahogany table until it rested in front of Jack.

On the front, in a bold, familiar script that Jack hadn't seen in years but recognized instantly, were his name and a set of instructions. The handwriting was his uncle's… strong, confident, with a slight rightward slant.

For Jack.

Please open this in private. This letter contains my own personal instructions for you, an explanation, and the wish I have for your future.

It was signed simply, *W. Halland.*

Jack stared at the envelope, his throat tightening. This was it. Not a legal document, not a deed or a title, but a direct message from the dead. A final word from the man who had just irrevocably shattered and remade his world. His heart gave a painful thud in his chest, a jolt of adrenaline and grief. This felt more real, more terrifyingly intimate, than the billions of dollars represented by the mountains of paper he had just signed.

Mr. Westmiller seemed to sense the shift in the room, the profound change in Jack's demeanor. "If you wish, we can all leave the room and give you the privacy to open it now," he offered, his voice softer, more pastoral.

Jack looked up from the letter, his gaze sweeping across the thirty expectant faces around the table. He saw their impatient, hungry curiosity. They wanted to know what was in it, what final piece of leverage or instruction the old man had left behind. In that moment, he felt a surge of defiance, a sudden need to reclaim some semblance of control.

"If it's all the same to you," Jack said, his voice surprisingly firm, "I think I need more privacy than that. And frankly, my head is spinning. Could we pick this up tomorrow?"

A subtle shockwave went through the room. A few of the investment bankers exchanged frustrated glances. One of the senior partners let out an almost inaudible sigh of impatience. They had cleared their schedules, flown in from other cities, all expecting to get down to the real business of strategy and liquidation today. Jack's quiet, polite dismissal was a power move he hadn't even intended, and it left them momentarily adrift. He didn't care. The thought of discussing business strategies after receiving this letter felt like a desecration.

Mr. Westmiller, however, merely inclined his head, a gesture of complete deference. The boy was learning. "Of course, Jack. Whatever you need." He turned his gaze toward the door. "Ms. Albright, would you please be so kind as to escort Mr. Halland to his suite at the Peninsula and see to it that he is checked in and has everything he requires?"

Ms. Albright, who had been standing silently by the wall, stepped forward. "Certainly, Mr. Westmiller. Please, Mr. Halland, if you would follow me."

Jack carefully picked up the letter, the heavy parchment cool and substantial in his trembling hand. He stood, his legs feeling unsteady beneath him. "Thank you all for your time," he said, the formal words feeling strange in his mouth. "I hope to see you all again tomorrow."

He shook Mr. Westmiller's hand once more, then turned and walked toward the door, following Ms. Albright. He didn't look back, but he could feel the weight of their collective gaze on him, a palpable force of frustrated ambition and calculating greed. The heavy door clicked shut behind them, leaving a room full of some of the most powerful people in the city to do the one thing they hated most: wait.

The moment the heavy conference room door clicked shut, the oppressive atmosphere lifted, and the elevator ride down felt like surfacing for air after being held underwater. The silence was a welcome respite, broken only by the soft, almost inaudible hum of the elevator's descent. Ms. Albright leaned against the polished wood paneling, turning to him with a look that was a complex mixture of appraisal and relief.

"You did a lot better in there than I expected," she whispered, her voice a conspiratorial murmur that made the small space feel even more intimate. "You held your own."

He looked at her, his mind still a chaotic jumble of figures and signatures. "They didn't talk about money," he said, the statement a question. "Not really."

A knowing, cynical smile touched her lips. "No, the direct talk of money comes later. That was the 'welcome to the family' portion," she explained. "But the hints were there. Did you see the looks on the faces of the investors from the venture capital firms? The partners from Sterling

Global? They were practically salivating. Each one of them sees you as a winning lottery ticket they just have to figure out how to cash."

He nodded slowly. He had seen it. The hungry, predatory gleam in their eyes, the way they sized him up as if he were a prize steer at auction. He thought back on the room, realizing with a start that the only two people, besides Ms. Albright herself, who had seemed genuinely supportive, who had looked at him like a person rather than a price tag, were Arthur Westmiller and his daughter. The older man had been firm, a steadying presence. And Constance... he pictured her again, her piercing green eyes, the regal set of her shoulders. She was a world away from Julie's girl-next-door familiarity, a different kind of beautiful that was both intriguing and deeply intimidating.

"So, what happens now?" he asked, the question feeling impossibly naive.

Ms. Albright's smile softened. "Now, you go to your hotel suite. You sit in a quiet room. You read the letter your uncle wrote for you," she said, her tone matter-of-fact, as if guiding a new client through a standard procedure. "And then, after you've done that, you decide what kind of man you're going to be."

He let out a short, humorless smirk. "Just how much are we talking about here? I mean, I lost count, but by the looks of it... it has to be many millions of dollars."

Her smirk returned, sharp and full of secrets. "With a 'B'," she said simply.

Jack stared at her, confused. "'A B'?"

She nodded, enjoying his incomprehension for a beat before delivering the payload. "Not millions, Jack. Billions."

The word hung in the air between them. *Billions.* The floor of the elevator seemed to drop out from under him. He leaned heavily against the cool, smooth wall, closing his eyes as the world tilted violently on its axis. He was a billionaire. Yesterday… no, *this morning…* he had been a boy on the verge of suicide, worried sick about the next electricity bill for a dusty, empty house. The sheer, brutal whiplash of it was enough to make him physically nauseous.

He opened his eyes and looked at her, his mind latching onto the one solid piece of information he had: her warning. "You said not to take the offer," he said, his voice barely a whisper. "What offer are they going to make?"

She leaned in closer, the scent of her subtle, clean perfume filling his senses. "They'll let you stew for a day. They'll hope the letter from your uncle is purely sentimental. Then, Mr. Westmiller, on their behalf, will present you with an offer designed to sound like all the money in the world to a boy like you," she whispered, her voice barely audible. "One point nine billion dollars. Cash. Wired to any account you want by the end of the week."

His heart hammered against his ribs, a frantic, trapped bird. A billion dollars. Nearly *two* billion dollars. The number was nonsensical, a figure from a fantasy. It wasn't just a lot of money; it was a SHIT ton of money. It was enough to solve every problem he'd ever had and every problem he could ever imagine.

"And… and what is it all actually worth?" he whispered back, his throat dry.

She leaned in so close her lips brushed against his ear, sending a shiver down his spine. Her voice was a wisp of air, a secret that could shatter worlds.

"Three hundred and fifty-six billion."

Then, she pulled back and, just as the elevator chimed, signaling their arrival at the lobby, she leaned in again and pressed a soft, brief kiss to his cheek. The doors slid silently open.

She walked out as if nothing had happened, leaving Jack to follow in a complete and utter daze. He felt the ghost of her lips on his skin, the impossible number echoing in his skull. Three hundred and fifty-six billion dollars. That wasn't a fortune; it was the GDP of a small country. He'd had the same stupid fantasy as everyone else… winning a few hundred million in the lottery would set you up for life. But this… this was astronomical. This was a number so vast it broke the very concept of money. He stumbled out into the grand lobby, a ghost in his own life, a boy who had woken up from one nightmare only to find himself in the middle of an incomprehensible, terrifying, and exhilarating dream.

The walk from the Art Tower to The Peninsula hotel was a journey of less than two hundred yards, but it felt like crossing a continental divide. The air shifted from the sharp, corporate energy of Century City to the tranquil, old-world luxury of Beverly Hills. Valets in crisp white uniforms glided silently to and from gleaming luxury cars. The hotel's grand, Renaissance-style entrance stood as a monument to a kind of quiet, established wealth that was utterly foreign to Jack.

He followed Ms. Albright through the revolving doors into a lobby that was both opulent and serene. A colossal floral arrangement, a vibrant explosion of lilies and orchids, stood as the centerpiece under a crystal chandelier. The air was cool and smelled of wealth and fresh flowers. Without breaking stride, she approached the check-in desk, where a poised young woman greeted her by name. The entire process was a discreet murmur of conversation that Jack wasn't privy to. A moment later, the desk clerk turned to him, her smile warm and genuine.

"Welcome to The Peninsula, Mr. Halland," she said, sliding a sleek, black keycard across the polished marble counter.

Jack managed a smile and a quiet thank you, the card feeling weighty and significant in his hand. He followed Ms. Albright… Ashley, he reminded himself… to a private bank of elevators reserved for the hotel's suites. As the ornate brass doors slid shut, encasing them in a small, paneled room of polished cherry wood, the silence felt charged. He looked at her, the whirlwind of the past few hours finally coalescing into a single, direct question.

"Okay, what the hell is going on?" he asked, his voice low.

She met his gaze, her expression perfectly placid. "What do you mean, Jack?"

A smirk pulled at his lips. He was done being passive. "Care to tell me why you kissed my cheek in the elevator back there?"

She didn't feign surprise. A slow, deliberate smile spread across her face. "There are two reasons for that," she said, her voice dropping to that same conspiratorial whisper. "One: in this new world of yours, it does not hurt to be on demonstrably good terms with the man who suddenly holds all the cards. And two…" She paused, her eyes raking over him with a frank, unapologetic appraisal. "I am single. And the opportunity to become intimately acquainted with one of the most powerful, and richest, men in the world is an opportunity no intelligent woman would ignore."

He chuckled, the sound humorless and shaky. The raw, transactional honesty of it was breathtaking. "Intimately acquainted?"

"I'm not looking for a wedding ring," she said with a dismissive wave of her hand. "But a mutually beneficial arrangement… a partner in bed and an ally in the boardroom now and then… could be very appealing."

He shook his head, feeling profoundly out of his depth. "Ms. Albright…"

"Ashley," she corrected him firmly.

"Ashley," he conceded. "I'm still trying to figure out what my name on a piece of paper means. I don't think I'm ready to just start… a mutually beneficial arrangement. I have… aspects of my own personal life I need to figure out first." The ghost of Julie, of her betrayal, of the whole tangled, painful mess, hung in the air between them.

She smiled, a flicker of something that might have been pity, or perhaps just impatience, in her eyes. "I understand." But her body language said otherwise. She took a step closer, erasing the space between them. Before he could process her intent, before he could form a protest, her lips were on his.

This was nothing like the brief, professional peck on the cheek. This was an invasion, a claiming. Her kiss was deep and demanding, a passionate exploration that swept away his half-formed objections. One of her hands came up to cup the back of his neck, her fingers tangling in his hair, pulling him deeper into the kiss, leaving him no room for retreat. He was going to resist, to push her away, but his resolve dissolved in the overwhelming sensory assault. Her lips were soft yet firm, and she tasted of coffee and something uniquely, intoxicatingly her own. After months of feeling nothing but a dull, throbbing ache of grief and loss, this raw, undeniable physical sensation was a shock to his system, a jolt of lightning that made every nerve ending crackle to life. It was fucking amazing.

She pulled back just enough to whisper against his lips, her breath warm and ragged. "How about we talk more in the morning?"

The elevator chimed, the doors sliding open to reveal not a hallway, but a private, exquisitely furnished vestibule. They were on the top floor. She took his hand and led him out, her touch sending another jolt through him. She stopped at a pair of large double doors. He fumbled with the keycard, his hands unsteady, and managed to unlock the door.

He pushed it open, and as he turned to face her, she kissed him again… a final, lingering press of her lips that was both a promise and a seal on the conversation.

"Read your uncle's letter," she whispered, her eyes dark and serious.

Then she turned and walked back to the elevator without a backward glance. The doors closed, and she was gone, leaving him standing alone on the threshold of a suite that was larger than his entire house, the scent of her perfume on his clothes and the taste of her kiss still burning on his lips.

Chapter 3.

The suite was an ocean of beige and cream, a vast, silent expanse of plush carpeting, fine silk, and polished wood. Jack barely registered the opulence… the grand piano in the corner, the floor-to-ceiling windows showcasing a breathtaking panorama of the city, the fresh flowers on every surface. He navigated the cavernous living room on autopilot and collapsed onto a sofa so large and soft it felt like sinking into a cloud. The heavy parchment envelope in his hand felt like it weighed a thousand pounds, a single object anchoring him to a reality that was rapidly unraveling.

His fingers, still trembling slightly from the emotional marathon of the day, broke the wax seal. The crackle of the old wax was a sharp, definitive sound in the quiet room, like a bone snapping, a point of no return. He carefully unfolded the single sheet of thick, cream-colored paper inside and was met with his uncle's familiar, confident handwriting.

Tucked within the folds of the letter was a single DVD in a slim paper sleeve. He slid it out. There was a single line written on the sleeve, in his uncle's same bold script:

To unlock my final words, you must first remember the beginning of your own heart. The password is the name of your first true love.

Jack's breath caught in his throat, a sharp, painful lurch in his chest. *Julie.* The name was a ghost, a wound, a constant, aching presence. How could his uncle have known?

Then, the memory surfaced, sharp and vivid. A strained family barbecue three years ago. The smell of charcoal and cut grass. He remembered proudly introducing a giddy, seventeen-year-old Julie to his mysterious, wealthy uncle from California. He remembered Uncle Will looking at her, then back at him, a warm, knowing smile crinkling the corners of his eyes... eyes so much like his own father's. "*You take good care of this one, son,*" Will had said, clapping him on the shoulder. "*First love is a powerful thing. Don't ever forget it.*"

It was a test. A final, deeply personal key to unlock the last secrets.

With a heavy heart and hands that felt strangely disconnected from his body, he set the DVD aside and turned his attention back to the letter itself. He began to read.

"Dear Jack,"

"There is so much to tell you, and I have so little time left to do so. By now, you will have survived a storm of paperwork and are the legal owner of my rather large and complex empire. But before we get to that, we must start at the beginning. The real beginning. The reason your father and I were at odds, the cause of the fight that tore our family apart... it was you."

Jack's breath hitched. The words seemed to leap off the page, charged with a terrible energy.

"Your parents... may God rest their souls... were wonderful people. Your mother was, and always will be, your mother. But the man you knew as your father... well, Jack, he was your uncle. I am your biological father."

The world stopped. The hum of the city outside, the soft whisper of the air conditioning, his own heartbeat... it all ceased. He read the sentence again, and then a third time, his mind refusing to accept the configuration of the words. It was a prank. It had to be part of the elaborate, cruel joke.

"You see, your father... my brother... could not have children. It was a source of great pain for them both. He came to me for help, a last resort. I knew how deeply important it was for your mother to conceive a child, to have a family. So, I did what a brother does. Your mother visited me in California for two weeks under the guise of a holiday. In that time, you were conceived. It was my brother's one condition that you never be told as long as he was alive, and I am a man who keeps his promises. When I received my diagnosis, I went to him. I begged him to let us tell you everything together. I wanted you to know me, to be prepared to inherit what I had built. That was three years ago. He refused. Now, they are both gone, and as you read this, so am I. There is no one left to be mad at, and for that terrible, empty reality, I deeply apologize."

"But there is one more thing you must do. Know that there is only one person left in this world whom I trust completely. Her name is Madeline. She will be everything you need... a guide, an ally, a confidant. But she will not come to you; you must go to her. She lives in France, near the village of Saint-Paul-de-Vence. She is a few years older than you, but she is the only one I trust to help you navigate what comes next. She is the key."

"The rest of the information, the more practical matters, you will find on the enclosed DVD."

It was signed, simply, *W. Halland.*

Jack let the letter fall into his lap. His father. His *father*. The word echoed in the silent, screaming cavern of his mind. He felt a dizzying wave of vertigo, a profound sense of dislocation, as if the very bedrock of his identity had turned to sand. The memories of the man who had raised him... his laugh, his advice, the way he smelled of sawdust and coffee... were now tinged with a tragic, noble lie. And his uncle... the distant, estranged figure from his childhood... was his father. A man he barely knew was the author of his existence.

Numbly, his mind still reeling from the bombshell revelation that the man who wrote the letter was not his uncle, but his father, Jack rose from the chair. He walked on autopilot across the plush, unfamiliar carpet of the hotel suite to the gleaming, black monolith of modern technology that was the state-of-the-art entertainment center. His fingers, feeling clumsy and foreign, fumbled for a moment before finding the button to open the disc tray on the sleek, minimalist DVD player.

With a sense of finality, he took the disc from its paper sleeve and slid it into the tray. The soft whir and click as it closed was the sound of a key turning in the final lock of his old life.

The massive television screen came to life with a soft hum, its perfect blackness replaced by a simple, elegant interface. In the center of the screen, a single text box appeared, a final gateway he had to pass through. Above it, a prompt glowed in clean, white letters:

To proceed, please enter the name of your first true love.

A fresh wave of pain and memory washed over Jack. It wasn't enough that he had to think of her; his father, in his infinite, cruel wisdom, was making him physically type her name, to acknowledge her importance as the key to unlocking these last secrets. He picked up the heavy, sleek remote, his thumb trembling slightly as he used the directional pad to navigate the on-screen keyboard.

It was a slow, painful ritual.

J…

U…

L…

I…

E…

He stared at her name, glowing on the screen, a ghost in the machine of his new life. He took a deep, shuddering breath and pressed the 'Enter' button.

The password box vanished. The screen flickered to life, and suddenly, he was there. His uncle… his *father*… was looking directly at him through the screen, his gaze so intense it felt as though he could see right into Jack's soul. He looked older than Jack remembered from that barbecue years ago, and thinner, the confident, easy smile unable to fully hide the deep lines of exhaustion and pain etched around his eyes. But it was unmistakably, undeniably him.

"Jack," his father's voice filled the room, a voice from beyond the grave. He then began to speak of the empire, of the complex web of companies and assets. "The men and women you met today are sharks, son. They smell blood in the water. They will offer you a lump sum, a number so large it will seem like a king's ransom. Maybe two or three billion dollars."

Jack's mind flashed to Ashley, to her warning. *$1.9 billion*. Close.

"Here is what you will do," his father continued, leaning into the camera. "You will accept their offer, but only under the condition that you retain full ownership of the Art Industries parent company... which includes the investment firms, the car dealerships, and the nine hotel and casino properties. Let them have the rest. The businesses you'll be selling are profitable, but they are headaches. They require a hands-on, active presence that you are not prepared for. The companies you keep are already run by loyalists, people who know my wishes and will run the businesses for you. After you sign the papers, your first stop is Monaco. The hotel and casino there holds a private vault in my name. Inside, you will find another DVD with further instructions."

He paused, and a roguish, familiar twinkle appeared in his eye... a look Jack had seen on his own face in the mirror. "Oh, and one last thing. I know Arthur Westmiller. He will have already tasked either his assistant, Ms. Albright, or his own daughter with getting close to you, to influence you. To seduce you, if necessary."

The blood drained from Jack's face. The memory of Ashley's passionate, calculated kiss felt like a brand on his skin.

"Now listen closely, because this is important," his father said, leaning into the camera, his voice dropping to a conspiratorial murmur. "Don't mistake their motives for love, but don't mistake them for enemies. While you cannot trust them personally, know this: when they are with you, when they fuck you, they will have your back one hundred percent. Their success is now tied to yours. For them to win, you have to win first."

He let that sink in before continuing. "You must understand the difference between the man and the firm. Arthur will play every angle. But his company, Westmiller and Sons, is trustworthy to the contract. They are the best at what they do, and as long as you retain them, the company will always look after you. It is in their absolute best interest to protect the empire. Your success is their success."

"So, my advice? Enjoy the perks. Let them get close. But you owe their hearts nothing," his father said with a shockingly casual grin. "And if, by some chance, one of them gets pregnant… that simply becomes another negotiation. A few million will make the problem go away and turn it into a very quiet, permanent arrangement."

He let out a short, hearty laugh, a sound that was both vibrant with life and chilling in its cynicism. And then, the screen went black, leaving Jack alone in the crushing silence of the suite, the ghost of his father's laughter still echoing in the air.

For the next hour, the sprawling, opulent suite became a self-contained universe of shock and recalculation. Jack paced the thick, soft carpet, the heavy parchment of the letter in one hand, his mind a frantic kaleidoscope of shifting realities. He read the letter again and again, each pass searing the words deeper into his psyche. *I am your biological father.* The phrase refused to settle, remaining an alien concept that warred with eighteen years of memory.

He returned to the massive television and played the DVD twice more, forcing himself to watch, to listen. The first time, he was just a son, stunned by the posthumous appearance of a father he never knew. The second time, he tried to be an heir, absorbing the cynical, Machiavellian advice. The casual cruelty of the words about Ashley and Constance, the cold calculation… it was jarring, yet a part of him, a newly awakened, pragmatic part, recognized the brutal logic of it.

He spread the summary documents out on the massive glass coffee table, the pages fanning out like a hand of impossible cards. He began to separate them, following the ghost of his father's instructions. He isolated the businesses his father had called "headaches"… tech startups with volatile projections, manufacturing plants with complex supply chains, media companies with fickle audiences. He did a rough, back-of-the-envelope tally of their listed asset values. Even his exhausted, untrained mind could see the number was staggering, somewhere in the fifty-billion-dollar range. He let out a dry, humorless laugh. They were going to offer him less than four percent of the value. The sheer audacity of it was almost impressive.

Then he turned to the keepers. The nine hotel and casino properties, including the one in Monaco with its secret vault. Their portfolio was valued at just over two hundred billion dollars. The investment firms, the quiet engines of the empire, held another hundred billion in assets under management. The car dealerships, a more tangible and understandable business, were valued at a few billion more. And then there were the personal holdings, a dizzying list of stocks, bonds, and properties that felt more like a dragon's hoard than a portfolio. He was going to follow the plan. He would play the part of the grieving, overwhelmed boy, accept their insultingly low offer, and walk away with the true heart of the empire, leaving them to fight over the scraps they thought were the prize.

He closed his eyes, the endless parade of zeroes behind the numbers swimming in his vision, a numerical migraine. And amidst this sea of incomprehensible wealth, there was the single, most important variable: Madeline. No last name. No address. Just a village in France. He pulled out his phone and searched for Saint-Paul-de-Vence. The images that filled his screen showed a picturesque, ancient walled town perched on a hill, overlooking the sparkling Mediterranean. It was beautiful, but it gave him no clue how to find one woman in a country of millions. The vault in Monaco, he realized, had to hold the key.

Utterly drained, physically and emotionally, he collapsed back onto the sofa. He didn't have the energy to find the bedroom, to undress, to pretend this was a normal night. With the documents spread before him like the map of a new and terrifying world, he surrendered to exhaustion, his mind finally shutting down.

But sleep offered no escape. His dreams were a feverish, chaotic theater where the three women who now occupied his waking thoughts took center stage.

The dream began in the snowbound park of his old life, the air biting and cold. Julie was there, her pregnant belly a stark, round silhouette against the white landscape. She was crying, her pleas echoing the voicemails he had ignored, but her voice was distorted, accusing. *"You left me,"* she wept, her tears freezing on her cheeks. *"You could have been a father."* The word twisted like a knife in his dream-self's gut. He tried to reach for her, to explain, but his feet were rooted to the frozen ground. Then Brian appeared, laughing, and wrapped his arms around Julie, pulling her away into a swirling blizzard until she was gone.

The scene dissolved, the snow melting away into the sleek, metallic confines of the elevator in the Art Tower. Ashley was there, her lips pressed against his, her kiss no longer just passionate but consuming, draining the very air from his lungs. Her hands were on his chest, but instead of caressing him, they were searching, patting him down like a security guard, her eyes gleaming with a terrifying, ambitious hunger. *"Three hundred and fifty-six billion,"* she whispered into his mouth, the words tasting of ash and expensive perfume. *"It's all just numbers, Jack. Let me help you count it."* She smiled, but her teeth seemed to sharpen, to lengthen.

Then the elevator opened not into the lobby, but into the vast, silent conference room. Constance Westmiller stood alone at the far end of the long mahogany table. The panoramic window behind her showed not the city, but a swirling, infinite vortex of stars. She wasn't smiling or speaking; she was just watching him with those unsettling, intelligent green eyes that seemed to see straight through his confusion and fear. She beckoned to him, a single, elegant gesture. He felt an irresistible pull, a need to walk towards her, to ask her what she knew, what she wanted. But as he took a step, the floor beneath him turned to glass, and he could see the dizzying, terrifying drop to the city miles below. He was paralyzed, caught between the insatiable hunger of Ashley and the enigmatic silence of Constance, haunted by the weeping ghost of Julie in the snow. He was surrounded, yet utterly, terrifyingly alone.

A sharp, insistent knock jolted him from the depths of the dream. Jack gasped, his body lurching upright on the sofa, a strangled cry caught in his throat. His heart hammered against his ribs, a wild, panicked drumbeat against the sudden, deafening silence of the suite. He was disoriented, the feverish images of his dream still clinging to him like a shroud. The pleading ghost of Julie in the snow, the rapacious hunger in Ashley's eyes, Constance's silent, unnerving judgment… it all felt more real than the opulent, sun-drenched room he found himself in.

Another knock, louder this time, more demanding. He shook his head, trying to clear the fog. He was in a hotel. Los Angeles. He looked at his watch, a cheap digital thing that looked absurdly out of place in these surroundings. 9:00 AM. He'd slept for hours, fully clothed on the sofa.

He pushed himself to his feet, his limbs stiff and heavy, and crossed the vast expanse of the living room. As he reached the door, he took a deep breath, steeling himself. He opened it.

Ashley stood on the other side, looking impossibly fresh and composed. She was dressed in a different, equally sharp outfit… a cream-colored silk blouse and tailored black trousers. A warm, predatory smile spread across her face as she took in his disheveled state.

"Good morning, Mr. Halland," she purred, her voice a low, intimate hum. She didn't wait for an invitation, stepping past him into the suite as if she owned it. He instinctively moved to the side to let her in, his mind still catching up. As she moved past, he hurried to the coffee table and snatched up the letter from his father, quickly folding it and shoving it into his back pocket. The last thing he needed was for her to see it.

She placed a large, expensive-looking garment bag on a chair and turned to him, her smile unwavering. "I took the liberty of doing a little shopping for you. A man in your position needs to look the part. I thought we could start with a suit that befits the businessman you now are."

Jack glanced into the bag. Inside was a charcoal grey suit of a fine, lightweight wool, a crisp white button-up shirt, and a bold, red silk tie... a power tie. He smirked, the gesture feeling more natural, more his own, than it had the day before. "I'm not really a suit and tie kind of guy."

"Perhaps not," she conceded, her eyes twinkling with amusement. "But today, you wish to make them sweat. You want to walk into that room and make them understand that the boy they met yesterday is gone. I can see you've been going over the assets," she said, her gaze flicking to the documents still spread across the coffee table. "So you know what's what. You know what it's all worth."

He nodded, his expression hardening.

"Your uncle... your father," she corrected herself smoothly, "made sure we at Westmiller and Sons knew how to take care of you. He paid our firm very well to ensure you get the absolute best counsel."

Jack smirked again, the memory of his father's cynical words from the DVD echoing in his mind. *Fuck them if you want...* "And Mr. Westmiller... he made sure you and his daughter would be very close to me, didn't he? Maybe closer than you would a normal client?"

Ashley's smile didn't falter, but her eyes sharpened. She glanced at the back pocket where he'd stuffed the letter.

"Will was always very thorough in his assessments of people," she whispered.

He was done playing games. He took a step closer to her. "So he was right? Your job is to insert yourself, get close, make sure I favor your firm?"

"Maybe a little of that," she admitted, her voice dropping to a husky murmur. She closed the remaining distance between them, her gaze hot and direct. "But I'm also interested in inserting myself more... personally."

He looked at her, at this beautiful, calculating, and undeniably desirable woman. A reckless, unfamiliar impulse took hold of him. "Take off your clothes," he said, the words leaving his mouth before he could second-guess them.

For the first time, a flicker of genuine surprise crossed her face. Then, it was replaced by a slow, smoldering smirk. She seemed to relish the command. "As you wish."

Slowly, deliberately, she shrugged off her blazer, letting it fall to the floor. She unzipped her trousers, sliding them down her long legs and stepping out of them with fluid grace. Now she stood before him in the silk blouse and a pair of chic, black panties. Jack's mouth went dry. He was a virgin. A boy who'd been haunted by a single, heartbreaking memory. And here, in front of him, was this goddess of a woman, disrobing at his command.

"Jack," she whispered, her voice a silken promise. "I can be everything you want." Her fingers went to the buttons of her blouse, undoing them one by one with agonizing slowness, her eyes never leaving his. With each undone button, more of her flawless, sun-kissed skin was revealed. The shirt came off, pooling at her feet. She was wearing a delicate black lace bra that did little to conceal her perfect, full breasts.

She walked toward him, and he found he couldn't move, couldn't breathe. Her hand came up, her cool fingers tracing a line from his collarbone down the center of his chest. He could feel the heat of her body, smell the intoxicating scent of her perfume. She leaned in and her lips met his, softly at first, a gentle, questioning touch. It wasn't the demanding, claiming kiss from the elevator; this was an invitation.

"You need to undress," she murmured against his mouth, her own lips warm and pliant. Her hands went to the hem of his wrinkled t-shirt and began to pull it over his head. As she did, she gently guided him backward, her body pressing against his, leading him away from the living room, towards the opulent marble bathroom. "We can shower," she whispered, a universe of promises in her voice. "And enjoy each other."

Chapter 4.

The bathroom was a sanctuary of gleaming marble and polished chrome. Jack, his mind still reeling from the encounter in the living room, followed Ashley as she led him by the hand into the shower enclosure. It was a space so vast it felt like stepping into another world, walled in by seamless glass. She turned a sleek, minimalist knob, and a warm, steady downpour instantly cascaded from the rain-shower head in the ceiling, filling the chamber with a cloud of billowing steam.

She was already wearing only her delicate black lace bra and panties, and the effect of the water was immediate and breathtaking. The fine lace became a second skin, the hot water tracing rivulets over her body, outlining every perfect curve. The sight of her, so exquisitely vulnerable yet so completely in command, sent a fresh jolt of adrenaline through Jack's system.

She pulled him closer under the spray, and the kiss she gave him was deep and possessive, tasting of water and want. The world outside the glass walls, outside this torrent of water and sensation, ceased to exist. There was only the sound of the drumming water and the intoxicating reality of her body pressed against his.

Her hands, slick and sure, moved to the hem of his t-shirt, peeling the soaking fabric up and over his head before letting it drop to the marble floor. Her fingers traced the muscles of his chest and abdomen, exploring him with a confident touch that both thrilled and terrified him. He was so lost in the sensation, in the heat of the water and the heat of her gaze, that when his own hands came up to try and unhook her bra, they were clumsy and useless. His inexperienced fingers fumbled with the wet clasp, unable to make it yield.

A low, throaty laugh rumbled in her chest, a sound of pure, sensual amusement. "It's okay," she murmured against his mouth, her lips curving into a smile. "Let me." She reached behind her back, and with a single, fluid motion, the clasp was undone. She let the soaked lace fall away, letting it join his discarded shirt on the floor.

The sight of her, unrestrained and magnificent in the cascading water, stole the breath from his lungs. This was real. The months of numb, hollow grief, the self-imposed isolation… it all felt like a lifetime ago, a story about a different person.

Then, she did something that shattered the last of his composure. Her lips left his, beginning a slow, torturous descent down his jaw, over his throat, and across his chest. Each kiss was a brand, a searing mark left on his skin. As she reached his waist, she sank gracefully, fluidly, to her knees before him on the wet marble floor. She looked up at him through the steam, her eyes dark and luminous, and in them, he saw a promise so profound it made his head spin.

He looked down at this incredible, powerful woman, willingly kneeling for him, and his mind, already reeling, went completely blank. She reached out, her hands wrapping around his length, stroking him gently, her touch both commanding and reverent. She leaned in, her tongue flicking out to taste him, a slow, sensual lick that sent shocks of pleasure coursing through his body. She took him into her mouth, her lips stretching around him, her eyes never leaving his as she began to suck him, her head bobbing in a rhythm that was both torturous and divine.

The sensation of her mouth on him, the heat, the wetness, the suction, it was all overwhelming. He could feel every inch of her, the way her tongue swirled around him, the way her cheeks hollowed out as she took him deeper, the way her hands worked in tandem with her mouth, driving him to the brink of madness. The water cascaded down on them, mixing with the droplets of pre-cum that leaked from his tip, the steam surrounding them like a cocoon, trapping them in this moment of pure, unadulterated pleasure.

She increased her pace, her head moving faster, her hands gripping him tighter, her mouth taking him deeper. The sound of her sucking him, the wet, obscene noises, mixed with the roar of the water, creating a symphony of sensation that threatened to drown him. He could feel the pressure building, the coil in his stomach tightening, his balls drawing up, ready to release.

He reached down, his hands tangling in her hair, not to guide her, but to hold on, to anchor himself as she took him to the edge and pushed him over. He came with a cry, his body shaking, his vision blurring, as she continued to suck him, milking him for every last drop, swallowing him down like he was the most delicious thing she had ever tasted.

Even then, the intimacy didn't cease. Her touch gentled, a soft and reassuring caress in the aftermath. When the tremors subsided and he could breathe again, he felt her hand on his arm, gently urging him to help her to her feet.

He stood, dazed and pliant, as she rose before him, her body slick and gleaming. Her eyes held a new kind of power, a deep satisfaction mixed with a clear, focused intent for what was to come. Without a word, she gently turned him around to face the cool marble wall, the warm water still sluicing down his back. Her body pressed against his from behind, her soft breasts against his shoulder blades, her hands sliding around his waist to find him again, already hardening once more under her expert touch.

Her lips were close to his ear, her whisper a hot, private secret in the steamy, loud enclosure. "This is just the beginning, Jack," she murmured, she turned him again and bent over before him, her hands guiding him, positioning him, preparing him for what she wanted, for what she knew he now needed. She reached down, taking him in hand, and guided him into her, the water cascading over them both as he filled her completely. He let out a low groan, the sensation of her around him unlike anything he had ever experienced.

She began to move, her hips rolling in a rhythm as old as time, driving him deeper and deeper into her. Her hands gripped his hips, her nails digging into his flesh as she used him for her pleasure, matching his thrusts with her own, meeting him stroke for stroke. The sound of their flesh slapping together mixed with the roar of the water, creating a symphony of primal need.

Jack's hands splayed against the cool marble, trying to find purchase as she took him on a ride that was unlike anything he had ever imagined. He could feel every inch of her, the heat of her, the wetness, the way her body clenched around him, milking him for all he was worth. He was lost in a haze of sensation, the water, the heat, the scent of her, all of it combining to drive him to the brink of madness.

"Is this what you want?" he growled, his voice low and husky, his body leaning over hers, his lips capturing her earlobe, his teeth nibbling gently. He started to move harder, deeper, his hips rolling in a steady, relentless rhythm, his body slapping against hers, the sound echoing in the steam-filled shower.

"Yes," she hissed, pushing back against him, meeting his thrusts with equal fervor. "Just like that. Don't stop."

Their bodies moved in sync, a primal dance, their breaths coming in ragged gasps, their hearts pounding in unison. The water cascaded down on them, the steam surrounding them, trapping them in their own private world of pleasure.

Jack reached around, his hand finding her clit, his fingers rubbing in tight, precise circles, matching the rhythm of his thrusts. He could feel her body tensing, her muscles coiling, her breath hitching as she climbed towards her peak again.

"Come for me," he whispered, his voice a low, commanding growl. "Let me feel you come undone around me."

And she did. With a cry that echoed off the marble walls, her body clamped down on him, her orgasm ripping through her, her inner muscles milking him, drawing him deeper, urging him to join her.

He let out a low groan, his body shaking as he found his release, his seed spilling into her, their bodies locked together in a moment of pure, unadulterated bliss.

They stayed like that for a moment, their bodies sated, their breaths slowly returning to normal. Jack pulled out, turning her around to face him. He kissed her, a soft, gentle kiss that was a stark contrast to the wild abandon of moments before.

"I told you," she said, her voice a low purr, a smirk playing on her lips. "This is just the beginning." And with that promise hanging in the air, she took his hand and led him out of the shower.

When Jack entered the conference room, the energy in the air shifted palpably. The day before, he had felt like an imposter, a piece of dirt tracked onto a pristine silver platter. Today, draped in a charcoal grey suit that felt like a suit of armor, he *was* the silver platter. The memory of the morning… of Ashley's body slick with water, of her passionate, claiming kisses, and the raw, physical power of their encounter… was a secret well of confidence he drew from now. He strode to the head of the table with a newfound assurance, and he could feel their eyes on him, assessing this new version of the boy they had met yesterday.

He caught the gaze of Constance Westmiller, who was seated directly across from him again. Her intense green eyes swept over him, and the corner of her perfectly sculpted lips tilted up in a slow, appreciative smirk. It was a look that acknowledged the change, a silent concession from one predator to another.

"Mr. Halland," Arthur Westmiller boomed, rising to shake his hand. The man's smile was wide, full of paternal pride. "I must say you look like a new man today."

"Thank your assistant for that," Jack replied, his voice even and cool. He let his eyes drift toward the door where Ashley stood, a silent and composed observer.

Mr. Westmiller's gaze followed his, and his smile broadened. "She is a very good assistant."

Jack smirked, the double meaning of the words a private, satisfying joke between the three of them. He thought of the shower they had shared just hours before and had to admit the man was not wrong. He took his seat, the leather sighing under his weight, and placed his hands on the vast mahogany table. "So, what is on the agenda today?"

As if a switch had been flipped, the thirty men and women around the table all sat up straighter, their polite morning chatter ceasing. The air grew thick with anticipation.

"Well," Mr. Westmiller said, gesturing to the men at the center of the table. "Now comes the financial part of this."

An older man with a placid, grandfatherly face and sharp, calculating eyes stood up, his smile radiating condescension. "Mr. Halland," he began, his voice smooth as honey. "We from the Western Investment Bank consortium wish to offer to buy your companies from you. A young man such as yourself shouldn't be saddled with such a burden. We want to save you the trouble of dealing with the headache of running these complex and demanding businesses."

Jack nodded slowly, letting the man's patronizing words wash over him. "I had a feeling," he said. "But what are you offering?"

"We wish to offer you quite a large lump sum of money to take these businesses off your hands," the man continued.

"Of course, all personal assets are yours... the houses, cars, the plane, and whatnot. But the businesses, we will gladly buy from you."

Jack remained seated, fixing the man with a level stare. "What are you offering?" he repeated, his voice quiet but firm, forcing the man to get to the point.

The banker's smile tightened slightly. "We will offer you one point nine billion dollars for all of it."

The number landed in the silent room. Jack felt the ghost of a laugh bubble in his chest. It was exactly the figure Ashley had whispered in the elevator. His father's prediction had been off by only a hundred million. He let a slow smirk spread across his face.

"One point nine billion," he mused aloud, his voice laced with amusement, "for over three hundred and fifty-six billion dollars' worth of business."

A wave of shock rippled through the room. Faces fell. The bankers and investors exchanged panicked, furious glances. They were stunned he knew the numbers.

"You know," Jack continued, his voice hardening, "yesterday, before I even knew what the hell I had, I would have taken that deal. But now..." He stood up, commanding the room's attention. He felt the weight of his father's instructions, a clear and steady path through this nest of sharks. "Here is my counteroffer. And believe me, it is more than generous of me to offer it."

He paused, letting them hang on his words. "You give me two-point-five billion. In return, I will sell you all of the companies *except* for the hotels, the casinos, the car dealerships, and the investment firms," he stated, listing the core assets his father had told him to protect. "And, of course, this building and all of Art Industries remains under my name."

He leaned forward, placing his palms flat on the table. "The net worth of the companies I'm offering you is fifty-two billion dollars. It can be yours for two-point-five billion. Nothing more, nothing less." He then sat down, the quiet click of his chair the only sound in the tomb-like silence. He glanced at Ashley, who gave him a subtle, approving nod. He saw Mr. Westmiller trying, and failing, to hide a proud smile.

"You can't be serious," a woman with a sharp haircut and a sharper voice snapped, her face flushed with indignation. "The offer is one-point-nine, and it is for *all* of your businesses."

Jack shook his head, a gesture of finality. "Then I hope you all have a good day, and I'm sorry for wasting your time."

The woman sputtered, her composure cracking. "What could you possibly know about running these businesses? You're a kid!"

Jack smiled, a genuine, disarming smile that seemed to infuriate her further. "You are right," he said calmly. "I am just a kid. I turned eighteen just six months ago. But I am banking on the fact that you will take the extraordinarily profitable deal I have offered you. Because if you don't, my first act as the sole owner of this empire will be to hire someone to run these businesses for me, and your window of opportunity will be gone forever."

The silence that followed Jack's ultimatum was so absolute it felt like a physical weight pressing down on the room. The thirty powerful men and women, who moments ago had viewed him as a child to be placated, now stared at him with a mixture of raw shock and grudging respect. He had not only seen their trap but had also turned it on them, and they were utterly unprepared.

To break the tension on his own terms, he slowly turned his head toward the door where Ashley stood. He gave her a small, almost imperceptible smile. "Ms. Albright," he said, his voice cutting through the heavy silence, "could you please get me some water?"

The request was simple, yet it was a clear demonstration of his new authority. Ashley's professional mask was perfect, but her eyes sparkled with a triumphant pride that was meant only for him. "Right away, Mr. Halland," she said smoothly.

She moved with fluid grace to the polished sideboard, where crystal glasses and bottles of mineral water were arranged. Every eye in the room followed her as she returned to the table and placed the bottle neatly in front of him. As she leaned over, the subtle, intoxicating scent of her perfume enveloped him for a moment. Her hand came to rest on his shoulder, her fingers pressing firmly into the fine wool of his suit. The touch lasted a few seconds longer than necessary, a warm, possessive gesture that was both a public claim and a private reassurance.

Across the table, Constance Westmiller, who had missed nothing, let a knowing, almost feline smirk touch her lips. She saw the gesture for the power play it was, a silent move in a game she was now also a part of.

One of the men, his face red with frustration, decided to make one last attempt to regain control. "Mr. Halland," he said, his voice strained, "we will go as far as to offer you two billion. That is our final offer. But we will insist on getting the hotels and casinos in that deal."

Jack twisted the cap off the water bottle, the sharp crack echoing in the quiet room. He took a long, slow drink, using the moment to steady the tremor he felt in his gut. He set the bottle down with a soft click and sighed, as if disappointed.

"You must take me for a fool," he said, his voice devoid of heat, which made the words all the more chilling. He looked around the table, meeting the eyes of the stunned investors one by one. "The casinos and hotels alone are valued at over two hundred billion dollars. The offer I gave you stands. Take it or leave it."

With that, he pushed his chair back and stood up, the motion fluid and decisive. The meeting was over because he said it was. He walked toward the door, his steps measured and confident.

"I will be going back to Washington tomorrow," he announced to the room without turning around. "I have some personal business to take care of. If I have not heard from you before I get on that plane, the deal is off the table permanently."

He opened the heavy door and walked out, not looking back, not giving them the satisfaction of seeing any hesitation. He didn't stop, heading straight for the gleaming bank of elevators, his mind a roaring tempest. He felt the bile rise in his throat. The adrenaline that had carried him through the confrontation was crashing, leaving him shaky and nauseous. Talking about billions of dollars, holding the financial fates of these powerful people in his hands, and trying to act like it was the most normal thing in the world was not as easy as the movies made it look. It was a terrifying, gut-wrenching performance.

The elevator chimed, the doors sliding open into an empty, silent car. He stepped inside, and as the doors closed, sealing him in the quiet, sterile space, his confident facade crumbled. He leaned his head against the cool, polished wall, his heart hammering against his ribs. He felt like he was going to puke. He took a deep, shuddering breath as the elevator began its smooth, silent descent, trying to quiet the storm inside him.

For two hours, the opulent hotel suite felt more like a gilded cage. Jack paced the vast living room, the city of Los Angeles a sprawling galaxy of indifferent lights below. He walked to the floor-to-ceiling windows, then turned and stalked back toward the grand piano he had no idea how to play. He was a ghost haunting a life that wasn't his yet, replaying every moment from the conference room.

The numbers were staggering, nonsensical. He, Jack Halland, who just a week ago was worried about a heating bill, had turned down one-point-nine billion dollars. Then he'd turned down two billion. The sheer insanity of it made his stomach churn again. He had bluffed, postured, and held a line he wasn't sure he even understood, and now he was left alone with the terrifying consequences.

A sharp, confident knock echoed from the door. He froze, his first instinct a flare of irritation. He was in no mood for Ashley's brand of "comfort" or another round of business.

"Open up, Mr. Halland." The voice was not Ashley's. It was a rich, melodic contralto laced with amusement. It was Constance Westmiller.

With a deep sigh, he crossed the room and pulled the heavy door open. "Miss Westmiller," he said, managing a tired smile.

She stood there, a vision of cool elegance in a dark green dress that perfectly complemented her auburn hair. She was immaculate, poised, and exuded a confidence that seemed ingrained in her DNA. She smirked, her green eyes dancing with a light he hadn't seen in the conference room. "So, that was quite a performance."

She didn't wait for an invitation, gliding past him into the suite as if she owned it, a faint, expensive scent of jasmine and sandalwood trailing in her wake.

He chuckled, closing the door. "You LA girls really know what you want, don't you?" he mumbled, the words a direct reference to Ashley's uninvited arrival that morning.

Constance turned, her expression unreadable, one perfectly shaped eyebrow raised. "And what, precisely, does that mean?" she asked, her tone dangerously smooth.

He saw he hadn't rattled her. "This morning, Ashley walked in just like you did," he clarified. "Not invited".

A slow, knowing smile spread across her face. "By all means, Mr. Halland, if you want me to leave, I can leave," she said, calling his bluff.

He shook his head, gesturing to one of the plush sofas. "Nah, it's alright. Had this been my private home, it might have been different".

"I'm sure," she said, the word dripping with irony as she gracefully sat down, crossing her long legs. "So, you left quite an impression on everyone when you left."

He let out a genuine, humorless laugh, sinking into the chair across from her. "I sure hope so. I almost puked in the elevator on the way down".

Her answering laugh was surprisingly warm and genuine. "You certainly kept your nervousness hidden well". Her expression turned serious. "Now, I have been sent here to talk to you. They want you to consider the two billion for the companies you offered. Nothing more, nothing less".

"You can tell them, 'no deal'," he said instantly.

She smiled, a flash of shared conspiracy in her eyes. "My father said you were smarter than they give you credit for. After you left, they went into a long, vicious argument".

He smirked, leaning forward. "And their best outcome after all that was to offer me two billion for a fifty-two-billion-dollar portfolio? That's not an argument; that's an insult".

"I told them you wouldn't accept," she said simply.

"And what will they do now that I've said no again?" he asked.

Without a word, she pulled a sleek, impossibly thin phone from her handbag. She dialed a number and placed the phone on the glass table between them, the speakerphone activated.

"Hi, Dad," she said. "I'm here with Jack. It's a no".

Arthur Westmiller's voice, weary and resigned, filled the room. "You were right, Constance. He's not bluffing".

"Mr. Westmiller," Jack interjected, his voice firm. "Tell them the price is two-point-five. It's not negotiable."

"Oh, they heard you, Jack," Westmiller replied. "You are on speakerphone with the entire consortium".

Jack felt a jolt of adrenaline. He smirked. "Well, unless they are calling back to accept my offer, this conversation is over." Before anyone could respond, he reached out and pressed the disconnect button on her phone, ending the call.

Constance stared at him for a long moment, her head tilted. Then she let out a low chuckle. "At first, I thought you were just a punk kid who stumbled into a fortune," she admitted. "But in the last few hours, you've proven, not just to my father but to me, that you are a lot more than that".

He smirked, a real one this time, feeling a surge of pride at her admission. "Tomorrow morning, I'm leaving. How do I get the private jet to be ready for me to use?" he asked, the question feeling both powerful and foreign on his tongue.

She didn't hesitate. She picked up her phone and dialed another number from memory. "Captain Mortensen, good evening," she said, her tone shifting to one of easy command. "I need the jet ready for Mr. Halland tomorrow morning at nine a.m. Please file a flight plan for Portland, Oregon… Yes, the G650. Thank you, Captain."

She hung up, placing the phone back in her bag as if she had just ordered a pizza. The casual display of power was more staggering to Jack than anything that had happened in the boardroom. She had the keys to a kingdom he was only just realizing he now ruled.

"Constance," Jack began, his voice low and steady, cutting through the fragile truce between them. He leaned forward, pinning her with a weary but direct gaze. "I told Ashley the same thing I'm telling you now. Let's stop playing games. Your job is to insert yourself, get close, and make sure I favor your father's firm, isn't it?"

She didn't flinch. A slow, enigmatic smile touched her lips. "That is what my father wants, yes," she conceded, her honesty disarming.

He smirked, leaning back in his chair. The admission was exactly what he expected. "And what do *you* want?" he asked, genuinely curious now.

Constance held his gaze for a long, silent moment, the air crackling between them. Her playful demeanor vanished, replaced by a raw intensity. "Honestly?" she asked, her voice dropping a register.

He nodded. "I'd prefer it. I'm getting tired of people trying to play me."

"Alright. Honestly," she began, her eyes unwavering, "at first, I saw you exactly as they did: a punk kid who stumbled into a fortune he didn't deserve."

"That makes two of us," he said quietly, the words tasting like ash.

"But the way you handled yourself today," she continued, ignoring his self-deprecation, "showed me you're more than that. I read up on you, Jack. I know about the accident. I'm sorry about your parents, about you being left all alone."

A wave of unexpected grief washed over him, hot and sharp. He swallowed hard, forcing back the lump in his throat as a tear threatened to escape. He just nodded, unable to speak.

"But you didn't give up," she pressed on, her voice softening slightly. "It's obvious you didn't just let the money go to your head. You went back to your suite last night and you *studied*. You absorbed the information, which makes me believe your father's letter said something profound. And then you walked into that room and you put that board of investors in their place. Many men would have been intimidated. They demand respect, they are power players, they are extraordinarily knowledgeable… but you knew what you had, and you used that knowledge to your advantage."

She paused, letting her assessment settle in the quiet room. He could only stare at her, surprised by the accuracy of her perception.

"So, what do I want?" she asked, circling back to his original question. Her voice was calm, deliberate, as if she were laying out the terms of a merger. "I want a husband. Someone that will stand up for what they believe in. Someone that can afford the good life and isn't afraid to live it. Someone that respects me enough to see me as a partner."

The world tilted on its axis for the second time in as many days. He blinked, certain he'd misheard. "You want me to marry you?" he asked, the words feeling absurd on his tongue.

She tilted her head, her expression deadly serious. "You desire me. I can see it in your eyes, just as I'm sure you can see it in mine. I may not be the only woman you ever have, but yes, Jack, I want you to marry me. I want to be the wife on your arm at events, parties, board meetings, and interviews. Your first wife." She delivered the last two words with chilling precision. "And in return for that position, I will let you fuck as many girls as you feel like. My only condition is that you listen to me if I tell you someone is not good for you… if a girl comes along with the wish to actually hurt you and use your position against you."

Jack let out a short, incredulous laugh. "Like what you're doing right now?"

She shook her head, her patience unwavering. "I'm being honest with you about my ambition. I want to be elevated. I want to be your first wife. But in exchange, I will give you something none of the others will: the truth. Always."

Jack leaned back, the sheer audacity of her proposal leaving him breathless. "We know nothing about each other," he said, his voice barely a whisper. "How can we possibly know if we'd match?"

In a single, fluid motion, Constance stood, crossed the space between them, and gracefully sat down in his lap. Before he could react, she wrapped a hand around the back of his neck, her fingers tangling in his hair. Her lips found his, and she kissed him… a deep, searching kiss that was not a fiery invasion like Ashley's, but a deliberate, consuming seal on her offer. It was a kiss that tasted of jasmine, ambition, and a startling, pragmatic passion.

She pulled back just enough to whisper against his lips, her breath warm. "Jack, you don't have to love me. Just take care of me, protect my position, and I will be the best partner you could ever ask for. I will fuck you every day if you have the need."

He looked into her stunning green eyes, seeing a universe of complexities he couldn't begin to fathom. "Constance," he whispered back, his own voice hoarse. "I'm not saying I don't want to… but I'm not ready to marry anyone. I have… personal issues I need to handle first."

Just as he finished speaking, a sharp, electronic chime shattered the intimate moment. Her phone, still in her purse, was ringing.

Chapter 5.

The deep, resonant hum of the Gulfstream's engines changed pitch, dropping to a throaty whisper as the plane descended through the familiar grey blanket of a Pacific Northwest sky. Jack sat back in the plush cream leather seat, staring out the window as the lush greenery of Oregon rushed up to meet them. He felt the whisper of the hydraulics, a gentle bump as the tires kissed the tarmac, and then the powerful, seamless deceleration as the jet slowed. He was landing in Portland.

Just the night before, he'd been in a world of glass and steel, a king in a borrowed suit. The investors, after a frantic series of calls, had capitulated. They accepted his offer. Two-point-five billion dollars would be wired to an account of his choosing before the end of the week, all in exchange for companies worth fifty-four billion. He had asked Constance and her father to handle the deluge of paperwork, a task they accepted with unnerving efficiency.

It was now Sunday. Constance had already given him access to one of his father's primary personal accounts, a "rainy day fund," she had called it. He'd logged in on his phone, his hand trembling as the number resolved on the screen: over six hundred million dollars. He had stared at it, a figure so vast it was meaningless, and remembered the gut-wrenching anxiety of seeing his old bank balance of $237.54. Constance had informed him there were over a dozen such accounts scattered across the globe, all holding substantial amounts.

His thoughts drifted to the previous night. Constance had been true to her word; she had not slept with him. But she had made it exquisitely clear what he would be getting if he accepted her marital proposition. After the phone call with the investors, she had stayed. The conversation had been a masterclass in seduction, a verbal dance that left him reeling before she had even touched him. When she did, it was with a purpose and skill that was terrifying. She had left him drained and hollowed out, her mouth working on him with an expert proficiency that made Ashley's passionate encounter feel clumsy by comparison. It wasn't an act of intimacy; it was a brand being seared into his flesh, a demonstration of her power. As he had filled her throat, his world collapsing in on itself, he had the distinct, chilling feeling that he was being played like a finely tuned instrument. Then, with a satisfied, knowing smile, she had left, but not before giving him the instructions for the jet he was now on.

The cold, transactional nature of his new life in LA felt a world away now, replaced by a familiar, stubborn ache. His thoughts, as they always did, returned to Julie. Pregnant with Brian's child. The phrase was a dagger he twisted in his own gut. And yet, beneath the layers of anger and betrayal, the stubborn, irrational love for her remained. It was a sickness, a poison he couldn't sweat out, and it was the real reason he was back.

The jet taxied smoothly to a private section of the terminal, far from the commercial hustle. As the cabin door hissed open, revealing a set of carpeted stairs, Jack stood. Outside, a sleek black limousine sat waiting on the tarmac. He recognized the driver, the same stoic man who had driven him to the airport what felt like a lifetime ago.

"Mr. Halland. Welcome back to Portland," the driver said, his voice imbued with a new layer of deference as he took Jack's suitcase.

Jack smiled, the suitcase itself a symbol of his transformation. The worn, battered duffel bag he'd left with was gone, replaced by a piece of expensive luggage. Inside were the new suit, shirts, and pants he'd bought, the first purchases of an entirely new life. He knew he needed more clothes, a whole new wardrobe, and for the first time, he could afford anything he wanted.

He slid into the cool leather interior of the limo, the door closing with a solid, satisfying thud.

"Where to, sir?" the driver asked, his eyes meeting Jack's in the rearview mirror.

Jack thought for a moment, the battle that had been raging in his mind coming to a head. His head screamed at him to go to the house, to lock the door and figure out his next move. But his heart, that stupid, broken, and hopelessly stubborn part of him, had other plans.

He gave the driver an address on Fourth Street, in the heart of their small, dreary hometown. He was going to see Julie.

The ride through his hometown was a new and deeply unsettling sensation. Jack sat cocooned in the silent, leather-scented interior of the limousine, watching the world of his youth slide by the tinted windows. He saw the corner store where he'd spent his allowance on candy, the park where he'd first held Julie's hand, the familiar, slightly worn houses and businesses he had known his entire life. A dizzying thought echoed in his mind: *I could buy all of it. I could write a check and own this entire street.* In two days, he had secured a profit of two-point-five billion dollars, a number that still felt like a line from a movie. This didn't even account for the fortune he still owned, the houses and condos scattered across the globe, or the private jet he had just disembarked from.

As the limousine glided to a silent stop, his heart began to hammer against his ribs. It was Julie's house, a simple two-story home that was so achingly familiar it hurt. He took a deep breath, steeling himself. The driver opened the door, and he stepped out into the cool, damp air. The weather had shifted since he'd left; the brutal snowstorm had given way to a warmer front, with temperatures in the high forties. The last remnants of the snow were melting away in dirty patches on the lawns. He looked around, his brand-new suit feeling alien in the humble neighborhood. Curtains twitched in the houses across the street. He saw faces pressed against the glass, their expressions a mixture of curiosity and awe at the sight of the sleek, black limousine.

The front door of the house opened, and Gloria Fredericksen stepped out. Her face, etched with worry lines he hadn't remembered, broke into a wide, relieved smile when she saw him.

"Jack," she breathed, rushing forward. He met her halfway and received his customary hug, a fierce, maternal embrace that felt like the first real thing he had touched since he left.

"Mrs. F., it is so good to see you," he said, his voice thick with emotion.

She held him at arm's length, her eyes scanning him from head to toe, taking in the expensive suit before flicking to the limousine. "What in the world happened to you? Julie came home the other day, completely distraught, said you left in a limousine. And now you're back in another one, dressed like you're going to a funeral?"

He managed a small smile. "A lot has happened, actually. And I'm here to see Julie. I need to… we need to clear the air."

Gloria's expression softened with understanding. She nodded. "Julie's not home right now, sweetie. She's at the doctor for a checkup."

Jack nodded, a flicker of relief warring with his resolve. He turned to the limo driver. "I'll call you when I need you again," he said, his tone firm. The driver nodded, got back in the car, and drove off, leaving Jack standing on the sidewalk, a strange silhouette of newfound wealth in his old world. "No need to warn her I'm here," he said quietly to Gloria.

Her smile was warm. "Can I offer you a cup of coffee while you wait?"

"Please," he said, the word coming out as a grateful sigh.

They entered the house, and as Jack sat at the familiar kitchen island, Gloria started to make coffee, the simple, domestic act a balm on his frayed nerves.

"So," she began gently, not looking at him. "What happened?"

Jack took a deep breath and the story spilled out of him. He spoke of his parents, of the gaping hole their death had left. He spoke of how deeply Julie had hurt him, all things Gloria knew. But then came the new information: the lawyer's call, the death of his uncle, the shocking inheritance.

"And now," he said, his voice breaking, "I'm the only Halland left." He felt her hand cover his on the counter. "I was ready to end it all, Mrs. F. Right before the call came, I was done."

He saw tears well in her eyes. She squeezed his hand tightly, knowing better than anyone the pain Julie's betrayal had caused him.

"What I discovered in L.A. was more than I ever expected," he continued, finding his composure. "I never have to worry about money again."

She smiled, a sad, gentle expression. "That's nice, dear," she said, her voice soft. He knew she couldn't possibly comprehend the scale of it.

As she turned to pour their coffee, a sudden impulse, born of affection and his newfound power, seized him. He pulled out his phone, his fingers flying across the screen in a text to Ashley. *"Please do me a favor. I want to know what is owed on the house at 1426 Fourth Street in my hometown, owned by Gloria Fredericksen. Find out if it can be paid off."*

The response was almost instantaneous. *"There is a hold on the loan. It appears to be three months in arrears."*

His jaw tightened. He typed back, *"Pay it off. In full."*

He watched the three dots appear and then vanish, replaced by a single, powerful word: *"Done."*

He put the phone away just as Gloria placed a steaming mug of coffee in front of him.

"Texting your girlfriend?" she asked with a teasing smirk.

"She wants to be," he admitted, staring into the black coffee. "But I'm still not sure what, or who, I want."

She smiled warmly at him, a mother's knowing look. "Julie?" she asked softly.

He smirked, but there was no humor in it, only a bitter, familiar pain. "She's still expecting Brian's spawn, isn't she?" he said, the harsh word hanging in the air between them. Gloria's smile faded as she nodded slowly.

"That is one of the things I came here for," Jack whispered, his voice raw as he stared into his coffee cup. "I need to have it cleared out. She hurt me, Mrs. F."

Gloria nodded, her heart aching for the boy she had known his whole life. Her eyes drifted to the window just as a familiar figure walked up the driveway. "Here she comes," she whispered, giving Jack's hand one last, quick squeeze.

The front door opened, and the sound of keys clattering into a bowl echoed from the hall. "Mom, I'm home," Julie called out, her voice weary.

"In the kitchen, dear," Gloria called back, her tone deliberately casual.

Jack did not turn. He sat with his back to the doorway, his shoulders rigid, every muscle in his body tensed for impact. He heard her footsteps, the soft shuffle of her shoes on the linoleum, and then a sudden, sharp intake of breath as she stopped dead in her tracks.

"Jack," she whispered, his name a fragile breath of disbelief and hope.

He turned slowly on the stool and looked at her. For a moment, his breath caught in his chest. She was just as beautiful as he remembered, her features etched in his memory. But the sight was violently distorted by the prominent, round swell of her belly beneath her maternity sweater. She was six months pregnant, a living, breathing monument to his heartbreak. The pain was so sharp, so immediate, it felt like the first day all over again.

"Julie," he said, his voice flat.

She rushed forward and wrapped her arms around him before he could react. He was stiff for a moment, then his own arms came up reflexively to hug her back. For an instant, it was just like it used to be… the familiar scent of her hair, the way she fit against him. But then his hands brushed the taught curve of her stomach, and the reality of their situation crashed down on him again, a cold wall of another man's child between them.

"What are you doing here?" she whispered into his shoulder.

He gently unwrapped her arms and set her back. "I came to talk to you," he said, his eyes avoiding hers.

Her mother quietly placed a cup of herbal tea on the island in front of Julie, offering her a small, sad smile. "I'll leave you two to talk. Jack," she said, her gaze locking with his, "you do not go before you say goodbye."

"I won't, Mrs. F.," he promised. She gave a single nod and walked out of the kitchen, leaving them in a charged, heavy silence.

Julie sat down on the stool next to him. He watched her, unable to look away from her stomach. She carried the pregnancy well, her natural beauty somehow amplified, and the sight filled him with a confusing mix of awe and deep resentment.

"I'm sorry," she whispered, her voice trembling.

He finally looked up, meeting her tear-filled eyes. "Sorry? And that's going to fix it?" he asked, his voice colder than he intended.

She shook her head, a single tear tracing a path down her cheek. "Nothing can change this."

"No," he agreed, the word like a stone. "You made a choice, Julie. And now you have to live with it."

She nodded, wiping at her eyes with the back of her hand. "I know. I… I plan on giving the kid up for adoption," she whispered, the confession so quiet he almost didn't hear it.

He stared at her, surprised. "It's your child," he said simply.

"But there's no love," she choked out. "He took advantage of me. He said all the right things, and as soon as I told him I was pregnant, he just… disappeared." Her tears were flowing freely now. "I can never have your love again. I know that. I broke your trust, and you stopped loving me."

Jack swallowed a thick lump in his throat. She had broken his trust, shattered it into a million pieces. But could he tell her she was wrong, that he had never stopped loving her? Could he give her that hope when he didn't know what to do with it himself? Instead, he changed the subject. "If you could, what would you want to happen to Brian?" he asked, his voice low.

A flicker of something dark and furious ignited in her eyes, replacing the sorrow. "I want him to fucking die," she hissed, the venom in her voice shocking him. "And you know what? I'm not the only one. There's another girl, over on Addison Street. She's seven months pregnant. It's his child, too."

A cold rage, something he hadn't felt before, settled over Jack. Without a second thought, he picked up his phone, his thumbs moving with a newfound purpose. He sent a text to Constance. *"Got any contacts with a private investigator?"*

The three dots of her reply appeared instantly. *"We use several in the firm."*

"I need to know the location of a Brian Nolan," he wrote. *"He used to go to high school here. Has left town because of responsibilities he did not want. Two girls pregnant with his children."*

"Finding a loser. Got it," she wrote back, the reply a perfect encapsulation of her cynical efficiency.

Julie had leaned over, reading the messages on his screen. "Who is Constance?" she whispered, and the anger in her voice was gone, replaced by a deep, familiar hurt.

"The daughter of my lawyer in L.A.," he said, the partial truth feeling like a profound lie. He didn't mention that the night before, this same woman had delivered a mind-blowing, world-shattering blowjob that was as much a power play as it was an act of pleasure.

With a sigh that carried the weight of the past six months, Jack took Julie's hand in his. It was small and warm, just as he remembered. He squeezed it gently. "I never stopped loving you," he whispered, the confession feeling like it was being torn from his soul.

She looked up at him, her eyes wide and glistening with fresh tears. "Never?" she breathed, the word a fragile prayer.

He shook his head slowly. "But that doesn't make it simple. Julie, you hurt me… bad."

She opened her mouth to speak, to apologize again, but he raised his free hand to stop her. "Wait," he said, his voice gaining a new firmness. She nodded, her lips trembling. "I need you to understand. I am not the broken boy you left in the park. I'm not the kid who stood paralyzed while you let Brian run his hands under your shirt and fondle you."

He took a deep, shuddering breath, the memory still a raw, open wound. "For months, I was completely alone. My parents died. You were gone. And I was honestly, truly, considering just killing myself."

Her hand flew to her mouth, a stifled sob escaping her. "Jack…" she whispered, her face pale with horror.

He held her gaze, forcing her to see the truth of his despair. "Then I got a call from a lawyer in L.A. My uncle died," he said softly. "My last living relative. I am truly alone in this world now. But… he left me what he called a small fortune. I can afford to do anything I want. I can go anywhere, live anywhere. I even have a private jet."

She stared at him, trying to process the impossible words. "And you came here?" she whispered, her confusion evident.

He nodded, his thumb stroking the back of her hand. "Like I said, I still love you. But everything is different now. We need to find out what we are to each other, or if we can be anything at all."

"I want you back," she said immediately, her voice fierce with desperation.

His gaze fell from her eyes down to her stomach, to the undeniable proof of her betrayal. "Julie," he said, his voice laced with a deep, quiet sadness. "He or she will never be mine."

She nodded, fresh tears spilling down her cheeks. "I know. And I'll give him up for adoption," she whispered. "I already have the paperwork."

A sharp pang of something he couldn't name went through him. "A boy?" he asked.

She nodded again. "It's a boy. And if I have to wait until he's born and gone to have a chance with you… I will. I'll wait."

Jack took another deep breath, the confession twisting in his gut. It was time for the new, hard truth. "There will be other girls, Julie," he said, his tone flat.

She looked at him, confused. "What do you mean?"

He pulled out his phone, his new reality feeling cold and alien even to him. He opened his banking app and turned the screen toward her. She leaned in, her eyes widening as they tried to make sense of the number displayed: $614,237,981.54.

"This is one account," he whispered. "I have dozens like it."

"Jack... how much are you saying is a 'small fortune'?" she stammered, her mind refusing to comprehend the string of digits.

He smirked, a bitter, humorless expression. "I just sold about ten percent of the businesses my uncle had," he said, the word 'father' feeling strange and new, so he didn't tell her that yet. "The deal was for two-point-five billion dollars."

Her face said it all. The boy she grew up with, her childhood boyfriend, was a billionaire. The concept was so vast, so world-altering, it was like telling her he was from Mars. "Jack..." was all she could whisper.

"So yes," he continued, pressing the harsh reality onto her. "There will be more girls. They will come from all over the world. I will fuck who I want, when I want. I will live with who I want. But I will only *marry* one woman, and she will have to accept all of it."

"But I want to be your only girl," she whispered, her plea a relic from a life that no longer existed.

He felt a flash of the old, white-hot anger in his chest. "And I wanted to be your only boyfriend," he shot back, his voice cutting.

He stood up abruptly, the moment broken. "I want you to think about everything I've said. The real world, Julie, not the fantasy. And don't worry," he added, his voice turning cold and efficient. "I will handle Brian. And you will not need to worry about your expenses anymore."

He walked to the doorway of the kitchen. "When you know what you want, and when you can accept all of it, we can talk again."

He saw Gloria sitting in the living room, her face etched with sorrow. She had heard it all. He walked over to her and bent down, hugging her tightly. "I paid off your house," he whispered into her ear. Then he kissed her on the cheek and walked out the front door before she could even react.

He didn't call for the limo. He walked down the quiet street toward his own empty house. It was only six blocks, but he needed the time, the cool air, the familiar cracked sidewalks to try and make sense of the hurricane raging inside him.

Chapter 6.

The six-block walk was a journey through a graveyard of memories. When Jack finally pushed open the door to his old house, the silence that greeted him was different. It wasn't the lonely quiet of grief anymore; it was the hollow, echoing silence of a lie. This was the house he was born in, the house where he took his first steps, the house whose every creak and groan was as familiar as his own heartbeat. But it was not the house of his father. He knew that now.

His gaze was drawn to the wall of the living room, to a large, framed photograph taken on a sunny afternoon just last spring. It was him on his graduation day, beaming in his cap and gown. On one side stood his mother, her smile radiant with pride. On the other side, his father... the man he now knew was his uncle... had an arm wrapped around his shoulders, his expression one of deep, paternal affection. They were supposed to be his role models, his anchors, the very definition of his world. And they had lied to him, every single day of his life.

He sighed, a long, shuddering breath that seemed to pull all the air from the room. And then, the grief curdled into a white-hot rage. It started as a low tremor in his hands and surged through him like an electrical current. With a guttural snarl, he snatched the heavy brass lamp from the end table beside him and hurled it with all his might at the smiling, deceitful faces in the photograph.

But before the lamp could complete its destructive arc, his strength gave out. His knees buckled, and he collapsed to the floor. The sound that ripped from his throat wasn't a word; it was a primal scream of pure, undiluted agony and betrayal. It was a sound of a world breaking, of a boy's heart shattering for the second, and final, time. He fucking hated them. He hated their love because it was built on a foundation of deceit. He hated their memory because it was a fiction.

Lying there on the dusty floorboards, gasping for breath amidst the wreckage of his emotions, a strange and terrible clarity emerged. He knew now what he wanted. If his life was to be built on lies, he would build a new one on brutal, absolute honesty. He wanted dozens of women. He would fuck them all. He would have kids with them all. But he would be honest. His children would know who he was, who their siblings were. They would all be one large, sprawling, unconventional family. He wanted a life teeming with people, with noise, with truth. He wanted to live, and he wanted to enjoy every last cent of his fucking money.

He looked around the room, at the furniture that now seemed like props on a stage set. This wasn't his home. It was a museum of a life that had never truly been his. He pulled out his phone.

"I'm ready to be picked up. My old house," he said into the phone, his voice a raw rasp.

"I will be there shortly, sir," the driver replied.

Jack hung up. He stood, his legs shaky, and immediately dialed Constance.

"Three things," he said, the moment she answered, dispensing with any greeting. "First, I will not marry you. Not now. Maybe later, as we get to know each other. But right now, I want to live. I want to have whoever I want, however I want."

There was a pause on the other end, then her voice, cool and pragmatic. "Okay, Jack. But my offer stands. I will not sleep with you until you marry me."

He smiled, a humorless, tight expression. It was her leverage. He respected it. "I understand that. Second, I want you to find everything you can on Brian Nolan. I want him in jail, and I want him hurting."

"I will inform the investigator immediately," she said, her tone all business.

"And third..." he paused, his voice faltering as he looked around the room one last time. "I want my old house sold. Or given away. Fuck it, I want it torn down. This is not my home." The last words were a choked, hurting whisper.

Her voice softened, the professional facade cracking for just a moment, replaced by genuine empathy. "Yes, sir," she said gently. She could imagine the hurt.

"You said I had houses and homes all over the world," he said, pulling himself together.

"Yes. I'll send you the list now."

"Any in L.A.?" he asked.

"Yes," she answered. "There is a large house on the beach in Malibu. It was one of his favorites."

"Send me the address," he commanded. "And Constance... thank you." The words were quiet, but sincere.

"Jack, we work for you," she said, and he could hear the truth in her voice. "We will always look after your best interests."

"Will you meet me at the house in Malibu?" he asked, the request a step beyond business.

"Of course," she said without hesitation. "If that is what you want."

He nodded to himself, a silent confirmation. At that moment, he heard a polite knock on the front door. The driver. "See you in L.A.," he said into the phone and hung up.

He opened the door and looked at the stoic driver, a man who had become an unwitting bookend to the death of his old life. "Take me back to the airport, please," he said.

"Of course, sir," the driver replied, nodding.

Jack stepped out of the house for the last time, not looking back. He entered the limousine, and as they drove off, he watched the familiar streets of his childhood disappear in the rearview mirror, turning to ash behind him.

As the Gulfstream banked south, climbing through the clouds and leaving the damp, grey skies of the Pacific Northwest behind, Jack felt a profound sense of release. It was as if the plane's powerful ascent was physically lifting a crushing weight from his chest. He had walked into that house in Washington a ghost, haunted by the memory of a boy who had been betrayed. He was leaving as something new, something harder.

He had finally confronted Julie, not with pleas or tears, but with the cold, hard currency of his new reality. For the first time in six agonizing months, the power dynamic had been entirely his. He had laid out his terms, his truth, and left her to grapple with the consequences of her choices. There was no clean closure, no happy ending, but there was a definitive end to his role as the victim. He had bulldozed the past.

A cold, thrilling clarity settled over him. He finally understood the cynical advice his father had left on that DVD. Money wasn't just for comfort; it was for control. It was a tool to sculpt the world to his liking. He could afford to be selfish now, and by God, he would be. The years of being the nice, romantic boy had ended with his heart shattered and his trust in ruins. Now, he would use his immense wealth and power to get exactly what he wanted. After all, what is the point of having a fortune if you are not going to use it?

His mind, now free from the mire of his old life, began to map out the future. A thousand thoughts, a million possibilities, swirled in his head.

Monaco: The first real quest. There was a vault there, a message from his father, the next level of this insane game he was now playing. He would go there soon.

Madeline: The name echoed in his mind, a tantalizing mystery. The woman in France his father had called "the key". Finding her felt like the most important piece of the puzzle, the one part of his father's plan that wasn't about business or revenge, but something more.

Los Angeles: But first, L.A. He wanted to live a little, to indulge in the hedonism he had only seen in movies. He wanted to explore the world of casual, meaningless pleasure he had been so staunchly against just a few days ago. Maybe fuck a girl or two, just to feel something other than pain.

He smirked, a genuine, predatory expression this time. A specific memory bloomed in his mind with vivid intensity: the image of the two women, the twins, he had seen when his cab first drove him into Century City. They had been ethereal, otherworldly goddesses, moving with a "perfect, hypnotic synchrony" that was both mesmerizing and unsettling. They radiated an "effortless, intimidating beauty," and back then, he had felt they occupied a different universe, one he could never hope to enter.

Now, the thought of them, or women like them, filled him not with inadequacy, but with a surge of ambition. He could afford to be with girls like that. He could enter that universe, not as a visitor, but as a king. The idea wasn't about love; it was about conquest, about claiming the life he had been so violently thrust into. He would find women like that, and he would enjoy every single moment of his new, unbelievable life.

As the private jet began its final descent into the sprawling urban galaxy of Los Angeles, Jack's mind was a whirlwind of calculated plans. The weight of his past had been lifted, replaced by the exhilarating, terrifying freedom of his future. A new, colder philosophy was taking root.

He considered the women who now orbited his new life. Constance, with her sharp mind and even sharper boundaries, had made it clear that her bed was off-limits until he put a ring on her finger. It was a power play he could respect. But Ashley… Ashley was a different story. He remembered the uninhibited fire of their encounter in the shower, a raw, physical release that had been intoxicating. He smirked. He would invite her to the new house in Malibu. He would fuck her again, enjoying the uncomplicated pleasure she offered. But not tonight.

Tonight, he had another idea, a new plan forming in his mind, and he was eager to see if it would work in his favor.

His thoughts, flitting between power plays and hedonistic desires, were suddenly grounded by a simple, practical problem. He didn't have a passport. The realization was almost comical. He had the means to go anywhere in the world... to the vault in Monaco, to find Madeline in France... but lacked the basic document to cross a border. He, Jack Halland, a boy who before this weekend had never even left Washington State, was a global power with no way to travel the globe. He made a sharp mental note: his first call to Mr. Westmiller would be about arranging a passport, expedited with the full force his new status could command.

The soft bump of the wheels hitting the tarmac pulled him from his reverie. The plane decelerated with a powerful, quiet efficiency and taxied toward a private hangar, away from the chaos of the main terminals. Through the window, he could see a black limousine already waiting on the sunbaked tarmac. He made another mental note: thank the pilot for his efficiency and for arranging the car. Good service deserved acknowledgment.

The jet door hissed open, and Jack stepped out into the warm, smog-tinged California air. And then he froze. Standing by the open door of the limousine was the same large, burly man with the salt-and-pepper buzz cut and the stony expression from Friday. The man who had looked at him, a boy in a worn t-shirt with a duffel bag, and told him to "piss off."

A slow, cold smirk spread across Jack's face. He wasn't angry this time. He was amused. "Yeah, I think that's a no," he murmured to himself.

He pulled out his phone and dialed.

"Mr. Westmiller," he said, his voice deceptively calm the moment the lawyer answered.

"Mr. Halland! Welcome back to Los Angeles! I trust…"

Jack cut him off. "I thought I made it exceptionally clear on Friday that I was treated with disrespect upon my arrival."

There was a sudden, tense silence on the other end. "You did, sir. And I was assured it was handled immediately," Mr. Westmiller said, his voice now laced with alarm.

"Then explain to me," Jack continued, his voice dropping to an icy chill, "why the *exact same driver* is standing right here, right now, waiting to pick me up again?" He knew he was being rude, but he didn't care. This was a lesson, and he had the money to afford to be a demanding teacher.

"Sir… I… I don't understand. I was told the man was reprimanded and that it would not happen again," the lawyer stammered, clearly flustered.

"'Not happen again' is insufficient," Jack stated flatly. "I want you to terminate whatever contract you have with this limousine service. Find me a new one. This company has demonstrated that it cannot be trusted to stand by its promises. I will not use them again."

"Right away, sir. I'll make the arrangements for a new car immediately."

"Good," Jack said. "I will wait in the jet until it arrives."

He hung up without another word, turned, and walked back up the stairs into the cool, quiet cabin of the plane, leaving the driver standing by the limo in utter confusion. The driver watched the young man in the expensive suit disappear, completely baffled. He didn't remember the face of the kid he'd dismissed two days ago. All he knew was that the client he was supposed to pick up on Friday, the important Mr. Halland, had never shown up. Now, for some reason he couldn't possibly comprehend, and he didn't even know of yet, his very presence on this tarmac had just cost his company its most valuable client.

As Jack settled back into the plush leather seat of the jet, the silence of the cabin a welcome refuge, his phone buzzed on the polished wood table beside him. He glanced at the screen. A new text message from Julie. Her name, which once would have sent a jolt of either pain or hope through him, now barely registered. He watched the notification for a moment, a ghost from a world he had already left behind, then deliberately looked away. He would deal with that later. Or never. Right now, he had a new life to build.

He picked up the phone and dialed.

"Mr. Halland," Arthur Westmiller answered immediately, his voice a mixture of apology and efficiency. "The new driver is on the way. I was told it would be no more than ten minutes."

Jack smiled, the power of having his needs met so swiftly a new and satisfying feeling. "Thank you, Arthur. I'm actually calling about a different matter." He paused, the practical absurdity of his situation dawning on him. "I've just realized... I don't have a passport. And I find myself with a sudden desire to travel the world and see my father's companies."

"Of course, sir," the lawyer replied smoothly. "We can begin the process immediately. With the right connections, we can have it expedited, but it will still take a little time."

"I understand," Jack said, his gaze drifting out the window at the endless L.A. sprawl. "I see myself being busy enough here for the foreseeable future that it won't be an issue."

There was a slight hesitation on the other end, and then Westmiller's voice returned, now tinged with a careful, personal curiosity. "So... my daughter informed me that she... proposed to you last night."

Jack let out a low chuckle, not of mockery, but of a man who appreciates a well-played hand. "You did tell her and Ashley to get close to me," Jack stated, his voice free of accusation. He wasn't angry; he was simply acknowledging the rules of the game he was now a part of.

Westmiller chuckled in return, a sound of genuine, relieved amusement. "I'm guessing your father's letter pointed out I would do something like that."

"He did," Jack confirmed. "He also told me that, despite your methods, you were trustworthy. And I know your firm relies heavily on me keeping you under retainer."

"It's true, and I won't lie about that," Westmiller admitted, his honesty refreshing. "Your father's business was the cornerstone of this firm. Yours is now its entire foundation."

Jack smiled. It was time to reward that honesty and secure his own position. "Do me a favor. Write up a new contract for Westmiller and Sons. Ten years. I will continue using your services under the current retainer." He paused, adding, "I also want a clear breakdown of the fee structure.

What the retainer covers, and what the charges will be for menial, day-to-day services... like me calling you to arrange a passport."

The silence on the other end was profound. "Ten years, sir?" Westmiller finally asked, his voice filled with astonishment.

"I assume you had a similar deal with my father," Jack said.

"Yes, sir. But only for three years at a time. He liked to keep us on our toes."

"Nevertheless," Jack said, enjoying the lawyer's shock. "Make it ten years."

"Yes, sir," Westmiller said, his voice imbued with a new, profound sense of loyalty.

"And Arthur," Jack added, shifting the final piece of their relationship into place. "From now on, call me Jack."

He could hear the smile in the older man's voice. "Thank you... Jack. I will."

Just as he spoke, Jack saw a new, pristine black limousine glide silently into the private hangar. "My ride is here," Jack said. He hung up the phone as he stood, feeling more in control than he ever had in his life. He exited the plane once again, descending the stairs to meet his future.

As he settled into the pristine, leather-scented interior of the new limousine, Jack gave the driver the address in Malibu that Constance had sent him. The car pulled away from the private hangar with a silent, powerful grace, merging onto the freeway. He leaned his head back and finally allowed himself to open the text from Julie. His thumb hovered over her name, a gateway to a world of pain he had just decided to leave behind. With a deep breath, he tapped the screen.

Her words appeared, a mix of surrender and a desperate, final plea. *"Jack… it sounds like you've made up your mind… and if you really love me… I will accept it all. Even the other women. But I want to know if I am just a woman for you… or if I will be your wife."*

He sighed, the question landing with the force of a physical blow. A wife. He hadn't thought that far ahead. He had been so focused on the anger, on the power, on the idea of a life free from the rules that had broken him, that he hadn't considered the ultimate endgame. Before he could process it, his phone vibrated again with a second message from her.

"Mom just told me you paid off the house. Jack, I can't thank you enough. Mom has been struggling so much since Dad left. I love you. Even if you don't marry me… I will always love you."

He closed his eyes, the messages burning behind his lids. Her unconditional love was the one thing he had craved for six agonizing months, and now, here it was, offered freely in the wake of his ultimatum. The city passed by the tinted windows in a blur of sun-drenched concrete and palm trees. The freeway began to hug the coastline, revealing the vast, glittering expanse of the Pacific Ocean. He opened his eyes, the deep blue of the water doing nothing to calm the storm inside him.

"What's our ETA?" he asked the driver, his voice rough.

"Fifteen minutes, sir," the driver replied.

Jack nodded, turning his attention back to his phone. He typed, deleted, and typed again, trying to find words that were both honest and non-committal. *"While I am not sure where I stand on 'wife' at the moment, I want you in my life. I hope you will accept things as they are for now."* He pressed send, the message feeling both kind and cruel.

Her response was immediate, a testament to her desperation. *"Jack, even if you only wanted me as a friend, I want to be there for you. I owe you that. I treated you wrong, and I will spend my life making it right."*

He smirked. It would never be truly right. The damage was done, the trust irrevocably broken. But he could see a path for her in his life. *"You will be so much more than a friend,"* he texted, the confession feeling like a final surrender to a truth he couldn't escape. *"I do love you."*

He put his phone away as he felt another message come in, ignoring it for now. He had said what needed to be said.

The limousine turned off the Pacific Coast Highway, climbing a winding road before pulling into a long, private driveway. At the end of it, perched on the cliffside with a breathtaking view of the ocean, was the house. It wasn't a mansion in the classical sense, but a stunning, multi-leveled marvel of glass, steel, and warm wood that seemed to grow organically from the rock. Terraces and infinity pools cascaded down toward the beach below. It was a masterpiece of modern architecture, and it was his.

Standing by the massive front door, a figure of poised elegance against the backdrop of the setting sun, was Constance.

Chapter 7.

The moment Jack stepped across the threshold of the Malibu house, the world outside ceased to exist. He wasn't just in a mansion; he was inside a masterpiece. The front door opened into a cavernous great room with ceilings that soared thirty feet high, crisscrossed with warm wooden beams. An entire wall was a seamless sheet of glass, revealing a jaw-dropping, panoramic vista of the sun setting over the Pacific Ocean. The rhythmic sound of the waves crashing on the beach below filled the space with a soothing, powerful hum.

"Holy hell," he whispered, the words utterly insufficient as he took in the minimalist furniture, the infinity pool that seemed to merge with the ocean, and the floating staircase that led to the upper levels.

Constance's low chuckle echoed in the vast space. "It is quite nice," she said, and he could hear the genuine admiration in her voice. "One of his favorites."

He turned from the view to look at her, a smirk playing on his lips. "So, you told your dad you proposed to me."

Her own smirk was immediate and sharp. "I did. I also told him you turned me down."

He chuckled, shaking his head as he walked further into the room, running a hand over a cool, marble countertop. "You know that's not true. I just told you I wasn't sure yet."

She laughed, a full, melodic sound. "To a girl like me, Jack, that's a rejection."

"Yeah, maybe," he conceded, turning to face her. "But not every girl proposes to a man she's known for less than twenty-four hours."

"Alright," she said, taking a step closer, her green eyes sparkling with challenge. "So, if I ask again in a month?"

Jack laughed aloud this time. "We have to actually get to know each other first, Constance."

She closed the remaining distance between them, her gaze hot and direct. She took his hand, her fingers cool and smooth, and deliberately placed it on her breast. Through the fine fabric of her dress, he could feel the firm swell and the rapid beat of her heart. "You know I will give you everything you could possibly want," she whispered, her voice a silken promise. "All you have to do is marry me."

His breath hitched. Acting on pure instinct, he leaned in and kissed her, a deep, searching kiss born of confusion, attraction, and a desperate need to silence her overwhelming proposition. It was a kiss of conflict, and when he pulled back, he rested his forehead against hers. "Constance… I'm not ready," he whispered, the admission costing him.

She chuckled softly, pulling away and looking at him with an amused fondness. "You are cute when you blush," she said. She reached into her handbag and pulled out a sleek, heavy set of keys attached to a simple leather fob. She pressed them into his hand.

"All yours," she said, her smile not quite reaching her eyes. "Well, all of this is yours. All except me."

She turned with a fluid grace and walked toward the massive front door. Just as she pulled it open, she paused and looked back at him over her shoulder.

"And by the way, Jack," she said, her tone casual, as if she were mentioning the weather. "I am more than willing to sign a prenuptial agreement. I'm not marrying you to take your money if we divorce. I'm marrying you for the life we'll have together. But," she added, a wicked glint in her eye, "I will expect to be spoiled."

And with that, she walked out, the heavy door closing with a soft, definitive click behind her, leaving him alone in the cavernous, silent house.

Jack stared at the closed door, her last words echoing in the space. "Are you fucking kidding me?" he mumbled to the empty room. The offer was staggering in its audacity and its brilliant, cold logic. A prenup. A way to protect his fortune. A way to have the beautiful, intelligent, ambitious partner without the fear of being taken for a fool. It was a tool, another piece of the billionaire's life he hadn't even considered.

And as the weight of her offer settled upon him, his thoughts, as they always did, drifted back to a small house in Washington. What would Julie say to that?

For the better part of three hours, Jack explored the Malibu mansion like an archaeologist discovering a lost city. Each room was a new revelation. He wandered through a state-of-the-art home theater with plush, reclining seats and a screen that took up an entire wall. He ran his hands over the cool, stainless-steel surfaces of a professional-grade kitchen, filled with gleaming appliances he had no idea how to operate. He found the master suite, a sprawling sanctuary of its own with a bathroom the size of his old living room and a bedroom where one entire wall was a sheet of glass, offering a view that made it feel as if the bed were floating over the ocean itself. This was his. The sheer scale of it all was overwhelming, a stark contrast to the solitary figure wandering its halls.

He slid open a massive glass door and stepped out onto a wide stone terrace. The salty tang of the ocean filled his lungs, the sound of the waves a constant, powerful rhythm. The private beach stretched out below him. To his left and right, the nearest houses were a few hundred feet away, affording a comfortable illusion of seclusion. The house to the left belonged to an older couple, who were quietly tending to a vibrant garden of coastal flowers. To his right, it was another world entirely. A group of younger people, mostly women his age and a few years older, were sunning themselves around a sparkling blue pool, their laughter carrying on the breeze. They were all, without exception, stunningly beautiful. A slow, predatory smirk touched Jack's lips as he thought of the kind of trouble he could get into now.

He turned and walked back inside, the decadent thoughts still swirling in his head, when his phone rang, the sound jarring in the quiet house. He pulled it from his pocket, not recognizing the number.

"Speaking," he said, his voice flat.

"Mr. Halland," a cheerful, professionally sharp female voice began, "this is Lori Decker from Twelve News. It has come to our attention that you are the sole heir to the fortune of the late William Halland, and we were wondering if we could interest you in an interview."

The words hit him like a slap. *Sole heir. Fortune.* The anonymity he hadn't even realized he cherished was already gone. Without a word, he jabbed the "end call" button on his screen and immediately dialed Arthur Westmiller.

"Care to tell me who gave the media my phone number, who I am, and what I just inherited?" he bit out the second Arthur answered.

"What?" the lawyer replied, the alarm in his voice immediate.

"I just got a call from Twelve News asking for an interview," Jack said, his voice tight with fury.

"What did you tell them?" Arthur asked, his tone urgent.

Jack smirked, a humorless, angry expression. "Nothing. I just hung up."

"Good. Well, maybe not good… that was rude… but it's better than the alternative," Arthur said, thinking fast.

"I don't want the world to know who I am," Jack shot back. "I was hoping to just live a rich, anonymous life."

"I'm afraid that boat has sailed, Jack," Arthur said gently. "If Twelve News already knows, others will too. Someone on the inside of the deal must have leaked it. This is too big a story to stay quiet for long."

Jack cursed under his breath, pacing the vast living room. "So now what?"

"You will need to stay out of the public eye for a while. Lay low. This will eventually blow over as they move on to the next story," Arthur advised.

"Stay out of the public eye? So I have billions of dollars, but I'm locked away in a gilded cage?" he said, the bitter irony stinging him.

"Sir, there are a few things you need to consider now," Arthur said, shifting into his role as consigliere. "A personal assistant to manage your schedule and your properties. A small, discreet security detail. Perhaps a personal trainer and a chef."

Jack snorted. "Seriously?"

"Yes, sir. Your father had all of those, and I can recommend you speak to his former staff. Though," Arthur added, his tone shifting to one of wry amusement, "from what I hear from Ashley and my daughter, there may be a few young ladies around the house soon, and I assume you don't want them being ogled by anyone other than yourself."

Jack thought about it. He wanted women around, and he sure as hell didn't want to share them or have them watched. "Okay, talk to me about an assistant."

"I know several excellent candidates who could be of interest to you, sir. Do you want me to arrange interviews?"

"If you could. But I guess it will have to be here, since I'm apparently locked in my own house for now."

"Very well, sir. Also, I will send Ashley to you with some groceries. I'm guessing there isn't much in the house since it has stood empty for a while."

Jack's anger began to subside, replaced by practical needs. "Yes, please. Tell her I'll need enough for a few days. Also, I want a new cellphone with an unlisted number for my personal life and a new laptop so I can access my online accounts securely."

"Yes, sir. I'll send her shopping right away. And by the way, sir... the wire transfer from the investors cleared this morning. You are officially a billionaire."

Jack was silent for a second, the word landing with a quiet, definitive thud. "Arthur," he asked, his mind already moving to his next desire. "Any of these assistant candidates' women?"

He could hear Arthur chuckle on the other end. "Yes, sir. Several of them. And I have no doubt they would be very willing to work *closely* with you. But a word of advice: they will throw themselves at you for the position. Don't let yourself get caught in a losing battle of sex for favors. That doesn't mean you shouldn't enjoy what they offer... just don't offer the first one the job. Make sure you interview them all."

Jack smiled, a real smile this time. "Thank you, Arthur." He hung up the phone and sank into one of the large, comfortable sofas. He closed his eyes and sighed, the scent of the ocean filling his new, empty home.

As the initial adrenaline of the day began to fade, Jack remembered the waiting message from Julie. He sank into a deep leather armchair that faced the ocean and opened the text.

"Jack... even if I am not your wife... I will always be yours. This is a promise I make now. I know I said that before... but I know I should have listened to you back then... but..."

The message stopped there, unfinished. He smirked. That final, hanging "but" bothered him. It was the precursor to an excuse, a justification he was no longer interested in hearing. He knew she was referring to Brian, to her moment of weakness, but her inability to even write the name felt telling. He decided to cut through the sentiment with a cold dose of his new reality, a test to see if she truly understood the world she was asking to re-enter.

"Tell me Julie... if I were to marry you... would you sign a prenup?" he texted.

He pressed send and put the phone away without waiting for a reply, the question hanging between them like a guillotine. He walked back to the massive glass door and sighed, looking out at the waves. His moment of peace was shattered. On the sand below his property line, two news vans were parked, their satellite dishes aimed at the sky. Camera crews with long-lens cameras were pointed directly at his house, and reporters were gesturing dramatically, speaking into microphones.

A sharp knock echoed from the front of the house. He turned, and through the frosted glass panels flanking the main door, he could see the unmistakable flashing lights of a camera. They were at his front door, too.

He felt a surge of panic and rage. He retreated upstairs to the master bedroom and dialed Arthur again.

"Send the cops here," he said, his voice tight. "I feel like I'm being invaded. There are reporters on my property... on the beach and on my front porch."

"Consider it done. I will have a private security firm on the way right away, Jack. They'll be more effective," Arthur's voice was calm and reassuring.

Jack hung up and, on a morbid impulse, turned on the large television mounted on the wall. He flipped through the channels, and there it was: a live shot of his own house, seen from the beach.

"We are standing here on the beach just a few feet from where the new heir of the Halland consortium now resides," a young, attractive reporter said into the camera, her face a mask of professional seriousness. "We have been told by a reliable source that Jack Halland, a young man of just eighteen, signed off on a deal today, selling a small portion of his inherited businesses for the staggering sum of two-point-five billion dollars. While our source remains unnamed, we know now that this is a great deal and a significant power move. The young Jack Halland, originally from Washington, is set to live a life of unimaginable luxury and wealth."

Jack stared at the screen. He admired her polished looks but already hated her guts. She spoke about his life as if it were a commodity, his privacy a triviality. His phone buzzed, and he picked it up, seeing Ashley's name.

"Jack," she said, her voice warm.

"Hey. When you get here, I don't think you'll be able to get in. The whole area is swarming with reporters," he said, the frustration evident in his tone.

"I heard," she replied. "But Mr. Westmiller already told me to inform you that the security team is on its way. Your front and back perimeters should be clear in less than an hour."

Jack sighed, a small bit of the tension leaving him. "Thank you."

"So," she said, her voice dropping into a low, flirty purr. "Need some company for the night once the coast is clear?"

He chuckled, the familiar game a welcome distraction. "Still trying to insert yourself into my life, Ashley?"

She laughed. "Jack, please. I'm already one of your favorite girls."

He smirked. She wasn't wrong. "And what does that mean for me?" he asked, playing along.

"A few nice dinners now and then," she purred. "A shopping trip sometime, some lavish gifts, and of course, great sex."

He laughed with her, enjoying her blunt honesty. "No request to marry me?" he teased.

"Gods no, Jack," she said with a genuine laugh. "I like you, a lot. But you will not be the only guy I fuck."

The light, playful mood shattered instantly. Her words were a splash of cold water, directly challenging the new rulebook he had just written for his life. "Ashley," he said, his voice suddenly cold. "If you're going to be my girl, I expect to be the only one fucking you. I have no interest in you risking some disease from another guy only to give it to me, and then I pass it on to whoever else I'm with."

There was a sharp intake of breath on her end. "Double standards? You can have a stable of girls, but I can't have more than one guy?" she shot back, her voice laced with disbelief and anger.

Jack snorted, his own anger rising. "Ashley, I can afford to be an asshole. I can afford to have my own ideas and my own rules."

The line went silent for a few seconds.

"So here's the deal," he said, pressing his advantage, his voice hard. "If you don't like the idea that I'm the only one you're sleeping with, then we don't need to continue this… flirting. I like you, Ashley. But that's my only demand."

He thought he might have pushed her too far, that she would argue or try to negotiate. Instead, he heard a sharp, definitive *click* as she hung up the phone.

He stared at the dead screen, surprised by the abruptness of her rejection. He sighed, running a hand through his hair. He was a billionaire, besieged by the media in his own home, and he had just been hung up on. "Great," he mumbled to the empty room. "Guess I won't be getting any food delivered."

The silence in the mansion was absolute, broken only by the distant, rhythmic crash of the waves. Jack stared at his phone, the dead screen reflecting his own grim expression. Ashley had hung up on him. It was a minor rejection, but it was the first time since his world had turned upside down that someone had so decisively refused him. He was still processing the unfamiliar sting of it when the phone rang again, shrill and demanding. He looked at the screen: *Constance Westmiller.* With a sigh, he answered.

"Miss Westmiller," he said, his voice flat and tired.

"What the hell did you tell Ashley?" she asked, her voice sharp and devoid of the playful warmth from their earlier conversation. It was the voice of a business partner witnessing a strategic blunder.

Jack snorted, a humorless puff of air. "I told her my demand if she wanted to be one of my girls."

"*Demands*?" she repeated, the word dripping with incredulity. "Jack, she's a person, not a company you're acquiring."

"Yes, demands," he shot back, his own irritation rising. "I believe my new position affords me the ability to have some."

"And just what was this brilliant demand?" she asked, her tone laced with sarcasm.

"That if she is fucking me, I will be the only guy she is fucking," he said, the words blunt and crude.

Constance was silent for a second, and he could almost hear the gears turning in her sharp mind. When she spoke again, her anger had cooled, replaced by a tone of frustrated analysis. "And let me guess, she accused you of having double standards."

"She might be right," he admitted, not caring. "But I can afford to have them. I'm young, I'm rich, and I want to live my life. And if that means I choose to fuck fifty girls, I will demand that for the time they are with me, I am the only one they fuck. It's a simple rule."

"Jack," she started, her voice now carrying a note of pity that infuriated him. "It's not a simple rule; it's a stupid one. You're not in your small town anymore. You're trying to apply the possessive logic of a high school romance to a world that doesn't operate that way. Women like Ashley aren't impressed by jealousy; they're insulted by the attempt to control them."

"It's not about jealousy," he lied, though a part of him knew it was. "It's about... safety. Logistics."

"Oh, please," she scoffed. "This isn't about logistics. This is about you getting your heart broken by one girl and now you're trying to put a leash on every woman you meet. Ashley was an asset. She genuinely liked you. She could have been a loyal ally, a confidante. You had her in the palm of your hand, and instead of closing your fingers gently, you squeezed so hard she had no choice but to bite you and run."

Her words hit their mark, each one a perfectly aimed dart. He was being analyzed, dissected, and found wanting.

"You're acting like the boy who was cheated on, not the billionaire who just strong-armed some of the most powerful investors in the country," she continued, her voice relentless. "You're letting your past dictate the rules for your new life, and frankly, it was a bad move."

"No, Constance," he finally snapped, his voice rising, the frustration boiling over. He was tired of being wrong, tired of being told what he was feeling. "I am done with this. I am done with all of you telling me how I should feel or act. These are my terms. This is my life. Either you all fucking accept it, or you can leave me the hell alone!"

He jabbed the end call button, silencing her mid-sentence. He hurled the phone onto the massive bed, where it bounced on the plush duvet. The house was silent again, but now the silence felt accusatory. He stood in the center of the vast bedroom, a king in his castle, who in the course of a single afternoon had managed to alienate the only two women who understood his new world. He had the power, he had the money, but he was utterly, furiously alone.

Chapter 8.

For hours, he did not move. He sat in the armchair in the deepening gloom of the master suite, a statue carved from misery and anger. The seven calls that made his phone vibrate across the bed went unanswered. The several sharp knocks that echoed from the massive front door downstairs went ignored. He was a prisoner in his own mind, the palatial mansion a silent, indifferent cell.

The words of the women he had met in this new life ran through his thoughts on a torturous loop. Constance's voice, sharp with a logic he couldn't refute: *"You're acting like the boy who was cheated on, not the billionaire..."* And Ashley's parting shot, a casual blade that twisted in a wound he thought was beginning to scar over: *"I like you, a lot. But you will not be the only guy I fuck."*

Those words hurt more than they should have. They were an echo of Julie's betrayal, the same casual disregard for his feelings, for his desire to be the one and only. The familiar, sickening pain of seeing her with Brian returned with a vengeance. He replayed every conversation he'd had since this whirlwind began, searching for a foothold, for a moment of clarity, but finding only more confusion.

He finally became aware of his surroundings when he realized the room was pitch black, save for the faint, distant glow of Los Angeles. He looked out the massive window. The beach was deserted, the ocean a black, churning void. On the perimeter of his property, he could see two men in dark uniforms walking in a slow, deliberate pattern. The security team Arthur had sent. Another layer of his new, isolated reality.

With a groan, he pushed himself from the chair and walked to the bed, picking up the phone. The screen lit up with a dizzying cascade of notifications. Seven missed calls: three from Constance, one from Ashley, two from Arthur, and the last one from Julie. He smirked, a bitter twist of his lips. Below the calls were twenty-eight text messages. He decided to face the firing squad one by one.

He opened Ashley's first. *"You hurt me, Jack. I thought we could be good together, but you want to put chains on me."* The next was colder. *"I have informed Constance and Arthur Westmiller that I no longer wish to work on your account."* He dreaded the third one. *"I would have fucked you seven ways to Sunday every single day. There would have been no one else, but I always like to keep my options open. Now, however, they are wide open."* He deleted the thread, the final, taunting words a bitter pill.

He scrolled past a string of texts from reporters, including one from the woman on the beach, who had audaciously attached a professional headshot of herself. He deleted them without reading.

Then he opened Constance's. The first was practical. *"Your food, cellphone, and laptop are by your front door since you did not answer your phone or the knocks on the door."* The second, sent an hour later, was different. *"Jack, please call me. The silence worries both my father and me."* He sighed, a flicker of guilt mixing with his anger.

Finally, he opened the four messages from Julie. His heart hammered in his chest. *"Fuck, Jack, I saw the news. And to answer your question... yes. I will sign any paper you want. A prenup, anything. To be with you, I would do anything."* A slow smile spread across his face, the first genuine one of the day. The next text arrived. *"Jack, I received a call from the police. Brian has been arrested. He was found by a private investigator, and your name was involved."* His smile widened into a dark, satisfied smirk. The third message followed. *"Jack, Mom is asking if you need anything. We will come to you if you need us."* Then the last, worried message. *"You are not replying. Did I do something wrong?"*

He looked at the screen, at her complete and total surrender, at her offer of unconditional support. He typed back a careful reply. *"Julie, I had a bad day. Having problems with some people down here. It's best if you and your mother stay away for the time being. But I promise you this: you and I, we are not done."*

He sent the message and walked downstairs, the vast, empty house echoing with his footsteps. He peered through the peephole. Seeing no one, he opened the door and quickly pulled in the half-dozen paper grocery sacks. As he carried them into the kitchen, he could tell some of the food… milk, cheese… had been sitting out in the sun too long and would have to be thrown out. But as he unpacked the bags, he noticed Constance had added a twelve-pack of beer. A small, knowing, and deeply insightful gesture.

Even though he was three years shy of being legal, he twisted the cap off a bottle and took a long, deep drink. The bitter liquid was a shock to his system. He leaned against the marble island, the condensation from the bottle cold against his hand, and let out a short, sharp laugh. It was far from his first beer, but god, he needed this one.

It was hours later, deep in the night, that Jack finally surrendered. He peeled off his suit, leaving it in a heap on the floor, and slid between the cool, high-thread-count sheets of the vast bed that was now his. The time on his phone glowed with an alien blue light: 2:17 AM. He was adrift in the center of an ocean of mattress, the sheer size of the bed making him feel small and untethered. He closed his eyes, the scent of the clean, unfamiliar linens filling his senses, and wished with every fiber of his being that this was all just a fucking bad dream, that he would wake up in his old room in Washington, the only horror being the lingering ache of a teenage heartbreak.

As sleep finally came, it offered no escape. It was a dark, suffocating tide that pulled him under, into the cavernous great room of the Malibu house. But in the dream, the glass wall didn't look out onto a tranquil ocean; it revealed a churning, black sea under a bruised and starless sky.

The three women in his life were there. Julie and Constance stood off to the side, their arms linked, their faces beautiful, painted with identical, mocking smiles. Between them and him stood Ashley. She was impossibly lovely, her eyes filled not with the flirty desire he remembered, but with a cold, terrifying purpose. She walked toward him, and he found he couldn't move, his limbs turned to lead.

"I like you, a lot, Jack," she whispered, her dream-voice a silken caress as she reached him. She placed her hands on his chest, her touch not one of passion, but of a surgeon locating an incision point. He watched in silent, paralyzed horror as her fingers phased through his skin, her expression never changing. He felt a grotesque tearing sensation, a wet, hollow pressure, and she pulled her hands back. In her grasp, she held his heart, a glistening, still-beating thing.

As Ashley examined his heart with detached curiosity, the laughter began. It was a duet of cruelty, Julie and Constance laughing at his evisceration, the sound echoing in the vast, dark room. Behind Ashley, a new figure materialized from the shadows. Brian. He was shirtless, his muscles gleaming, his face a mask of smug satisfaction. His hands slid around Ashley's waist, pulling her back against him. He groped her ass, his eyes never leaving Jack's, a triumphant smirk on his lips.

"Maybe I'll fuck her like I fucked Julie," Brian's voice whispered, the sound crawling directly into Jack's ear.

A scream built in Jack's throat, a desperate, silent roar of rage and terror. He wanted to scream at Brian, to pull Ashley away from him, to save her, to get the fuck away from all of it. He was being dismantled, his past and present tormentors united in a single, perfect tableau of his own powerlessness.

He woke up with the scream tearing from his own throat, a raw, ragged sound that shattered the profound silence of the mansion. He lurched upright in the massive bed, drenched in a cold sweat, his heart hammering against his ribs as if trying to escape. The sheets were twisted around his legs. The ghost images of the nightmare… Ashley's cold eyes, Brian's smirk, the sound of that laughter… still clung to the shadows of the room.

"Fuck," he gasped, running a shaking hand through his damp hair. He was alone. Utterly alone in a palace he now owned. And in that terrifying moment of clarity, he realized the ultimate, cruel irony of his new life. The three women who dominated his thoughts… Ashley had abandoned him, Constance was a potential adversary, and the only one still talking to him, the only one offering him comfort, was Julie. The one who had started it all. The one who had hurt him the most.

The frantic, ragged breaths from his nightmare eventually subsided, replaced by the deep, oppressive silence of the mansion. Sleep was a lost cause now. Jack sat on the edge of the enormous bed, his head in his hands, the ghost images of his dream… Ashley's cold eyes, Brian's smug face… still clinging to the shadows of the room. He was exhausted, but his mind was a hornet's nest of anger, fear, and a bitter, burgeoning cynicism.

He was contemplating the absurdity of his new life when a sound, sharp and alien, shattered the quiet. A polite, electronic chime from the front door, followed by a firm, decisive knock.

He froze, his muscles tensing. Who the hell would be here? It was early, the sun just beginning to cast a pale, golden light over the ocean. The security guards were supposed to be keeping people away. His first instinct was that it was another reporter who had somehow slipped through the new perimeter. A fresh wave of irritation washed over him.

The doorbell chimed again, more insistent this time. He wasn't going to ignore it. He was done hiding. With a groan, he pushed himself off the bed. He caught his reflection in a full-length mirror… a sweaty, shirtless boy in rumpled boxer shorts, his hair a mess, his eyes wide and haunted. He looked like a victim. He refused to be seen that way.

He stalked into the cavernous master bathroom, the cold marble floor a shock to his bare feet. He leaned over the wide basin and splashed his face with icy water again and again, the shock chasing away the last dregs of his nightmare. He stared at his reflection, at the pale, tired face looking back at him. He saw the boy from Washington, but something else was there now, too… a harder set to his jaw, a colder light in his eyes.

He walked back into the bedroom and found the expensive suitcase he had arrived with, still lying open on a luggage rack. He pulled out the new, clean clothes he had bought… a pair of dark trousers and a simple, crisp white shirt. As he dressed, it felt like he was putting on a costume, a uniform for the role he was now forced to play: Mr. Halland.

Now looking composed, he walked down the floating staircase, the sound of his footsteps echoing in the cavernous great room. As he reached the bottom, he pulled out his phone to check the time, and saw a new text message. It was from Constance.

"First assistant interview today at nine am."

He stared at the message, then at the time on his phone: 8:54 AM. They hadn't even waited a full day. The relentless pace of his new life was already set.

"Well, she is punctual," he mumbled to himself, a humorless smirk touching his lips.

He reached the massive front door and called out, his voice steady and controlled. "Who is it?"

A clear, confident female voice replied from the other side. "Mr. Halland? My name is Fiona Johnson. Mr. Westmiller sent me to talk to you."

Jack took one last, deep breath, smoothing the front of his shirt. He was no longer the boy who woke up screaming. He was the employer. He was the one in charge. He turned the heavy lock and pulled the door open.

Standing on his porch, silhouetted against the bright morning sun, was a young woman who was so breathtakingly beautiful it took him a moment to process. She was tall and slender, with cascades of honey-blonde hair and intelligent blue eyes. Dressed in a sharp, impeccably tailored navy-blue business suit, she held a leather portfolio in one hand and offered him a polite, professional smile that didn't quite mask the ambitious glint in her gaze. She was the first candidate. The game had already begun.

"Come in, please," Jack said, stepping back to hold the massive door open.

Fiona Johnson walked in, her professional smile unwavering, though her eyes widened almost imperceptibly as she took in the cavernous great room and the stunning, sun-drenched view of the Pacific. She moved with a practiced poise, her heels clicking softly on the polished marble floor. "Thank you, Mr. Halland."

He guided her toward the living area, a space dominated by two oversized, cream-colored recliners facing each other in front of the glass wall. It felt less like a living room and more like a therapist's office or a negotiation chamber. He gestured for her to take one, and he sat in the other, sinking into the plush leather. "So, you're here for the assistant position?" he asked, getting straight to the point.

She nodded, placing her leather portfolio neatly in her lap. "Yes, sir. Mr. Westmiller told me a bit about the position. As I understand it, I will be working very closely with you, running your schedule, arranging appointments, and managing the day-to-day logistics of your homes."

Jack nodded slowly, studying her. She was a fortress of professionalism. It was time to test the walls. "There's more to it than that," he said, his voice low and serious. "You'll need to know everything about me. My finances, my travel, my social engagements. Everything I do. There can be no secrets between us."

She met his intense gaze without blinking. "So I was told, sir. Discretion is one of my primary qualifications."

He leaned forward slightly, a ghost of a smirk on his lips. "And your... personal preferences?" he asked, the question deliberately ambiguous and loaded with unspoken meaning.

Fiona's polite smile tightened, becoming a hard, thin line. A shield of ice seemed to descend over her blue eyes. "Mr. Halland," she began, her voice suddenly devoid of all warmth. "While I understand that in positions like this, a certain... intimacy can be presumed, I would like to make my position unequivocally clear. I am not inclined to participate in that sort of behavior. In fact, I find the idea of men touching me to be utterly revolting."

The statement was so blunt, so shocking, it almost made him laugh.

"However," she continued, her confidence unwavering, "I can assure you that even though I have no desire to have sex with you, I will be the most efficient, loyal, and capable assistant you could ever think of having. My professional capabilities are entirely separate from my personal inclinations."

Jack kept the smirk on the inside. *Yeah, right.* The speech was too polished, too prepared. He didn't believe a word of it, but he found her angle fascinating. A woman who claims to be repulsed by men would be the perfect person to vet the women he *did* want to sleep with. A beautiful, untouchable gatekeeper.

"I appreciate your candor, Ms. Johnson," he said smoothly. "And I will, of course, take that into consideration when I make my final decision."

Her composure finally cracked. A flicker of genuine disbelief crossed her face. "You seem to misunderstand, sir," she said, her tone suddenly condescending. "I *am* your assistant."

Jack actually snorted, a short, sharp burst of derisive laughter. "That would be a no," he said, enjoying the look of shock that washed over her. "You see, you are the *first* candidate I am interviewing. There will be others to talk to before I make my decision."

"I was led to believe this was a done deal!" she huffed, her voice rising as she shot to her feet. The poised professional had vanished, replaced by an indignant, spoiled woman who had just been denied something she thought she was owed.

"That may be," Jack said calmly, not bothering to stand. "But it was not a deal made by me."

She huffed again, her face flushed with anger and embarrassment. Without another word, she turned on her heel and stormed out, her sharp, angry footsteps echoing through the mansion until the heavy front door slammed shut behind her.

Jack chuckled to himself, pulling out his phone. He sent a quick text to Constance.

"Candidate number one. Arrogant and a terrible liar. It's a no."

After the high-stakes drama of the interview and its aftermath, a profound exhaustion settled over Jack. He walked upstairs, the silence of the mansion a stark contrast to the chaos in his head. All he wanted was a shower, a simple act of normalcy to wash away the lingering grime of his nightmare and the tension of the morning.

He undressed, letting the expensive new clothes fall to the floor, and walked into the vast marble bathroom. He turned the sleek chrome handle, and a torrent of hot water cascaded from the ceiling, instantly filling the glass enclosure with a thick cloud of steam. But as the steam swirled around him, it conjured an unwelcome ghost. The image of his dream… of Ashley, her hands on his chest… flashed in his mind. The memory of her touch, both in the dream and in reality, was a brand he couldn't ignore. He felt a sudden, desperate urge, a need to fix the mistake he had made.

Stark naked, with the bathroom fogging around him, he grabbed his phone from the vanity. His fingers were trembling slightly as he dialed her number, half-expecting her not to answer.

She picked up on the third ring. "Mr. Halland," she said, her voice a wall of ice. "I believe I made it quite clear that I am no longer involved with your account."

"Ashley... I owe you an apology," he said, the words feeling clumsy and inadequate.

There was a profound silence on the other end, so long he thought she had hung up again.

"I treated you wrong," he continued, his voice softer, more vulnerable than he intended. "And I understand why you're angry. But this is all new to me, and I have... issues. Baggage."

He heard her sigh, a long, slow exhalation that seemed to carry some of her anger away with it. "Jack," she said, her voice losing its hard edge, "Constance told me about your old girlfriend. About what happened."

Relief washed over him. He wasn't just a rich asshole to her anymore; he was a person with a history. "I know what I said was harsh," he admitted, leaning against the cool marble wall as the steam enveloped him. "But it's true. I don't feel comfortable knowing the girls I'm with are with other men."

"Jack, if I'm fucking you, I'm not just going to go around and fuck everybody," she said, a hint of frustration in her voice. "But it's nice to have the *option*. It's about the freedom. What if Mr. Right is out there, and I miss him because I'm in a non-exclusive arrangement with a billionaire who has fifty other girls?"

He smirked, a real, tired smile this time. "What if *I* was Mr. Right?" he asked, the question a half-serious probe.

She actually laughed, a genuine, warm sound that made his stomach flutter. "You could be. But I'm not ready to get married, Jack. And neither are you."

He snorted. "You're right. I'm only eighteen."

A beat of silence passed, and then her voice dropped to a conspiratorial whisper. "So, you miss me?"

"Fuck, you have no idea," he breathed, the confession torn from him. "This is the hardest phone call I've made in years."

She laughed again, a sound of victory this time. "Okay, Jack. If we fuck, I will still not work on your contract at Westmiller. That's a professional boundary. But… I will advise you when you need it. Off the books."

An idea, bold and audacious, crystallized in his mind. "What if you were my assistant?" he asked.

Her laughter was sharp with disbelief. "And quit my job with Westmiller and Sons? Are you insane?"

"Why not?" he pressed.

"Jack, they pay me well. Very, very well. I have a career there."

"I'll give you a million a year," he said without a moment's hesitation, the number sounding both absurd and perfectly natural on his tongue.

The silence on her end was absolute. He had dropped a bomb, and he waited for the fallout.

"You're serious?" she finally whispered, her voice filled with shock.

"Completely," he said, his own confidence surging. "There will be another administrative assistant, one of the people your old firm is sending over. But I trust you, Ashley. You were willing to walk away from all of this because of your own principles. I admire that. I need someone like that by my side."

"But if I'm your assistant, why hire another one?" she asked, her mind already working through the logistics.

He smiled. "You won't be a normal assistant. You'll be with me. Everywhere I go. The other one will be the gatekeeper, the scheduler, the one who handles the mundane. And she will answer to you. And to me."

He was offering her a position of immense, unparalleled power. His chief of staff. His right hand.

"Jack," she said, her voice now deadly serious. "If I do this, you will sign a contract with me. A personal services contract. Ten years minimum."

"Deal," he said instantly. "And I'll pay Westmiller for the loss."

Her laugh was triumphant. "When do you need me?"

He smirked, feeling a surge of power and desire. "Two hours ago."

"I'll be there soon," she said, and hung up.

A wide grin spread across Jack's face. He had won. He immediately dialed Arthur Westmiller.

"Jack," the lawyer answered, his tone relieved.

"Arthur," Jack replied, enjoying the use of the older man's first name. "I regret to inform you that you no longer have Ashley Albright working for you."

"And why is that?" Arthur asked, a note of caution in his voice.

Jack smiled. "Because she is now my personal assistant. I'll hire another one from the candidates you're sending over to handle the administrative work."

Arthur Westmiller burst out laughing, a deep, booming sound of genuine admiration. "You sweet-talked her? Convinced her to leave a partner track position?"

Jack chuckled. "You could say that. So, I'm offering to pay you for your loss. I know there are expenses involved in losing a woman of her caliber. Say, a million dollars, to give you a chance to hire someone new."

"That is very generous of you, Jack," Arthur said, his voice filled with respect. "And though it is entirely unnecessary, I will accept."

"I thought you might," Jack said.

They said their goodbyes, and Jack finally ended the call. He placed the phone on the dry vanity and stepped under the torrent of hot water, a king who had just successfully poached his rival's most valuable knight. The water washed over him, and for the first time since he'd arrived in this new world, he felt like he was finally cleaning away the past.

Chapter 9.

Getting dressed when your entire wardrobe consists of two suits makes the choice of what to wear remarkably easy. As Jack pulled on the trousers from the day before, he made a mental note to have Ashley, his newly hired and most important asset, arrange for a complete overhaul of his closet. He needed clothes for this new life… casual clothes for the beach, sharp outfits for meetings, comfortable things for just existing in this palace he now called home.

He picked up his new phone and saw a text from Julie had come in during the night. He opened it, his heart giving a familiar, painful lurch.

"Jack… I am so glad you are not mad at me… and I hope we can see each other soon. This pregnancy is killing me for several reasons. One, it is not your child… and God, I wanted it to be. Two, I will not keep it, so I feel like I am just carrying it for nothing. And three… it prevents me from flying to L.A. right now to come and be with you."

He smirked, a sad, complicated expression. He would answer her later. He needed to process the raw, painful honesty of her message. He went downstairs and started a cup of coffee. He was relieved to find his father had owned a Keurig, with a neatly stacked library of coffee pods beside it. It was a small, mundane detail that made the man he never knew feel slightly more real.

With the hot coffee in hand, he walked to the glass wall overlooking the back of the property. He could see his two security guards walking their patterns along the edge of the sand. Further down the beach, he saw some of the girls from the house next door. Two of them, standing on their own private stretch of beach, were pointing up towards his house, directly at him. On impulse, he lifted his coffee cup in a silent greeting. To his surprise, they both giggled and waved back enthusiastically. He smiled. *Maybe... just maybe he could fuck one of them sometime,* he thought, the idea feeling less like a fantasy and more like a future possibility.

A firm knock on the front door pulled him from his reverie. He walked over and looked through the peephole. It was Ashley. A wide grin spread across his face as he unlocked and opened the door.

She hurried in, her arms laden with grocery bags, and the moment the door clicked shut behind her, she dropped everything. The bags tumbled to the marble floor with a soft thud as she launched herself at him, her arms wrapping around his neck, her mouth finding his in a deep, hungry kiss that tasted of coffee and want.

"You better not be lying about your offer," she whispered against his lips, her breath warm and ragged.

He kissed her again, pulling her flush against him. "Every word was the truth," he confirmed.

She pulled back, a triumphant, brilliant smile on her face. From her designer handbag, she pulled out a thick stack of papers bound in a blue legal folder. "Arthur drew up the contract right after you talked to him," she said, her smirk returning. "He almost fell out of his chair when I told him what you were offering to pay me."

Jack laughed, taking the contract from her. He leaned against the wall, flipping through the pages. Most of it was standard legal jargon, but a few highlighted clauses caught his eye. "What is this one?" he asked, pointing.

Her smile was sharp and knowing. "That says that if you marry me during the term of this contract, you are still obligated to pay out the remainder of my salary as a lump sum. So if we get divorced, I have the money to live. It also states that I agree, in the event of a marriage proposal from you, to sign any prenuptial agreement you see fit."

He smirked, impressed by her foresight. She was playing chess, not checkers. "And the other one?" he asked, pointing to the next highlighted section.

"That," she said, her voice dropping slightly, "is the child provision. It states that should I have a child with you, I will commit to a conclusive blood test proving it is yours. In turn, you will pay a one-time, tax-free trust settlement of fifty million dollars to ensure the child is cared for, privately and luxuriously, for the rest of his or her life. It relinquishes me from all parental duties and you from all future financial obligations."

Jack smiled. Cold, clean, and brutally efficient. "Any others I need to know?"

She pointed to the last one, her finger tracing the words. She leaned in close, her voice a low whisper in his ear. "For the duration of this ten-year contract, I promise to only fuck you, unless you give me explicit, written permission otherwise."

He grabbed her, his hand tangling in her hair, and kissed her hard. He pulled back, his eyes searching hers. "And if Mr. Right comes along?" he asked, testing her.

She smiled, a slow, sensual expression that made his pulse race. "In ten years, we might just be ready for that next step... Mr. Right," she whispered.

Jack felt a surge of triumph. He had won. He took the offered pen. He signed his name on the line, the signature of a boy now legally binding him to a future he couldn't have imagined a week ago. Ashley signed her own name with a confident flourish. They each took a copy of the contract, a document that was both a declaration of employment and the most intimate of treaties.

Ashley's touch was electric, her fingers burning a trail across Jack's chest as she leaned in, her voice a husky whisper. "Now what's first on the agenda?" she purred, her eyes glinting with a hunger that matched his own. Jack's response was a predatory smile as he captured her hand, his grip tight and dominating. He yanked her towards the sofa, a dark, secluded spot where no prying eyes could intrude on their privacy.

He pushed her down onto the cushions, his body covering hers as he kissed her with a ferocity that left her dizzy. His lips devoured hers, his tongue invading her mouth, exploring every inch. His hands were everywhere, tearing at her clothes with a desperation that spoke volumes about the extent of his desire. He pushed her pants down roughly, exposing her already soaked pussy to his eager gaze.

Turning her around, he bent her over the arm of the sofa, her ass presented to him like an offering. "Now you're going to get what I've been craving for the past twenty-four fucking hours," he growled, his voice hoarse with need. He quickly shed his own pants, his cock springing free, hard and throbbing. He rubbed the head against her wetness, coating himself in her juices before plunging deep into her with one powerful thrust.

"Fuck!" Ashley screamed, her body arching back to meet his. "Yes, Jack, yes!" She was soaking wet, her pussy clenching around him, trying to milk him dry. He began to move, his hips slamming against her ass, his balls slapping against her clit with each brutal thrust. The room filled with the sounds of their frenzied coupling… the wet slapping of flesh, their ragged breaths, and their desperate moans.

Jack's hands gripped her hips, his fingers digging into her soft flesh as he pounded into her. He leaned down, his chest pressing against her back as he whispered in her ear, "You feel so fucking good, Ashley. So tight, so wet. I could stay buried inside you forever." His words sent shivers down her spine, and she came undone, her body convulsing around him as she screamed her release.

But Jack wasn't done. He pulled out, his cock glistening with her juices, and turned her to face him. He kissed her again, his tongue exploring her mouth as he walked her backwards until she was sitting on the sofa. He pushed her legs apart, exposing her swollen, glistening pussy to his hungry gaze. He knelt down, his tongue licking a path from her ass to her clit, making her cry out in pleasure.

He sucked on her clit, his tongue flicking against the sensitive nub as he inserted two fingers into her tight channel. He curled his fingers, hitting that spot inside her that drove her wild. She bucked against his hand, her body begging for more. He added another finger, stretching her, preparing her for his cock. "Jack, please," she begged, her voice a desperate whimper. "I need you inside me. I need you to fuck me."

He stood up, his cock throbbing and leaking pre-cum. He positioned himself at her entrance, his eyes locked on hers as he slowly pushed into her. Inch by inch, he filled her again, stretching her, completing her. She wrapped her legs around him, urging him deeper. He began to move, his hips rolling as he fucked her slow and deep. He leaned down, capturing her mouth in a passionate kiss as their bodies moved in sync.

Jack's hands roamed her body, squeezing her breasts, pinching her nipples, leaving a trail of fire in their wake. He broke the kiss, his lips trailing down her neck, her collarbone, until he reached her breasts. He took one nipple into his mouth, sucking hard, his tongue swirling around the sensitive bud. He bit down gently, making her gasp as he marked her as his. He moved to the other breast, giving it the same attention, his hands squeezing and kneading her flesh.

Ashley's body was on fire, her blood boiling with desire. She could feel her orgasm building, her body tightening as she climbed higher and higher. Jack could feel it too, his cock swelling inside her as he chased his own release. "Come for me, Ashley," he growled, his voice a low rumble in his chest. "Let me feel that tight pussy milk me dry." And she did. Her body exploded, her inner muscles clenching around him, her juices gushing out, soaking them both.

The sensation sent Jack over the edge. With a roar, he thrust deep into her, his cock pulsing as he filled her with his hot seed. He collapsed on top of her, his body slick with sweat, his breath coming in ragged gasps. She wrapped her arms around him, holding him close as they both came down from their high.

Jack rolled off her, pulling her into his arms as he lay on his back. He kissed the top of her head, a contented smile on his face. "Best fucking assistant ever," he murmured, his eyes already drifting closed. Ashley snuggled into his chest, a satisfied smile playing on her lips. "I aim to please, boss," she replied, her voice drowsy with satisfaction.

The initial, frenzied storm of their passion had subsided, leaving a warm, languid intimacy in its wake. They stood together under the heavy spray of the rain shower, the water sluicing over their sated bodies. Ashley leaned her head against Jack's shoulder, her fingers tracing idle, delicate patterns across his chest. The silence was comfortable, broken only by the drumming of the water on the marble floor.

"So, Jack," she whispered, her voice a low, sultry purr that was barely audible over the shower's roar. "Now that the first item on the agenda is… handled… do you have any actual work for me?"

He chuckled, a deep, contented sound. He turned, pulling her fully against him, her slick skin sliding against his. "Yeah, I do," he whispered back, his lips close to her ear. "But I needed this first. I needed *you*. To feel something real after the last few days."

She hugged herself tightly against him, a gesture of profound, unguarded affection. "Me too," she confessed. "More than you know."

"I'll need clothes," Jack said, a practical thought breaking through the haze of pleasure. He smiled. "I have exactly two suits, and after today, they are both not exactly clean anymore."

She smiled back, already shifting into her new role. "Okay. Suits, casual wear, beach wear, formal wear? What are your sizes? Any brands you like or hate? We'll need to do a full overhaul of that empty closet."

"All of it," he said. "A full overhaul. And everything else. Food, drinks, whatever you think I could possibly need to actually live in this place." He soaped his hands and began to gently wash her back, his touch now tender and slow.

"I'll have to go into town for a proper shopping run," she said, leaning into his touch. He soaped her body, his hands running reverently over her shoulders, her stomach, and then her chest. She moaned softly as his thumbs brushed against her nipples, her head falling back against his arm.

"Did you get the new cellphone and laptop?" she asked, her voice slightly breathless.

He nodded. "Yeah. They're with the groceries. I just haven't set them up yet."

"And that new phone will be for personal stuff?" she clarified.

"Exactly," he confirmed. "I need to reach out to a few people, give them a number that isn't going to be plastered all over the news by tomorrow."

She kissed his neck softly. "Julie?" she whispered, the question gentle, without a hint of jealousy.

He nodded, the simple movement a heavy confession. "I love her," he whispered, the words tasting of truth and pain. "Always have, always will."

Ashley was quiet for a moment, processing this. "Do you think she'll hurt you again?" she asked, her voice laced with genuine concern.

He shook his head, a weary but certain gesture. "No. I believe her. She's hurting like I was. Well, not exactly like I was, but she's lost and alone. I get it."

"And her baby?" Ashley asked, her voice soft.

"She's giving him up for adoption," he said.

Ashley nodded slowly against his chest. "I can see that. It's a hard situation." She tilted her head back to look him in the eyes, her expression serious. "Jack, just be sure you want this. Be sure you're ready for all of it. I never want to see you get hurt like that."

He pulled her into a deep, searching kiss, a kiss of gratitude and trust. "That's why you're here, Ashley," he said against her lips. "To make sure I don't fuck up."

She smiled, a slow, wicked grin spreading across her face. "And to fuck you," she whispered, her eyes sparkling.

He chuckled and nodded, the sound echoing in the steamy chamber. "Yeah," he said. "Lots, and lots of that."

The warm, lingering afterglow of their shower left them in a state of tranquil intimacy. Dressed now in the clean, simple clothes he'd arrived in, Jack sat on one of the plush sofas, nursing the cold beer Constance had thoughtfully provided. Ashley, having organized the groceries in the vast, empty kitchen, came and curled up beside him, her head resting on his shoulder, her fingers tracing idle patterns on his chest. The setting sun painted the room in hues of orange and gold.

"By the way," she whispered, her voice a sultry purr against his skin, "Constance told me to remind you that your next interview is tomorrow morning at nine a.m."

He felt her smile against his neck.

"She also said to promise you that this one, unlike the last one, actually likes men," Ashley continued, her eyes twinkling with amusement. "And that she is very interested in being a 'true assistant'… in every way you might want."

Jack smirked. "And you know her?"

"I know her," Ashley confirmed. "Her name is Jenny. And trust me, she will be a lot to handle… she's smart, she's ambitious, and she doesn't miss a trick. But if she works for you, if you earn her respect, she will be fiercely loyal."

He nodded, taking a slow drink of his beer. "Arthur's advice was to talk to them all. He said there were others."

"There are," Ashley said, sitting up slightly to look him in the eye, her expression shifting from playful to serious. Her role as lover receded, and his new Chief of Staff emerged. "There are six candidates in total that Arthur vetted based on their résumés. But now that I am your assistant, Jack, my first official duty is to tell you that four of them are not right for you."

He raised an eyebrow, intrigued. "And why is that?"

"Because Arthur is a brilliant lawyer, but he's a sixty-year-old man who only sees what's on paper. I know these girls, or at least their type," she said, her voice dropping to a conspiratorial tone. "Two of them are what we call 'aspirational influencers.' They see you as a meal ticket to a lifetime of yacht parties and Instagram content. Their only loyalty is to their own brand. The other two," she paused, her expression hardening, "are far more dangerous. They're the ones who see you as a husband. And if you have a relationship with them and *don't* propose, they will be the first to claim rape and abuse when you try to end it. They'll see it as their golden parachute."

He frowned, a cold knot forming in his stomach. "Why would Arthur even send them to me?"

She shook her head. "He doesn't know their motives like I do. I went to school with one of them. I've worked with the other three at different events and firms before I started at Westmiller. I've seen how they operate. Arthur sees a summa cum laude graduate from UCLA; I see a predator in a designer suit."

He nodded, a chill running down his spine. He was out of his depth, and he knew it. "And the other two? Jenny is one of them?"

Ashley's smirk returned, sharp and confident. "Yes. Jenny Johnson and another woman named Maya, Maya Alvarez. They are both beautiful, incredibly intelligent, and ruthlessly ambitious. But their ambition is different. They aren't looking for a husband or a life of leisure. They're looking for the job of a lifetime. This job," she whispered, leaning in to kiss him softly. "They want to be attached to power. Their loyalty is guaranteed because your continued success becomes the foundation for their own."

He processed her words, the cynical logic a perfect echo of his father's advice. This was the game. He now had a player on his side who knew the other team's playbook. He put his beer down and took her hand, his expression firm and decisive.

"Well, as my new Senior Personal Assistant," he said, testing out the title, "I expect you to call Arthur Westmiller first thing in the morning. Tell him that I have reviewed the candidate list, and I will only be speaking to Ms. Johnson and Ms. Alvarez. The other four interviews are to be canceled immediately."

Her smile was dazzling, a mixture of pride, respect, and arousal. "As you wish, boss," she said, her voice a low, throaty murmur. She leaned in and kissed him again, a slow, deep kiss that sealed their new partnership, a complex treaty of business, pleasure, and power.

That night, Jack slipped into bed, his arms wrapped around Ashley's naked body. He pulled her close, her back pressed against his chest, his cock already hardening against her soft ass. She wiggled against him, a soft moan escaping her lips as she pushed back, encouraging him. He reached around, his hand cupping her breast, his fingers teasing her nipple until it was a hard peak. He pinched it gently, making her gasp as he ground his cock against her.

He trailed kisses down her neck, his stubble rough against her soft skin, leaving a path of goosebumps in his wake. His other hand snaked down her stomach, his fingers dipping into her wetness, coating himself in her juices. He circled her clit, making her buck against his hand, her breath coming in short gasps. He slipped two fingers into her tight channel, curling them to hit that spot that drove her wild. He fucked her with his fingers, his palm grinding against her clit with each movement.

Ashley reached behind her, her hand gripping his cock, stroking him slowly as he continued to finger-fuck her. He groaned in her ear, his teeth nipping at her lobe as he increased his pace, his fingers scissoring inside her, stretching her, preparing her for his cock. She turned her head, capturing his lips in a passionate kiss, her tongue exploring his mouth as their bodies moved in sync.

Jack broke the kiss, his breath ragged as he positioned himself at her entrance. He pushed into her slowly, inch by inch, feeling her stretch around him, her tight pussy gripping him like a vice. He began to move, his hips rolling as he fucked her slow and deep. His hand snaked around, his fingers finding her clit, rubbing it in slow circles as he pounded into her.

Ashley's body was on fire, her blood boiling with desire. She could feel her orgasm building, her body tightening as she climbed higher and higher. Jack could feel it too, his cock swelling inside her as he chased his own release. "Come for me, Ashley," he growled, his voice a low rumble in his chest. "Let me feel that tight pussy." And she did. Her body exploded, her inner muscles clenching around him.

The sensation sent Jack over the edge. With a roar, he thrust deep into her, his cock pulsing as he filled her with his hot seed. They both collapsed, their bodies slick with sweat, their breaths coming in ragged gasps. Ashley snuggled into his chest, a satisfied smile playing on her lips as they both drifted off to sleep, their bodies still joined, their hearts beating in sync.

Jack's dreams were a vivid, erotic fantasy. He was in a large, opulent bedroom, a king on his throne of a bed. Ashley was there, her lips wrapped around his cock, her head bobbing up and down as she took him deep into her throat. He could feel her tongue swirling around his shaft, her hands cupping his balls, rolling them gently as she sucked him off.

Julie was there too, her lips on his, her tongue exploring his mouth as she straddled his chest, her pussy grinding against him. He could feel her wetness, her heat, as she rubbed herself against him, her moans filling his ears. He reached up, his hands squeezing her breasts, his fingers pinching her nipples, making her cry out in pleasure.

In the background, Constance stood naked, her body on display, her hands roaming her curves as she moaned his name. "Jack," she called, her voice a sultry purr. "Fuck me, Jack. I need you inside me." He looked at her, his cock throbbing in Ashley's mouth as he imagined taking Constance from behind, her ass pushing out, begging for his cock.

There were other women too, their faces blurry, their bodies perfect. They were all there for him, their hands and mouths exploring his body, their moans and whispers of pleasure filling the air. He was a king, a god, and they were his for the taking. He could feel their lips on his neck, his chest, his stomach, his cock, his balls. He was surrounded by pleasure, drowning in it, and he never wanted to surface.

Ashley's mouth on his cock was driving him wild. He could feel his orgasm building, his balls tightening as she took him deeper, her fingers digging into his thighs as she bobbed her head faster, her saliva coating his cock, making it glisten in the low light. He looked down at her, her eyes locked on his as she sucked him off, her tongue never stopping its relentless assault on his shaft.

He came with a roar, his cock pulsing as he filled her mouth with his hot seed. She took it all, swallowing every drop as she continued to suck him, milking him for all he was worth. He collapsed back, his body sated, his mind blown as he drifted deeper into his erotic dream, his women surrounding him, their bodies pressing against his, their lips on his, their hands exploring him, their moans of pleasure filling his ears.

Jack jolted awake, his body tensed, his heart pounding in his chest as he surfaced from his erotic dream. He took a moment to orient himself, his breathing ragged as the remnants of his fantasy clung to him like a second skin. He became aware of the warm, soft body pressed against him, the gentle rise and fall of Ashley's chest, and the reality of his situation dawned on him. He was hard, painfully so, and Ashley was grinning at him, her lips glistening with a secret smile.

" Quite a compliment, waking up with you hard against my ass," she whispered, her voice a husky purr that sent shivers down his spine. "I had to give you what you needed." She licked her lips slowly, sensually, her eyes never leaving his as she crawled up his body, her naked flesh pressing against him, igniting every nerve ending. She straddled his hips, her wet pussy pressing against his cock, and he groaned, his hands gripping her thighs, his fingers digging into her soft flesh.

She leaned down, her lips capturing his in a deep, passionate kiss. He could taste himself on her, the salty, musky flavor of his own desire, and he didn't care. He kissed her back, his tongue exploring her mouth, his body aching with need. "Fuck, Ashley," he whispered against her lips, his voice hoarse with desire. "I've never woken up like that before. Never had a blowjob from someone I woke up with. I have never tried that before." His confession hung in the air, a testament to the intensity of their connection.

Ashley smiled, a wicked, knowing smile that promised more. "Happy to assist," she whispered, emphasizing the word 'assist,' a reminder of her role, of their dynamic. She kissed him again, her body grinding against his, her breasts pressing against his chest, her nipples hard and begging for attention. He reached up, cupping her face, his thumbs brushing against her cheeks as he deepened the kiss, his body begging for more.

She broke away, her breath ragged, her cheeks flushed. "You have two hours before the interview," she reminded him, her voice steady despite the desire burning in her eyes. She stood up, her body glowing in the soft light, a vision of pure sex and temptation. She held out her hand, helping him up, her touch sending electric shocks through his body.

"Go shower," she instructed, her voice firm yet gentle. "I'll go buy some clothes and return before she comes." She turned to leave, her hips swaying with each step, her naked body a feast for his eyes. She picked up her clothes, her movements graceful and efficient, and began to dress, her eyes never leaving his.

Jack watched her, his body aching with need, his mind a whirl of desire and confusion. He turned and headed to the bathroom, his steps heavy, his body throbbing with unspent desire. He turned on the shower, the steam filling the room, a stark contrast to the cold reality of their situation. As he stepped under the spray, the hot water cascading over his body, Ashley stuck her head in, her eyes sparkling with mischief.

"Jack, I know you're not old enough, but should I get more beer?" she asked, her voice teasing, a reminder of their age difference, of the power dynamic between them. He chuckled, a deep, rumbling sound that echoed in the small room. "Please," he replied, his voice hoarse, his body still aching with need. She smiled, a slow, sensual smile that promised more to come.

"Be right back," she said, her voice a sultry purr as she left, the door clicking shut behind her. Jack leaned against the cool tiles, his body under the hot spray, his mind a whirl of erotic images and sensations. He took a deep breath, his body finally beginning to relax as he let the water wash over him, cleansing him, preparing him for the day ahead.

Chapter 10.

The shower was a sanctuary, a chamber of steam and roaring water that felt worlds away from the cold, haunted silence of his past life. Jack stood under the torrent, letting the near-scalding water beat against his shoulders and back, willing it to wash away more than just the sweat of his nightmares. He wanted it to peel back the very memory of the boy who had stood paralyzed in the park, the boy who had crumpled on a dusty floor in Washington, the boy who had woken up screaming in this very house. The water sluiced over him, and with it, the ghosts of the last few days seemed to retreat, leaving him feeling scoured, raw, and strangely new.

When he finally twisted the sleek chrome handle, the sudden quiet was just as profound as the noise had been. He stepped out onto a plush, dark grey bath mat that felt like a cloud under his bare feet and wrapped himself in a towel so thick and heavy it felt more like a robe. He caught his reflection in the fogged-up, wall-sized mirror. Wiping a clear patch with his hand, he stared at the face looking back. It was still his, but the haunted, hollowed-out look in his eyes was being replaced by something harder, more calculating. Arthur's voice echoed in his mind. *A personal trainer... a chef...* He looked at his own lean, almost lanky frame. He wasn't a boy anymore, not really. He was a billionaire. An emperor of a kingdom he didn't know how to rule. He needed to look the part. The suggestion wasn't about vanity; it was about armor.

"Not a bad idea," he whispered, the words fogging the small patch of clear glass.

"What's not a bad idea, boss?"

He turned. Ashley was leaning against the bedroom doorframe, a vision of casual power in dark jeans and a simple white blouse that somehow looked more expensive than his entire old wardrobe. She was holding a shopping bag, and her lips were curved into a knowing, appreciative smile as her eyes roamed his naked body, lingering for a moment before meeting his gaze.

"If you greet your next interviewee like that," she said, her voice a low purr as she sauntered into the room. "The job discussion might get… accelerated."

He felt a flush creep up his neck but covered it with a smirk. "First of all…" he began, walking towards her, making no move to cover himself.

She laughed, a throaty, genuine sound. "First of all, what?"

"Arthur suggested I get a personal trainer. And a chef," he explained, stopping just before her.

Ashley nodded, her expression shifting from lover to chief of staff. "I know a few," she said. "The best, actually. People who are discreet and used to our kind of lifestyle… the lifestyle you are looking for. I'll vet them personally."

"Of course you do," he said, the corner of his mouth twitching. She handed him the bag from a high-end boutique he'd never heard of. He pulled out a pair of soft, tailored linen trousers and a fine-gauge cashmere sweater in a deep charcoal grey. The fabric felt impossibly soft against his skin as he dressed, a new uniform for a new life.

"Any last-minute advice before I start the interview?" he asked, pulling the sweater over his head.

Ashley closed the space between them, her hands coming up to straighten the collar of his new sweater. Her eyes, sparkling with a potent mix of business and pleasure, locked onto his. "If she offers to fuck you," she whispered, her breath warm against his lips before she kissed him, a quick, sharp press that was both a promise and a command, "take the offer."

She turned to leave, and he caught her hand. "Where are you going?"

She looked back at him, her smile brilliant and competent. "I only bought what you need to survive today. The house is a shell. You need everything. Food, toiletries, a bar worthy of the view. I need to go buy the rest," she said. "Your job is to handle Jenny. My job is to build your world." And with that, she was gone.

Jack stood alone in the master suite and chuckled, a rough, uncertain sound. He was sure she was just jesting… but then again, she knew his plans. She knew he wanted to explore this new, hedonistic side of his life, and she had already agreed to it. He shook his head, the lines of his old morality blurring into the opulent, sun-drenched reality of his new one. He headed down the floating staircase, the cool metal a stark contrast to the warmth of the California morning, and made his way to the kitchen to make a cup of coffee before the next phase of his impossible life began.

The sharp, confident knock on the front door echoed through the vast space at precisely nine a.m. Jack, who had been nursing his coffee while staring out at the waves, felt a jolt of nervous energy. He set his mug down, smoothed the front of his cashmere sweater, and walked to the door, his bare feet silent on the cool marble. He took a steadying breath, reminding himself that he was the one in charge, and pulled the heavy door open.

The woman standing on his porch, silhouetted against the brilliant morning sun, made the breath catch in his throat. Ashley had told him she was beautiful, but the word was a pale, insufficient descriptor. Before him stood a goddess forged in fire and nerve. A riot of fiery red hair was cropped into a sharp, audacious pixie cut that framed a face of stunning contrasts. Her eyes were the color of moss after a spring rain, intelligent and alive, and a playful constellation of freckles was dusted across the bridge of her nose and high on her cheekbones. She was dressed in a flawlessly tailored suit of deep forest green, the jacket unbuttoned to reveal a glimpse of a cream-colored silk blouse. She was professionalism and provocation in one perfect package.

"Mr. Halland," she said, her voice a smooth, confident melody. "Jenny Johnson." Her smile was wide and dazzling, but it was her eyes that captured him. A spark of something knowing, a glint of playful challenge, danced in their green depths as she looked him over. She was sizing him up, and she was not intimidated.

She held out a hand, and he took it. Her grip was firm, her skin warm. "A pleasure to meet you, Ms. Johnson," he said, his own voice sounding steadier than he felt. He stepped aside, gesturing her in.

"Can I offer you a cup of coffee?" he asked as she walked past him, a faint, intriguing scent of citrus and spice trailing in her wake.

She turned, taking in the cavernous room and the ocean view with an appreciative but unimpressed air. She belonged in places like this. "Please," she said, her smile widening.

"And how do you like it?" he asked, moving toward the kitchen island.

"Black, please. With two sugars," she replied, her gaze following him.

He chuckled as he placed a pod in the Keurig. "Dark and sweet," he mused aloud.

Jenny slid gracefully onto one of the bar stools, crossing her long legs. The glint in her eyes intensified. "I've been told I am, too," she said, her voice dropping a half-octave, turning the simple statement into a silken promise.

Jack's fingers fumbled for a moment as he opened the cabinet for the sugar. He set the jar on the counter as the machine hissed, filling a sleek black mug. He placed it in front of her, then retrieved his own, leaning against the counter opposite her. The air between them crackled with unspoken possibilities.

"So," he began, deciding to meet her challenge head-on. "Tell me about yourself, Ms. Johnson."

She took a delicate sip of her coffee, her eyes never leaving his over the rim of the cup. "Well, Mr. Halland," she began, setting the mug down with a soft click. "The professional summary is that I graduated summa cum laude from Wharton, managed a sixty-million-dollar emerging markets portfolio by the time I was twenty-five, I'm fluent in French, Japanese, and passable in Russian, and I can have a Gulfstream G650 fueled and ready to fly to Monaco with less than two hours' notice."

She paused, letting the weight of her competence settle in the air. "But I have a feeling that's not the part of my résumé you're most interested in."

Jack raised an eyebrow, staying silent, letting her lead.

"My real expertise," she continued, leaning forward slightly, her voice becoming more intimate, more conspiratorial, "is in understanding the unique pressures and... needs... of a man in your position. My philosophy is that a true personal assistant, a *real* one, anticipates and fulfills *all* of the client's requirements. The loyalty has to be absolute. There are no half-measures."

She picked up her mug again, her painted red nail tracing its edge as she held his gaze. "My previous employers had certain... appetites. For discretion, for companionship on long trips, for stressful late-night work sessions that required a certain kind of... release."

She leaned forward, the glint in her eyes blazing now, a direct, searing look that was both a challenge and an invitation. "My most recent employer, for example. A woman. A brilliant, ruthless titan in the private equity world. Her appetites weren't for men, but she still required companionship. Loyalty. And yes, after a seventeen-hour day thrashing the competition, she required release."

Jenny's lips curved into a subtle, knowing smile. "Sometimes that meant my ensuring her favorite girl was on a private jet to meet us in Zurich. Sometimes it meant me, personally, making sure she was relaxed enough to sleep. The gender, the preference... that's all irrelevant, don't you think? The *principle* is what matters. I believe that pleasure is just another form of logistics, Mr. Halland. And I am an exceptionally talented logistician."

She took another slow sip of her coffee, the picture of composure, then placed the mug down and met his stunned gaze.

"You're in the process of building an empire," she finished, her voice a velvet hammer. "You don't need someone who just manages your schedule. You need a partner. Someone who understands that your success, your power, your... *satisfaction*... is the only metric that matters. That's who I am."

He held her gaze, letting the silence stretch, a subtle test of his newfound authority. "And do you understand," he began, his voice low and even, "that Ashley Albright is the supervising assistant? She is in charge. You will follow her instructions, and you will follow mine."

A slow, knowing smile spread across Jenny's face, the glint in her eyes turning from playful to conspiratorial. "Ashley?" she whispered, the name a soft, resonant note in the air. He saw a flicker of understanding, of rivalry, of a history he was only just beginning to uncover.

Jack simply nodded. "She told me about you."

Jenny's smirk was sharp and predatory. "Did she now," she purred, her tone dripping with insinuation.

He chuckled, feeling a strange sense of power in being the nexus between these two formidable women. "There is one more interview I have to conduct. I believe you know her as well. Maya Alvarez."

The smile never left Jenny's face, but it changed, becoming something nostalgic and edged with competition. "Oh yeah," she whispered, her gaze drifting for a second as if seeing a ghost. "I know Maya, alright. The three of us... we had big plans back in school. Plans to run this town."

She pushed her coffee cup aside and, in one fluid, unhesitating motion, stood from the stool. Her fingers went to the buttons of her silk blouse. "I'm guessing," she said, her eyes locked on his as she undid the first button, "that Ashley is more than just an assistant."

His answering smirk was all the confirmation she needed. The blouse came open, revealing a simple, elegant lace bra that did little to conceal the perfect curves beneath it. She shrugged off her suit jacket, letting it fall onto the stool, and then slipped the silk from her shoulders.

She walked around the polished marble counter, her movements deliberate and hypnotic. The sound of her knees meeting the floor was a soft, definitive thud that echoed in the silent, sun-drenched kitchen. She looked up at him, her expression a potent cocktail of ambition and desire.

"This," she said, her voice a husky murmur, "is just the beginning of what I will offer as your assistant."

Her cool, professional fingers were on his belt, unbuckling it with practiced ease. She tugged down the zipper of his trousers and freed him, his cock springing hot and hard into the cool air of the room. Her lips were on him instantly, a wet, searing heat that stole the air from his lungs. She took him deep, her throat accepting all of him, and he let out a choked whisper.

"Fuck..."

She smiled around him, a subtle shift of her lips that sent a jolt of pure electricity through his system. His hands, acting on their own accord, found their way into her short, fiery red hair. The strands were soft, silky. He didn't force her, but his fingers tightened, his hands guiding her head back and forth in a rhythm that matched the frantic pounding in his own chest. A low, guttural moan vibrated from her throat, traveling directly up his shaft, and he knew he wasn't going to last. The feeling was too intense, too overwhelming. It was a system overload, a blinding rush that obliterated thought.

He grunted, his hips bucking involuntarily, and he came with a choked cry, filling her mouth with his release.

"Fuck… Jenny…" he gasped, his voice dry and raw.

She didn't pull away. She continued to stroke him with her tongue until the last tremor subsided, then kissed the sensitive tip of his cock, licking away the last drop of cum with a deliberate, proprietary flick.

She looked up at him, her green eyes blazing with triumph. "I do hope you consider me for the position," she whispered.

Slowly, she rose to her feet, wiping the corner of her mouth with the back of her hand. She leaned in and gave him a slow, deep kiss that tasted of him, of coffee, and of victory. "I really hope so," she whispered against his lips.

She turned and picked up her blouse. He watched her, his mind still reeling. The freckles he had noticed on her face were not confined there. They spilled from her collarbones down her chest, a beautiful, scattered constellation that dusted the pale, soft swell of her perfect breasts. It was fucking sexy.

She put on her shirt and jacket with the same unhurried grace she had taken them off. "Tell Ashley I hope to hear from her soon," she said, her voice once again cool and professional. She walked to the door, then paused and smiled back at him over her shoulder, a final, devastating smirk. And with that, she was gone.

He stood there for a long moment, his heart still hammering. He finally looked down, tucked himself back into his pants, and zipped them up, his hands shaking slightly. He leaned against the counter, a hollow laugh escaping him.

"Fuck," he said to the empty, magnificent room. "Having money really does change your whole fucking life."

An hour later, the quiet of the mansion was broken by the sound of the front door opening. Ashley stepped in, followed by a silent, efficient procession of four large men in discreet dark polo shirts and cargo pants, his new security detail. They were laden with shopping bags from high-end grocers and boxes from electronics stores.

"Living room for the electronics, kitchen for the rest," Ashley commanded with an easy authority. The men nodded, depositing their burdens with quiet precision before seeing themselves out. The house was no longer just a shell; it was being stocked for a king.

"Who was that?" Jack asked, walking out from the kitchen.

Ashley turned, a playful smirk on her lips. "The security guys. Getting them to do a little heavy lifting saves on delivery fees."

He shook his head, a small smile playing on his own lips. "How did it go with Jenny?" she asked, her eyes dancing with amusement.

"She was... a strategic weapon disguised as a bombshell," Jack said, the words feeling accurate.

Ashley let out a low, appreciative laugh. "So, did she make her closing argument?"

He smirked, running a hand through his hair. "She did blow me," he admitted, his voice a low murmur.

Ashley's laugh was full and triumphant this time. "Now *that's* more like it. She knows how to seal a deal." She began unpacking a box of new kitchenware, her movements deft and purposeful. "By the way, I spoke to Arthur. Maya Alvarez will be here tonight at six."

He looked at her, surprised. "Tonight?"

She nodded, not looking up from her task. "I figured if we get the assistant hired, we can start thinking about more important things. Like getting you out of this house." She started to unload bags of fresh produce, and he moved to help, but she waved him away with a flick of her hand.

"Ah-ah," she chided gently. "Not your job, remember? You hired an assistant to do this."

He leaned against the counter, crossing his arms. "And are you going to wipe my ass for me, too?" he teased.

She finally looked up, her gaze hot and direct. "If you ask for it nicely, assisting is my job," she said, her voice a silken promise. She turned back to her work, leaving him to ponder the dizzying implications of their arrangement.

Jack grabbed a cold beer from the now-stocked fridge and walked out onto the expansive back balcony. He sank into a cushioned lounge chair, the sun warm on his face, the sound of the waves a constant, soothing roar below. He heard a splash and a burst of feminine laughter from the property next door and glanced over. A half-dozen girls were in and around the pool, a vibrant tableau of sun, water, and youth. He recognized two of them from the day before.

One of them, a stunning brunette in a tiny bikini, saw him looking and her face lit up. She whispered excitedly to her friend, who also turned to stare.

"Mr. Halland!" the brunette called out, her voice carrying easily on the breeze. "Come join us!"

He chuckled and shook his head, raising his beer in a salute. "Sorry, girls! Maybe some other time!"

The brunette didn't miss a beat. She hopped out of the pool, water streaming from her tanned body, and started walking purposefully across the lawn that separated their properties. A security guard stepped forward, moving to intercept her.

"Let her through," Jack called out, his voice calm but firm. It was his first real command to his new staff. The guard turned, saw Jack, and gave a single, professional nod before stepping aside.

The girl, hurried up the short steps to his balcony, slightly out of breath. "You're really him," she said, her eyes wide. "Jack Halland."

He nodded and took a slow sip of his beer. "I am Belinda," she said, extending a wet hand. He took it briefly.

"So, you live there?" he asked, nodding toward the neighboring mansion.

She laughed, a bright, practiced sound. "God, no. It's my parents' house. We're just crashing here for the break."

"Too bad," he said, letting a hint of disappointment color his tone.

Her smile was immediate and predatory. "We're here for two more days, if you feel like coming over," she offered.

He looked her up and down, making his appraisal obvious. "And the guys I saw here the other day?"

She waved a dismissive hand. "Classmates. They think they have a shot."

He smirked. "Yeah. I know the type. I *was* one of them before all this."

Her flirty expression faltered, replaced by genuine curiosity. "You really went from nothing to… this, didn't you?"

He looked out at the ocean, his own expression hardening. "I really don't feel like talking about that."

She recovered instantly. "I get it. Well, I meant it, you know. Come over anytime. I'll make sure you have a *great* time," she said, her emphasis leaving no room for doubt. She turned and ran back across the lawn, rejoining her friends who immediately swarmed her for details.

He chuckled to himself, taking another drink. "Probably a gold digger," he whispered to the ocean.

"Oh, she absolutely is," Ashley said, stepping silently onto the balcony beside him. She sat down in the adjacent chair and handed him a fresh, condensation-beaded beer. "Her father runs a mid-tier media company. They're comfortable, not wealthy. Belinda's trust fund is barely six figures. Her only path to this lifestyle is marrying it."

He looked at her, then back at the pool, where Belinda was now acting out her conversation with him for her rapt audience. "Yeah, I had a feeling."

"It's three o'clock," Ashley said, her tone shifting back to business. "Three hours until Maya arrives."

Jack nodded, taking a long drink of the fresh beer. He smiled, but there was no humor in it. "You know what I never expected when all of this started?"

She shook her head, waiting.

"Being stuck in my own house. I have all this money, but because someone couldn't keep their mouth shut, I can't go anywhere. It's a security risk."

"I know," she said softly. "But there are ways around that."

He looked at her, intrigued. "Explain."

Her playful smirk returned. "You have a helicopter pad on the roof. You have a fleet of private cars with tinted windows. You have a security team that can clear a path anywhere. And there is always, always a masquerade ball happening somewhere in L.A."

He smiled, a genuine one this time. "Yeah, but if everyone is wearing a mask, how do I know who I'm dancing with? Or kissing? Or wanting to invite home?"

Ashley laughed, a real, warm sound. "That's what talking is for, Jack. You flirt. You charm them. You discover who they are." She tilted her head, her expression softening. "You really have no true concept of dating, do you?"

He felt a blush creep up his neck and shook his head. "Julie and I were together for three years before she…" He stopped himself, the words catching in his throat.

Ashley reached out and took his hand, her touch surprisingly gentle. "Jack… you never really went on a first date, did you?"

He just shook his head, unable to speak.

She gave his hand a final squeeze and stood up, all business once more. "Go get ready for your interview. I'm going to do some research."

He nodded, stood, and headed back inside, leaving her to her work as he went to wash away the day and prepare for the night.

Chapter 11.

As the clock on Jack's new phone read exactly 6:00 p.m., a firm, punctual knock echoed from the front door. He heard Ashley's soft footsteps on the marble floor as she went to answer it. He remained in the great room, a silent observer, trying to project an aura of calm command he was only just beginning to feel.

He watched as Ashley pulled the heavy door open and a genuine, brilliant smile lit up her face. The woman standing on the threshold was her equal in beauty, but where Ashley was warm sunshine and sharp confidence, this woman was cool moonlight and sleek sophistication. Her raven-black hair was cut into a severe, elegant bob that framed a face with high cheekbones and intelligent, dark almond-shaped eyes. She was wearing a simple but exquisitely tailored black sheath dress that hinted at a stunning figure beneath its professional lines.

"Maya," Ashley whispered, pulling the woman into a genuine embrace that still held a flicker of old rivalries.

Maya returned the hug, her eyes scanning the cavernous room over Ashley's shoulder before landing on Jack. "What are you doing here?" she asked, her voice a low, smooth alto.

Ashley stepped back, her smile turning sly. "I'm his Senior Personal Assistant. His right hand."

Maya's perfectly sculpted eyebrows rose a fraction. "So, there's no position?" she asked, her gaze flicking back to Jack, reassessing the situation.

"There is," Ashley said, taking her friend's hand and leading her inside. "Mr. Halland is building an empire. He's going to need all the help he can get. I can only keep track of so much. We need someone to work under me, to follow instructions from both of us."

Maya's lips curved into a knowing smirk as she looked from Ashley to Jack, who was now walking toward them. "You're fucking him?" she whispered, the question blunt and direct.

Ashley's laugh was rich and unapologetic. "Are you kidding? He's eighteen, built like a goddamn statue, and is a fucking machine in bed. You can bet your ass I'm fucking him."

Maya's answering laugh was a low, throaty chuckle. "So he's hands-off, then?"

"No," Ashley's tone became serious, a quiet warning between friends. "He is most definitely not hands-off. But he demands respect, Maya. First and foremost, you remember he is the boss. He's not a predator, but he's also not a monk. Be straight with him. He respects honesty. If you fuck him, it's because you want to, not because you think it's a requirement for the job."

Maya nodded slowly, her dark eyes absorbing the strategic advice. Just then, Jack reached them. He had showered and changed into dark trousers and a simple, crisp black button-down shirt that clung to his lean, muscular frame. As Maya's eyes swept over him, he saw a flicker of surprise, an acknowledgment. *Ashley wasn't kidding,* the look said. *He is a stud.*

"Mr. Halland," Ashley said, her professional mask slipping back into place. "May I introduce you to my friend, and our next candidate, Maya Alvarez." She stepped aside.

Jack extended his hand. "A pleasure to meet you, Miss Alvarez." Her hand was cool and smooth in his, her handshake firm. The brief touch was like an electric current.

Ashley closed the door, giving Jack a subtle, knowing glance before saying, "I'll be upstairs if you need anything." She left them alone in the vast, silent room, the setting sun painting the ocean outside in fiery strokes of orange and pink.

Jack guided Maya toward the pair of sofas near the glass wall. "Please," he said, indicating for her to sit before taking the seat opposite her.

"So, Miss Alvarez," he began, his voice a low, steady baritone that he was growing into. "Tell me about yourself."

She smiled, a slow, captivating curve of her lips. She didn't launch into her résumé. Instead, she appraised him openly, her gaze lingering on his broad shoulders and the strong line of his jaw.

"I think Ashley might have undersold you," she said, her voice dropping into a more intimate register. "She said you were a force to be reckoned with. She neglected to mention you were also… so visually compelling. It's a powerful combination."

Jack felt a warmth spread through his chest at the direct, intoxicating compliment. "And you, Miss Alvarez, are you more than just your Stanford Economics degree and your impressive work in tech acquisitions?" he countered, letting her know he'd read her file.

Her smile widened. "Much more," she confirmed. "My real talent isn't just managing acquisitions; it's managing access. Getting you into places others can't, and more importantly, keeping others away from you when you desire privacy. I know how to become invisible. I know how to make problems… disappear. A man in your position will attract an endless stream of problems. I'm the person who ensures they never reach you."

She leaned forward slightly, the movement causing the fabric of her dress to tighten across her chest. "I understand you're building a life that will require… a unique skill set from your staff. Absolute loyalty. Unflinching discretion. And a partner who is not shocked or intimidated by your desires, whatever they may be." Her dark eyes held his, and in their depths, he saw a cool, thrilling promise. "I wouldn't be wasting your time, Mr. Halland, if I wasn't fully prepared to be that partner. And frankly," she added, her voice a near-whisper as her gaze dropped to his mouth, "I wouldn't mind at all."

He chuckled, a low, dangerous sound. He leaned forward, resting his elbows on his knees, turning this interview into an interrogation. "Let's test this theory of yours, Miss Alvarez. Say I desired to fuck a girl… that brunette from the pool next door, for instance… right here on this sofa. What is your logistical solution?"

Maya's smile didn't falter. She didn't even blink. "My function would be to ensure the… transaction… was seamless and private. I would confirm the young lady's willingness, handle any necessary arrangements, ensure you were not disturbed by phone calls or visitors, and then be available for your post-engagement debriefing. Unless," she paused, letting the word hang in the air, "I was invited to join."

His smirk widened. "Invited?"

"If my presence were requested to enhance the experience, Mr. Halland, then my presence would become part of the logistical solution," she stated, her voice a cool, silken whisper. "I am, as I said, adaptable to any requirement. My position is not contingent upon making myself personally available for you to enjoy… but if that is what you had in mind, I will gladly provide it."

The air crackled. This was a game of high-stakes poker, and she had just raised him. He decided to show her his hand.

"To be fair," he said, his voice dropping conspiratorially, "your competition, Miss Johnson, has already set a rather high bar. She gave me a mind-blowing blowjob right where you're sitting."

Maya's eyes flared with a competitive fire. A slow, predatory smile spread across her face. "Then," she whispered, her voice a velvet caress, "in the interest of a fair and thorough hiring process… you'll need a direct comparison."

Before he could even process the audacity of her words, she slid gracefully from the sofa to her knees, the fabric of her expensive dress rustling softly against the marble floor. She moved with the fluid, deliberate grace of a predator. He watched, mesmerized, as she reached for him, her cool, manicured fingers deftly unbuckling his belt and unfastening his trousers.

She pulled his cock from his pants, and as she did, Jack's gaze instinctively shot toward the massive glass wall. Outside, the sun was setting, and by the shimmering turquoise water of the neighboring pool, the party had frozen. Six beautiful girls in bikinis were standing or leaning against the edge, their drinks forgotten, their mouths slightly agape. They were watching. All of them. And he realized in a dizzying rush of pure adrenaline that he didn't want them to stop. This wasn't just sex; this was a coronation.

Maya leaned forward, her dark hair brushing against his thigh, and took him into her mouth. The sensation was electric, a slow, deep suction that was vastly different from Jenny's fiery enthusiasm. Maya's technique was a masterclass in control, her tongue swirling, her throat opening, taking him deeper than he thought possible. A throaty purr rumbled from her chest, and the sound drove him insane. His hands tangled in her hair, his fingers gripping the soft strands as he began to guide her, pushing himself deeper into the wet heat of her mouth.

He was the director of this scene, and the girls by the pool were his captive audience. He saw one of them... a stunning blonde in a blood-red bikini... whisper something to her friend, her eyes wide with a mixture of shock and arousal.

"I hope you swallow," he groaned, the words a low, guttural command meant as much for the girls watching as for the woman at his feet.

That was all it took. The combination of Maya's expert mouth, the public display of dominance, and the raw, pent-up energy of the last few days sent him over the edge. He came with a sharp, ragged cry, his body seizing as he flooded her throat. She took all of it, swallowing every drop without breaking rhythm, her hand stroking the base of his shaft until the last tremor had subsided.

When he was done, she licked him clean with a deliberate, final caress of her tongue, tucked him neatly back into his pants, and rose to her feet as if nothing had happened. He was breathing heavily, his mind reeling, his eyes still locked on the girls next door. He could clearly read the words on the lips of the girl in the red bikini as she turned to her friend: "Oh my God, that was so hot."

"I'll let you be the judge," Maya whispered, her voice smooth and steady.

He finally tore his gaze away from the window and looked at her, his heart still hammering. "That," he said, his voice hoarse, "was fucking fantastic."

She smiled, a victor's smile. "I'll let you know tomorrow," he managed. "Or rather… Ashley will call you."

She nodded, leaned in, and kissed his cheek. "Next time," she whispered in his ear, her breath hot and promising, "I'm fucking you." Then she turned and walked out of the house, leaving a stunned silence in her wake.

Jack leaned his head back against the sofa, a disbelieving chuckle escaping his lips.

"How much of that did you see?" he asked, not needing to look.

He heard a soft laugh from the direction of the grand staircase. He turned his head. Ashley was leaning against the archway, her arms crossed, a look of profound amusement on her face.

"All of it," she said.

He laughed and pushed himself off the sofa, heading for the stairs. She met him at the bottom, wrapping her arms around his neck and pulling him into a deep, possessive kiss.

When she finally pulled back, her eyes were sparkling. "So," she asked, her voice a low, teasing whisper. "Who will it be, boss?"

The first thing Jack became aware of was the warm, soft weight of Ashley's leg thrown possessively over his own. The second was the pale, golden light of the California morning filtering through the sheer curtains, painting the opulent bedroom in hazy stripes. The air was still and thick with the lingering, musky scent of their lovemaking, a testament to a night spent exploring every boundary of pleasure until exhaustion had finally claimed them.

A shrill, unwelcome intrusion shattered the peace. A phone was ringing, sharp and insistent, on the bedside table. Before Jack could even formulate a thought, Ashley moved with the swift, silent grace of a cat. She was already sitting up, the silk sheet pooling around her waist, as she plucked his phone from the charger.

"Mr. Halland's office," she said, her voice instantly transformed… cool, crisp, and utterly impersonal. It was the voice of the impenetrable fortress she was now paid to be. Jack propped himself up on his elbows, a smirk playing on his lips as he watched his new assistant in her natural habitat.

There was a pause as she listened. "I do apologize," she continued, her tone bordering on bored. "But at this time, we are not at liberty to comment on the financial or personal affairs of Mr. Halland." She waited another beat, then with a soft, final click, ended the call.

She placed the phone back on the table and turned to him, the professional mask melting away to be replaced by a look of wry amusement. He tilted his head.

"Channel Eight News," she said, answering his unspoken question. "They're getting aggressive."

He shook his head, a wave of irritation washing over him. "Any idea who leaked my name to the press?"

She shrugged, stretching her arms above her head in a move that made her breasts press against the thin sheet. "There were thirty people in that meeting, Jack. It could be any of them, which means we have to assume it was *all* of them. From now on, information is compartmentalized. No one gets the full picture but you and me."

He nodded, appreciating the strategic coldness of her thinking. She was worth every penny.

Her eyes sparkled with a teasing light. "So, speaking of the full picture… have you made your decision?"

He snorted, running a hand through his messy hair. He knew exactly what she was asking. Jenny or Maya. The fiery, audacious redhead who had offered him pleasure as a logistical solution, or the cool, sophisticated raven-haired woman who had offered him power as a form of intimacy. It was a choice between two perfect, intoxicating flavors of his new life. The problem was, the old Jack would have been paralyzed with indecision. The new Jack was starting to realize that the very nature of choice had changed for him.

He looked at her, a slow, dawning realization spreading across his face. "And I can only hire one?" he asked, the question a genuine test of the new rules of his universe.

Ashley's answering laugh was low and delighted. She leaned over and kissed him, a slow, lingering kiss. "Who said that?" she whispered against his lips.

He smiled. Of course. He was the one who made the rules now. He watched as she pulled out her own phone, her thumb hovering over her contacts, ready to execute his command.

"So, both of them?" she asked, a delicious, conspiratorial smirk on her face.

He closed his eyes for a second, the sheer audacity of it all sinking in. "What am I paying them?"

"Half of what I'm getting," she said, as if discussing the price of coffee.

"So if I hire both… it's a million a year in staff salary," he mused aloud. The number felt both absurd and completely trivial.

"Alright," he said, his eyes snapping open, his voice firm and decisive. "Hire them both."

Ashley's smirk widened.

"Give them their first assignments," he continued, enjoying the feel of command. "Have Jenny go to Westmiller's office. I want one of my personal cars brought here. The Aston Jack DB11. And have Maya go to the store. I have a craving for candy. Black licorice."

Ashley chuckled, already typing. "Yes, sir."

He watched as she made the calls, her voice a model of efficiency as she dispatched his two new employees on their respective missions… one of power, one of personal whim. He had just spent a million dollars as casually as he used to spend five on a comic book.

He laid his head back against the mountain of soft pillows and let out a long sigh. The morning sun was warm, the woman in his bed was a goddess, and two more were now officially on his payroll. And yet, as the machine of his new life whirred to life around him, his thoughts drifted north, to a small, quiet house in Washington. The image of Julie's tear-streaked face, her raw vulnerability, was a dull, persistent ache behind the glittering facade of his new reality. He wondered how she was doing.

The rich, dark coffee was a world away from the instant brew of his past life, and Jack savored the taste as he sat at the gleaming marble kitchen island. The chaos of the morning… the phone calls, the interviews, the hirings… had settled into a quiet hum of purpose. Ashley, having finished her own calls, approached him with a sleek, black slate of glass and metal in her hand. It wasn't just a phone; it was a scepter for his new kingdom.

"So, I have your new personal phone set up and secured," she said, her voice a low, professional murmur. She placed it on the counter in front of him. "It's completely unlisted and encrypted. A ghost."

He picked it up. It felt cool and substantial in his hand. "Thank you."

"I took the liberty of programming in the essential numbers," she continued, a small, intimate smile playing on her lips. She tapped the screen, bringing up the contact list. "There's mine, of course." Her finger traced her own name. "Jenny's and Maya's," she added, her tone now professionally neutral. "Constance's," she said with a note of respect for a powerful peer. She paused, her eyes meeting his, full of understanding. "And, of course… Julie's."

A wave of quiet gratitude washed over Jack. Ashley wasn't just his assistant or his lover; she was a strategist who understood the entire battlefield, including the parts that had nothing to do with business. He gave her a small, appreciative nod.

He tapped on Julie's name, his thumb hovering over the message icon. This was the first official act on this new, secret channel… the line connecting his new world to the last, most important piece of his old one. He typed, the words feeling both affectionate and deliberate.

"Hey babe… this is my new number. It is very important that this number stays between you and me. Only those I have a very deep, personal relationship with get this number. xoxo J"

He hit send and watched the screen. The three dots of her reply appeared almost instantly, a frantic, eager dance.

"Secret phone… staying off the radar… very smart. I'll delete the text and save the number. It's safe with me. Always. xoxo J."

A slow smile spread across Jack's face. He looked up at Ashley, who was watching him with a knowing expression. "New rule," he said, his tone suddenly serious. "This number is for us. The inner circle. If you receive a message from me, or send one, we do not use names. Just the first letter of your name. You are A."

Ashley's smirk was immediate and sharp, her mind instantly probing the logistics. "And how do you plan to differentiate when you have both a Jenny and a Julie in your life?" she asked, one perfectly sculpted eyebrow raised.

He smiled. She was already proving her worth, thinking three steps ahead. "Maybe two letters," he countered smoothly.

She laughed, a low, appreciative sound. "So Jenny is JE, and Julie is JU," she confirmed, accepting the new protocol. She was falling into line, not just as his assistant, but as his co-conspirator.

Jack nodded, his attention returning to the phone. He typed out the new directive to Julie.

"Two letters. You are JU. Not just J."

The reply was instantaneous: a single, happy smiley face. It was an emoji of complete and total acceptance. She wasn't questioning his strange new rules; she was just happy to be included, happy to be his. He looked at the phone in his hand, at the short, coded list of the five women who now formed the core of his new universe. He was building his own world, with its own private language, and they were all, in their own ways, agreeing to live in it.

Chapter 12.

The grand front door swung open before Jenny's hand even reached the bell. Ashley stood there, leaning against the doorframe with a coffee mug in her hand, a welcoming smile on her face that was equal parts friendly and proprietary. For her first day, Jenny had dressed for action, wearing impeccably tailored white trousers and a simple silk camisole under a sharp, open blazer. She looked less like an assistant and more like a corporate raider ready for a hostile takeover.

"Miss Boss," Jenny said with a theatrical bow, her green eyes sparkling with mischief. "And where might one find Mr. Boss this fine morning?"

Ashley laughed, a full, genuine sound that echoed in the sun-drenched foyer. "He's in the office, wading through deeds and titles for estates in countries he's never heard of. He's discovering the true meaning of 'more money, more problems.'"

She stepped back, and Jenny walked in, her gaze sweeping the room. "So, what's our first order of business? World domination? Or just brunch?"

"Infrastructure," Ashley stated, her tone shifting seamlessly from friend to manager. "Our job is to build the machine that allows him to be him. We handle the world so he can conquer it. First up: domestic staff. He needs a chef and a personal trainer, immediately."

Jenny's smirk was instantaneous. She knew this world and its players. "You're thinking of Milly for the kitchen, and it has to be Haley for the gym, right?"

Ashley nodded, her expression turning grim. "Haley will be easy. But Milly… she won't take my call. So if you could…"

Jenny let out a low groan. "She's still furious about the Rothschild gala, isn't she? Ash, you didn't steal her sous-chef; he quit because she threw a truffle slicer at his head."

"She sees it differently," Ashley said with a sigh. "And when she hears I'm going to be her boss's boss, her ego might not be able to handle it. But she's the best damn cook on the West Coast, and Jack deserves the best."

"Leave it to me," Jenny said, her confidence radiating. This was her first test, a delicate negotiation, and she relished the challenge. She pulled her phone from her bag. "Speaking of which, what's this 'JE' stuff you texted me this morning?"

Ashley smiled. "The Boss's new protocol. It's his private phone, inner circle only. He wants total security, so initials, no names. You're JE, I'm A, Maya's MA, and so on."

Jenny's smirk returned, but it was softer now, more insightful. "Got it. I'm guessing being splashed all over the news hit him harder than he expected."

"You have no idea," Ashley confirmed with a solemn nod. It was a silent acknowledgment between two women who understood the price of that kind of fame.

With that, Jenny gave a small nod, turned, and walked toward the glass wall overlooking the ocean, already dialing. She was no longer a friend visiting; she was an asset being deployed, ready to handle the first of many impossible tasks in her new, extraordinary job.

The coffee, hot and black, was a welcome anchor in the swirling chaos of Jack's new reality. He sat at the massive glass desk in the home office, a room that felt more like a corporate command center than a study. Before him lay a mountain of deeds and trusts, a paper empire that seemed to grow with every file Ashley opened. The initial list from the conference room had been a mere appetizer. This was the overwhelming main course.

"Why in the hell," Jack groaned, rubbing his temples as he stared at two separate deeds, "did he own two multi-million-dollar apartments in the exact same building in Beijing?"

He heard a soft snort from the doorway. Ashley leaned against the frame, a knowing smirk on her face. "Because, like you, he appreciated women."

Jack looked up, an eyebrow raised.

"In Beijing, he had a stable of three," Ashley explained, her tone as matter-of-fact as if she were discussing stock prices. "They lived together in one apartment. He kept the other one pristine for when he was in town. They would… visit… when he requested company."

He let out a short, sharp laugh. "Complicated."

"Sell them," he said decisively, pushing the two deeds into a pile to his left. "Both of them."

Ashley nodded, making a note on a tablet. He was pruning his father's messy, complicated life, choosing his own path. He pulled up the next file, a glossy portfolio for a sprawling beachfront villa in Brazil.

"This is a house…" he said, stating the obvious.

Ashley came to look over his shoulder, her scent… a clean, expensive mix of citrus and ambition… enveloping him for a moment. "One of the bigger ones," she confirmed. "And one of the most expensive to hold on to."

"Can we not just pay it off? Own it outright?" he asked, the logic seeming simple to him.

She smirked, a look of a seasoned veteran explaining the grim realities of the world to a rookie. "That's not the problem. The problem is the local *cartel*. Your father had an arrangement. A sizable yearly payment was made to them as a retainer for their non-interference. You stop paying, the house disappears. They'll strip it to the foundations overnight."

He looked at the numbers. The house had cost millions. The annual "security" payment was almost half a million. He shook his head in disgust. This wasn't an asset; it was a ransom.

"Let them have it," he said, his voice cold. He didn't just put the deed aside; he dropped the entire glossy portfolio into the wastebasket with a soft thud. It was a statement. He would not be extorted.

One by one, they went through the properties. Forty-six in total, scattered across the globe like the whims of a lonely, powerful man. Jack was ruthless. He wanted jets and five-star hotels, not permanent anchors in countries he'd never seen. He was building his own kind of empire, one that was lean, mobile, and free of the ghosts of his father's messy entanglements.

A soft knock on the office door made them both look up. Jenny stepped in, a brilliant smile on her face. Behind her, a half-step back, was Maya, her presence a cool, collected shadow. The room's energy instantly shifted, a complex calculus of power, lust, and burgeoning loyalty now that his entire senior staff was assembled.

"Boss," Jenny said, her green eyes sparkling.

"Mr. Halland," Maya purred, her voice a smooth, dark contrast.

Jack smirked, leaning back in his chair. The memory of both of them, on their knees before him, was a fresh, potent brand in his mind. And they both knew it.

"My car is in the garage?" he asked, looking at Jenny.

She nodded, holding up a set of keys that bore the heavy, silver Aston Jack crest. "The keys will be on the board by the door," she confirmed.

He nodded, then turned his gaze to Maya. She stepped forward and placed a simple paper bag on his desk. "As you requested, boss."

He smiled, reached into the bag, and pulled out a piece of black licorice. He popped it into his mouth, closing his eyes as the intense, bittersweet flavor of anise hit his tongue. It was a taste of his childhood, a simple pleasure in a world that was no longer simple.

"Damn, that is good," he moaned softly. He saw the three women exchange a look of shared, private amusement.

"So, I've been thinking," he said, opening his eyes and sitting up straighter. "This place is huge. I'm going to need a maid or two to keep it clean."

"Live-in maids?" Jenny asked, ever the logistician.

It was Ashley who answered, asserting her position as chief of staff. "Yes. As the three of us will be living here as well, our jobs are twenty-four-seven." She looked at Jenny and Maya. "There are suites for you both on the master floor, right next to his. My room is across from the master suite." She smirked. "Though I haven't moved any of my things in yet."

Jack smiled. "Take today, girls. Go get what you need to move in. Your cars can go in the main garage when you're done."

They all looked at him, a flicker of concern crossing their faces. "Mr. Halland, you need one of us by your side at all times," Maya said, her voice firm.

He chuckled, the sound genuine. "I managed just fine on my own before all of this. I'm sure I can handle a few hours."

Ashley held his gaze for a long moment, then nodded, conceding the point. "Promise you'll call if there's any sign of trouble."

"I promise," he said.

Then, in a move that both shocked and thrilled him, they each came forward to say their goodbyes. Maya leaned in and pressed a cool, promising kiss to his lips. Jenny followed, her kiss warmer, more playful, ending with a soft nip on his bottom lip. Finally, Ashley gave him a deep, lingering kiss that was both a claim and a promise of what was to come.

They left, and he was alone again in the silent, magnificent house. He leaned back in his chair and chuckled, a rough, incredulous sound.

His life sure as hell had changed.

The silence in the mansion was a new and welcome sensation. For the first time since he had inherited this ludicrously opulent life, the house was truly his. The constant presence of lawyers, assistants, and candidates had been replaced by a profound, peaceful quiet, broken only by the hypnotic rhythm of the waves crashing on the shore below. Jack put the last of the property deeds into a neat pile. He had made his decisions, pruning the tangled branches of his father's empire, and a sense of clean, decisive control settled over him.

He walked to the massive glass wall of the office, which offered a panoramic view of the coastline, and leaned against the frame, feeling the afternoon sun warm his face. His gaze drifted to the house next door. The kaleidoscope of colorful bikinis was still gathered around the shimmering pool. He could hear their laughter, a bright, carefree sound that felt like it belonged to another universe… a universe that was now, impossibly, within his reach. He thought of Belinda's bold, flirtatious invitation, the predatory thrill of knowing he was now the prize they all wanted.

A slow smile touched his lips. The thought of conquest, of indulging in the simple, uncomplicated hedonism they represented, was a powerful lure. But as he watched them, his thoughts drifted from the abstract fantasy to the stunning, complex reality of the women who were now truly in his life. He thought of Ashley, of the fierce loyalty in her eyes and the comforting warmth of her body pressed against his in the dark. He thought of Jenny, of the audacious fire in her soul and the memory of her lips, a promise of wild, untamed pleasure. He thought of Maya, of her cool, strategic mind and the intoxicating allure of the power she wielded so effortlessly.

They were the pillars of his new reality, three distinct, powerful forces that he had, against all odds, brought into his orbit. For the first time since a phone call had shattered his world, he didn't feel alone. He felt a strange, burgeoning sense of contentment. He had a team. A family, of sorts. He was safe.

It was in that precise moment of newfound peace that the world tore itself apart.

A flicker of movement in his periphery, high up on the terracotta roof of the neighboring property. A human-shaped silhouette where there should only have been sky. Before his brain could even process the incongruity, a sharp, flat *crack* ripped through the peaceful soundscape of the ocean. It was a sound utterly alien to this place, a sound of pure violence.

Time seemed to warp. He saw a spiderweb of cracks blossom instantly on the glass wall in front of him, originating from a single, star-shaped impact point. In the next millisecond, the entire wall didn't just break; it imploded with a deafening roar, a crystalline tsunami of tempered glass flying inward.

Simultaneously, a force like a sledgehammer slammed into his left shoulder. The impact was so violent it lifted him off his feet, hurling him backward like a ragdoll. His body crashed into the massive glass desk, and it didn't just break; it shattered, disintegrating under his weight in a second explosion of splintering wood and shrieking glass.

He landed hard on the floor amidst the wreckage, a searing, white-hot agony consuming his shoulder and spreading like fire across his chest. The air was knocked from his lungs in a pained gasp. He heard muffled shouts from outside... his security team, already reacting... followed by the sound of more gunshots, a frantic, deadly exchange.

He tried to push himself up, but his left arm wouldn't respond. He looked down and saw the dark, rapidly spreading stain on his shirt, the warm, sticky wetness of his own blood pooling on the shards of glass beneath him. The edges of his vision began to blur, the sounds of the gunfight fading into a dull, distant roar. The world was narrowing, collapsing into a tunnel of darkness. His last conscious thought was a silent, desperate mantra of three names... *Ashley, Jenny, Maya, Julie...* before the blackness swallowed him whole.

A steady, rhythmic, and deeply annoying beep was the first thing to pierce the thick, murky fog in his head. It was an anchor to a reality he had no desire to rejoin. He tried to open his eyes, but his eyelids felt like they were sealed with lead. A dull, throbbing sledgehammer pounded behind his eyes, and his entire body felt pinned to a rough, starchy surface by an immense, invisible weight.

"Fuck..." he groaned, the sound a dry, sandpaper scrape in his own throat.

Instantly, a hand was on his, cool and soft, its touch instantly grounding him in the sea of pain and confusion.

"Jack..." a voice whispered, a familiar, hoarse whisper thick with exhaustion and relief. Jenny.

His eyes finally fluttered open, a painful, bleary process. The world was a smear of blurry shapes and sterile, fluorescent glare. He could make out the hazy silhouette of fiery red hair beside him, the scent of her perfume a faint, welcome ghost in the antiseptic air.

"What the hell happened?" he managed to ask, his own voice sounding alien to him.

A plastic cup with a straw was immediately at his lips. "Sip slowly," she urged.

The water was blissfully cool, a miracle that soothed the raw scrape of his throat. As he drank, the world began to sharpen, the blurry shapes resolving into a grim tableau. He was in a private hospital room, hooked up to a symphony of beeping machines. And he wasn't alone. Jenny sat vigilant in a chair pulled right up to his bed, her eyes red-rimmed and shadowed with fatigue. On a small sofa against the far wall, he saw Maya and Ashley, slumped together in an exhausted, unguarded sleep. They weren't in their power suits or designer dresses, but in simple, rumpled clothes, their professional masks completely gone, looking young and vulnerable. They hadn't left him.

He looked back at Jenny. "You were shot," she whispered, her voice cracking.

The memory slammed into him like a physical blow. The flicker of movement. The shattering glass. The searing, white-hot agony. "The roof… the house to the right," he rasped.

She nodded, squeezing his hand. "He's dead," she said, her voice chillingly final. "Security got him before he could take a second shot."

"Who was it?"

"They don't know," she said, shaking her head. "No papers, no wallet, fingerprints burned off. A ghost. The police said it was a professional."

Of course it was. His eyes drifted past her to the silent television mounted on the wall. The screen was filled with dramatic, choppy footage from a news helicopter, showing his house, his beautiful new home, cordoned off with yellow police tape like a common crime scene. The camera zoomed in on the shattered window of his office. Then the footage cut to a grainy cell phone video of him, a bloody, unconscious figure on a gurney, being rushed into an ambulance as police and his own security team swarmed the property. A bold, sensational headline scrolled across the bottom of the screen: *BILLIONAIRE HEIR GUNNED DOWN IN MALIBU MANSION.*

"Fuck," he muttered, a fresh wave of nausea washing over him. The world knew. His privacy was gone forever. "My phone… I need my phone. Julie… she needs to know I'm okay." He tried to sit up, a move that sent a fresh explosion of fire through his shoulder, making him cry out.

Jenny's hand was instantly on his chest, gently pushing him back down. "Shhh, it's okay. Ashley already called her," she said, her voice soft and soothing. "She told her you were stable and that we'd let her know when you woke up. She handled it."

He sagged back against the pillows, a strange mixture of relief and resentment welling up inside him. His life was no longer his own to manage.

"Jack… you are so lucky to be alive," Jenny whispered, leaning closer. "The police said guys like that, with that kind of rifle, from that distance… they don't miss."

A grim smirk touched his lips. "I saw him," he said, the memory fuzzy but present. "A shadow. I was moving when he fired. That's why he missed."

"That's what they think, too," she confirmed, her eyes wide. "They found the shooter's camera. The recording shows you turning at the exact moment he pulled the trigger. You saved your own life."

He nodded, the information doing little to comfort him. He was alive because of a half-second of instinct.

Jenny leaned forward then, her face softening, the professional composure crumbling away to reveal the terrified woman beneath. She framed his face with her hands and kissed him, not a kiss of seduction or power, but one of frantic, desperate claiming. It was a kiss of pure relief, and he could taste the salt of a single tear that escaped her eye and ran down her cheek.

"We thought we lost you," she whispered, her voice breaking as she pulled back, resting her forehead against his.

The simple, unvarnished honesty of her fear cut through his pain. He was weak, his body a wreck, but he could feel the life, the warmth, returning to him through her touch.

"Glad you didn't," he whispered back. And for the first time since waking up, he truly was.

He leaned his forehead against Jenny's, the intimacy of the moment a fragile shield against the throbbing pain in his shoulder and the relentless beeping of the machines.

"It's been on a continuous news loop for almost sixteen hours," Jenny explained softly, pulling back just enough to look him in the eyes. "Every channel. They're calling it the 'Malibu Ambush.'"

He let out a low groan, the sound rattling in his chest. "The house is compromised," he rasped, the words feeling strategic and cold on his tongue. "As much as I love the beach, it's a security nightmare. I need something safer. A fortress in the sky. A penthouse."

Jenny's lips curved into a sad, knowing smile. "Ashley suggested the same thing right before she finally crashed."

His gaze drifted to the sofa where Ashley and Maya slept, a tangle of limbs and exhaustion. A fierce, protective ache spread through his chest, momentarily eclipsing the physical pain. "This is going to hurt," he said, looking back at Jenny.

She understood instantly. It wasn't the gunshot wound he was talking about. "Wake them up," he whispered.

Jenny nodded and moved to the sofa. She placed a gentle hand on Ashley's shoulder. "Ash… Maya…" she said softly. "He's awake."

Ashley's eyes snapped open, a brilliant, alert blue, the fog of sleep vanishing in an instant. She surged to her feet in a desperate, fluid motion and rushed to his bedside. Her lips found his in a kiss that was frantic and wet with unshed tears. She wrapped her arms around him, a crushing embrace of pure relief, and he gritted his teeth against the fresh explosion of fire in his shoulder. It was worth it.

Maya was right behind her, her usual cool composure gone, replaced by a fierce, quiet intensity. Her kiss was less frantic than Ashley's but just as desperate, a silent testament to her terror.

"God, Jack… I was so scared," Ashley whispered, pulling back, her face pale and tear-streaked. Her rock-solid assistant persona was gone, revealing the terrified woman beneath.

He managed a weak nod. "I know… I'm sorry…"

"Don't," Ashley said, her voice instantly firm, her grip on his hand tightening. "First off, you are not to blame for this. Second, a man in your position… you do not apologize for being the target of cowards."

Jack felt a ghost of a chuckle escape him. "I do," he said, his voice soft but clear, "to the ones I love."

The words stopped her dead. He watched as the strategic, professional mask she was trying to rebuild crumbled again, and a fresh tear traced a path down her cheek. In the quiet of the room, he saw Maya and Jenny exchange a look of profound, stunned respect. He had just defined the terms of their new relationship, and it wasn't based on a paycheck.

He took a breath, the effort immense, and shifted into the role he now had to play: the boss. "We need to find a new place to live. But until we do, get a hotel suite. A fortress. Presidential suite level, high above L.A., and completely discreet."

Ashley nodded, the tears gone, replaced by a steely resolve. Beside her, Maya was already tapping his instructions into a tablet.

"And I want a new security team," he continued, his voice hardening. "These guys dropped the ball. Big time."

"Mr. Westmiller is already handling it," Ashley confirmed. "This was a huge blow for everyone. He also said… some of the investors from the buyout have come forward. They're making noise, claiming that if you die, your assets are in chaos and they can move to take over your businesses."

A cold fury settled in Jack's gut, eclipsing the pain. The vultures were already circling. He looked at Jenny. "I want Constance Westmiller here. Now."

Jenny nodded once, her expression grim, and walked out of the room, already dialing.

He turned back to Ashley. "Thank you… for calling Julie."

Ashley's expression softened. "Of course. Do you want me to call her now? Let her know you're awake?"

He nodded, a wave of exhaustion washing over him. Ashley squeezed his hand, then she too left the room to make the call.

Maya stepped closer, all business. "The penthouse, sir. Any specific requirements?"

He managed a weak smile. "Two, maybe three floors. Large, extravagant, defensible. And I want a pool on the roof."

Maya's lips curved into a confident smirk. "I know someone who specializes in exactly that kind of property. Off-market, of course." She dialed a number on her own phone. "I'll handle it." She gave him a final, assessing look, a silent promise of her competence, and then she too was gone, her voice a low, commanding murmur as she walked into the hallway.

Jack leaned his head back against the stiff hospital pillow, alone again in the sudden quiet. The room was a command center that had just emptied, his three lieutenants deployed to wage his wars. His shoulder was a universe of fire, and he was so fucking glad to be alive. But a cold, terrifying question echoed in the beeping silence.

The shooter was a ghost. The investors were vultures. Who the hell wanted him dead?

Chapter 13.

They say money can buy anything. After three days in the sterile, beeping quiet of a hospital room, Jack had discovered the one thing his billions couldn't purchase: a shield from the world's ravenous curiosity. His discharge was not a quiet departure; it was a media circus. The journey from his room to the hospital's private garage was a nightmarish gauntlet. A cacophony of shouted questions rained down on him, a desperate, verbal assault from a pack of reporters. The air crackled with the blinding, concussive flash of a hundred cameras, each one trying to capture a piece of his pain. He felt like a caged animal on display, and all he wanted was to dig a hole and disappear into the sweet, anonymous darkness.

But Ashley had a plan.

She was a human shield, her body a formidable barrier between his wheelchair and the clamoring mob, while his new security detail formed a grim, human phalanx around them. She guided him into the subterranean garage, where not one, but six identical, blacked-out limousines sat with their engines rumbling in unison… a show of force and misdirection.

The moment the heavy door of their designated car closed, the chaotic symphony outside was instantly silenced, replaced by the cool, tomb-like quiet of the leather-scented interior. Ashley leaned back against the plush seat, a triumphant, brilliant smile on her face.

"The decoys are all taking different routes," she explained, her voice calm and steady. "One is heading back to the mansion in Malibu, one north, one west, one south, one east. They'll draw the majority of the pack. We'll circle a few blocks, let the last of our friends get bored, and then head for the hotel in Hollywood."

With that, the six limousines peeled out of the garage simultaneously. Jack watched on a small screen displaying the news feed, a smirk touching his lips as he saw the frantic scramble of reporters jumping into their vans, peeling off in pursuit of the wrong phantoms. One news van, persistent, latched onto them.

"Once they get word that one of the cars is heading to Malibu, they'll abandon us," Ashley said with unshakable confidence. "They always go for the most obvious story."

She was right. Twenty minutes later, after a dizzying series of turns through downtown L.A., the van's tracker on their screen abruptly changed course, speeding toward the coast. Ashley gave a sharp double-rap on the glass partition, the signal to their driver. It was time to go home… or to the closest thing he had to one now.

"Jenny and Maya are already at the penthouse suite," Ashley said, all business now. "The hotel has its own security on our floor, and ours are sweeping it now. We'll be secure." He nodded, a wave of gratitude for her competence washing over him. "Constance also assures us they have a firm lead on who hired the shooter," Ashley continued, her eyes fixed on a text message. Her playful smirk vanished, replaced by a grim, hard line. "Remember a Mrs. Falcor from the investors' meeting?"

He remembered. She was the one with the sharp, condescending eyes who had dismissed him as a "kid." He had proved her wrong, but it seemed she hadn't taken the lesson well. "What about her?" he asked.

"She's still not happy about the revised price. The extra six hundred million you extracted wasn't just a financial loss for their consortium; it was a public humiliation. She was outmaneuvered by an eighteen-year-old, and her ego couldn't absorb the blow."

He felt a cold knot form in his stomach. "So she paid some hitman to get rid of me?"

Ashley nodded grimly. "The police found financial links. She's being arrested as we speak. Constance is making sure every news outlet has a camera there when they lead her out in handcuffs. It's a message. A public execution of her reputation. The message is simple: you come at the king, you don't miss. And if you do, we will burn your world to the ground."

Jack smirked, but there was no humor in it. He remembered his last, angry words to Constance. He'd been a brute. He needed to apologize. But Ashley's own words echoed in his head: *A man in your position… you do not apologize.*

"Is she still mad at me?" he asked quietly.

Ashley shook her head, her expression softening. "No. She said she actually understands you better now."

His last words to her had been, *"Either you all fucking accept it, or you can leave me the hell alone!"* He sighed. "I yelled at her."

"She told me," Ashley confirmed. She paused, a sly look entering her eyes. "You know, you could marry her. It would be a hell of an alliance."

He smirked. "And then I couldn't marry you."

She laughed, a genuine, warm sound. "Who knows? Maybe in our world, bigamy will become legal."

He shook his head, the banter feeling good, normal. "Not ready for that." But as he said it, the reality of the last few days crashed down on him. The bullet. The pain. The darkness. His near-death experience wasn't an abstract concept anymore. He'd stared it in the face. If he had died, there would be no Halland left.

Ashley saw the change in him, the sudden shadow that crossed his face. "Tell me," she whispered, leaning closer.

He looked at her, his eyes wide with a sudden, existential terror. "If I had died," he whispered, the words tasting like ash, "everything my father built… it would be gone. The name Halland would be nothing but a footnote in a dusty legal document, a ghost on a stock ticker. Vultures like Falcor would have picked the bones of his empire clean."

"So you need to insert yourself more," she offered gently. "Add your name to foundations, to buildings…"

He shook his head, his gaze intense. "No," he said, the realization hitting him with the force of a physical blow. "I need an heir."

She kissed him then, a soft, lingering press of her lips against his. "Think about it before you do anything," she whispered. "And talk to us. All of us. We're here to guide you. That's the job."

Just then, the limousine glided down a ramp into a private, subterranean parking garage. They had arrived at their new fortress.

The days that followed were a waking nightmare, a claustrophobic siege played out on a loop on every news channel in the country. The penthouse, intended as a fortress in the sky, had become a gilded cage. Its sweeping, floor-to-ceiling windows, once offering a god-like view of Los Angeles, were now shrouded in heavy, drawn curtains to thwart the long lenses of the news helicopters that circled like vultures several times a day. The muffled roar of their blades was a constant, maddening reminder of the privacy he had lost forever.

Constance had visited, a cool, calming presence amidst the chaos. She had sat across from him, her green eyes assessing his bandages and the new, hard set of his jaw, and assured him with a quiet sincerity that she was not mad about their last, heated conversation. "I don't get 'mad,' Jack," she'd said, a small, wry smile on her lips. "I reassess. And my assessment of you has only grown." She had reiterated her offer of a strategic marriage, an alliance that felt more pertinent now than ever, and had left him with a cool, deliberate press of her lips to his cheek, a sealing of their unspoken pact.

But while his new life in L.A. was a whirlwind of security briefings and power plays, the news from Washington was a slow, unfolding tragedy relayed through texts from Julie's mother. At seven months, something had gone wrong. The baby, a boy he would never have known but whose existence had caused him so much pain, had died in her womb. The doctors, Gloria wrote, believed it was due to the immense stress and shock of the last few weeks. The news hit Jack with a complex, gut-wrenching cocktail of emotions: a shameful, fleeting wave of relief, instantly drowned by an overwhelming guilt for that relief, and a profound, aching sorrow for Julie's unimaginable pain.

Then came the news of the surgery. He had paced the length of the penthouse like a caged tiger, his healthy arm clenched into a white-knuckled fist, while she was under the knife. His power, his billions, were utterly useless. He couldn't be there. He couldn't hold her hand. All he could do was ensure she had the best care money could buy and wait, tormented by his powerlessness. His three assistants watched him, their usual playful banter silenced by the raw, unfiltered love they saw etched on his face. It was Jenny who had whispered to Ashley, "When this is over, we should have her come here. She can move in with us."

In the nights, they had organized themselves into a silent, intuitive rotation of care. It wasn't just about sex; it was a form of therapy, of grounding him in the living world. Ashley, his chief of staff, would climb astride him, her movements slow and controlled, a tender ministration designed to give him release without aggravating the fiery agony in his shoulder. Jenny, his spark of fire, would let him take his frustration and rage out on her, bending over the sofa as he fucked her from behind with a primal urgency that left them both breathless and spent. And Maya, his cool strategist, would offer a different kind of solace, pulling him into a missionary embrace filled with slow, deep kisses, a quiet reassurance of human connection.

On the third morning, Ashley was fielding the twentieth call from a tabloid reporter when another call came through on her personal cell. She answered it, her voice warm and professional. "Gloria, it's so good to hear from you. How is she?"

Jack watched as the color drained from Ashley's face. He saw her professional mask crack, her knuckles whiten as she gripped the phone tighter, the blood turning to ice in her veins. He knew, with a certainty that chilled him to the bone, that the nightmare wasn't over.

She listened for another minute, her eyes wide with horror, murmuring quiet assurances before finally hanging up. She stood frozen for a moment, her back to him, clearly struggling to compose herself.

"Jack…" she finally whispered, turning to face him. "Julie is out of surgery. She's stable."

He saw the lie of omission in her eyes. "What is it?" he asked, his voice low and steady. "What aren't you telling me?"

Ashley walked over to him, her movements stiff. She knelt before his chair and took his hand. "There were complications during the surgery," she whispered, her voice a hoarse, broken thing. "A hemorrhage. They had to… Jack, they had to perform a hysterectomy to save her life."

The words didn't register at first. They were just sounds.

"She'll never be able to have children," Ashley clarified, her voice cracking as a single tear escaped and traced a path down her cheek.

The world tilted and went silent, the muffled roar of the helicopters outside fading into a dull ringing in his ears. His legs gave out, and he collapsed into the nearest armchair, the breath knocked out of him. It wasn't just the baby. It was the choice. The future. The one thing she might have wanted for herself, gone forever. It was a loss so profound, so absolute, it was incomprehensible. It was a cruelty on a cosmic scale, and it was tied, however indirectly, to him.

He buried his face in his hands, a strangled, guttural sob tearing from his throat.

"Jack…" Ashley whispered, her hand on his good shoulder.

He shook his head, unable to speak, unable to even look at her. "I need to be alone," he finally choked out, his voice hollow, devoid of all feeling, a dead thing in the silent, opulent room.

She hesitated for only a second, then squeezed his shoulder and stood. He heard her open the door to the office, heard the soft, whispered exchange as she told Jenny and Maya what had happened. Then, he heard the three of them walk out, and the heavy door clicked shut, leaving him entombed, alone with a grief so vast it threatened to swallow him whole.

The silence in the presidential suite was absolute, a sterile, soundproofed quiet that felt a thousand feet removed from the sprawling, indifferent city below. This was his new fortress, a gilded cage of polished marble, abstract art, and floor-to-ceiling windows that were already shrouded in heavy, blackout curtains. Jack stood in the center of the vast living area, the faint, clean scent of the hotel's air freshener a poor substitute for the salty tang of the ocean he'd grown used to. He was safe, but he was trapped, and the news about Julie was a living, screaming entity trapped in the gilded cage with him.

His eyes fell on the suite's private bar, a gleaming, polished mahogany structure backlit and stocked with dozens of top-shelf liquors he didn't recognize. He walked over to it, his movements stiff and robotic. He had never been a drinker, had never felt the need. But the pain inside him was a roaring inferno, and he desperately needed something to quench the flames. He reached for a heavy crystal decanter filled with amber liquid... whiskey.

The glass stopper came free with a soft *pop*. He ignored the rows of sparkling highball glasses, lifted the decanter directly to his lips, and took a long, desperate swig. The whiskey was a violent, fiery revolt in his throat, a brutal shock to his system that made him double over, coughing and gasping. But the burn was real. It was a clean pain, a physical agony that momentarily eclipsed the emotional torment. He straightened, his eyes watering, and took another, deeper drink.

The opulent room began to swim, the sharp lines of the furniture blurring into soft, tilting waves. His legs felt like they were made of rubber. He stumbled backward, a clumsy, uncoordinated fall, and crashed into a delicate, expensive-looking armchair. There was a splintering crack, a sickening crunch of breaking wood, as the chair disintegrated under his weight. He landed in a heap on the plush carpet, surrounded by the wreckage.

The door to the suite's living area burst open. Ashley was there first, her face a mask of alarm, with Jenny and Maya right behind her. They saw him sprawled on the floor, soaked in spilled whiskey amidst the splintered remains of a designer chair that likely cost more than his old car.

"For fuck's sake," Ashley whispered, a breath of pure frustration and deep concern. She and Maya were at his side in an instant, flanking him, supporting his dead weight as they hauled him to his feet. He was limp, his head lolling, his body radiating the unfamiliar heat of alcohol.

Ashley's eyes, sharp and commanding, met Jenny's. "You take him. Master bathroom. Shower him, get him sobered up, and put him to bed." She then turned to Maya, her voice all business. "We'll handle this. Call the hotel manager, tell them an accent chair had an… unfortunate accident. Arrange for immediate payment and discretion. I don't want a whisper of this leaving this floor." Maya nodded, the cool-headed fixer already pulling out her tablet to manage the fallout.

The master bathroom was a luxurious cavern of Italian marble and swirling steam, the air thick with heat and moisture. Jack was slumped against Jenny's naked body, her soft, steady form the only thing keeping him upright under the relentless torrent of hot water. He was barely conscious, his eyes glassy and distant, his body a dead weight against hers. His hand moved in a drunken, clumsy grope, searching for her breast, his touch uncertain and needy.

Jenny looked down at him, her expression a complex mix of pity and tenderness, her eyes reflecting a depth of emotion that belied her young age. "You sure you can handle me right now, boss?" she whispered, her voice a gentle tease designed to pull him back from the edge of his despair. She knew he was hurting, that his mind was a whirl of pain and confusion, and she wanted to ease his burden, if only for a moment.

A lopsided, boyish smile touched his lips, a faint echo of his usual charm, and he leaned in, kissing her with messy, open-mouthed passion. His lips were soft, his kiss desperate, and she could taste the salt of his tears on her tongue. She laughed softly, a sound of pure affection, her hand sliding down his body, her fingers wrapping around his cock. It was an act of mercy, not seduction, a silent promise to take care of him, to help him find a moment's peace.

She knew he needed the oblivion of orgasm to finally let go of the pain and sleep. With a gentle touch, she guided him to turn so that he was facing the wall, his hands braced against the cool marble for support. She lowered herself to her knees on the wet marble floor in front of him, the water cascading over her back, her body a silhouette of curves and shadows. She looked up at him, her eyes locked on his, and she took him deep into her mouth, her lips stretching wide to accommodate his length.

Her actions were efficient but tender, a clinical application of pleasure designed to drain the pain from him. She sucked him deep, her cheeks hollowing as she created a tight seal with her lips, her tongue swirling around his shaft, tasting him, exploring him. She bobbed her head, her movements slow and deliberate, her hand gripping the base of his cock, her fingers squeezing and stroking in time with her mouth.

Jack's breath hitched, his body tensing as he fought to maintain control. He looked down at her, his eyes filled with a mix of surprise and gratitude, his hands reaching out to tangle in her hair, his fingers gripping her scalp, holding her to him. She took him deeper, her nose touching his pelvis, her throat relaxing to accommodate his invasion, her eyes watering from the effort.

She pulled back, her lips popping off his cock with a wet sound, her breath coming in short gasps. She looked up at him, her eyes filled with determination, and she took him deep again, her hand working in tandem with her mouth, her other hand reaching up to cup his balls, rolling them gently in her palm.

Jack came with a short, shuddering release, his body convulsing, his cock pulsing as he spilled his seed down her throat. A broken sound of grief and tension left his body, a raw, primal cry that echoed off the marble walls, a testament to the pain he had been carrying. Jenny swallowed every drop, her hand gently milking him, coaxing every last bit of pleasure from his body.

"There, boss," she whispered, her voice a soft, soothing melody as she stood up, her body pressing against his, her arms wrapping around him in a tight embrace. She kissed his forehead, her lips lingering, her breath warm against his skin. "Now you can sleep," she murmured, her voice a lullaby, a promise of peace and respite from his pain. She held him there, under the hot water, her body a shield against the world, her love a balm to his wounded soul.

She finished washing him, dried his pliant body with a thick, monogrammed hotel towel, and led him to the enormous king-sized bed. He collapsed into the crisp, five-star linens and was gone before his head hit the pillow.

Jenny stood over him, gently brushing a damp strand of hair from his forehead. She hated herself for the sharp pang of jealousy she felt for the girl who could cause him this much pain, but she also ached for him. Against all logic, she was falling for this broken boy-king.

The bedroom door opened softly, and Ashley stepped in. "How is he?" she whispered.

"Sleeping," Jenny replied, her voice soft. "He'll be out for a while."

"Did you take care of him?" Ashley asked, the question a practical one between caregivers.

"Just a blowjob," Jenny confirmed quietly. "He needed it."

Ashley looked at her friend, at the unguarded, loving way she gazed at their sleeping boss. "You're starting to love him," she stated, not as an accusation, but as a sad, undeniable fact.

A single tear escaped Jenny's eye, and she gave a small, defeated nod.

"Yeah," Ashley sighed, her own voice heavy with a shared secret. "Maya, too."

The confession hung between them. They were all falling.

"He has no idea, does he?" Jenny whispered, looking at Jack's peaceful face.

"No," Ashley replied, her gaze dark and prophetic. "But he will." She put an arm around Jenny's shoulder. "Come on. Let's leave him to his rest. We have his world to run in the morning."

Chapter 14.

The first thing Jack learned when he woke was that sleeping between three naked, warm, and beautiful women was the very definition of heaven. The second thing he learned was that a whiskey hangover was a particularly vicious kind of hell. A low groan escaped his lips as he tried to shift, the slightest movement sending a jackhammer pounding behind his eyes and a wave of nausea through his gut.

A set of soft lips immediately found his, silencing the sound. "Morning, boss," he heard Jenny whisper, her fiery hair a stark, beautiful contrast to the white of the hotel pillows.

Another set of lips brushed against his cheek, cool and deliberate. "Good morning, Mr. Halland," Maya's smooth alto voice murmured from his other side.

Then, a third kiss, deeper and more possessive, landed squarely on his mouth. "Morning, Jack," Ashley whispered, her body pressed flush against his back.

He forced his eyes open, a painful process that felt like peeling back sandpaper. The opulent hotel suite swam into bleary focus, but all he could truly see was the tangle of pale limbs and different shades of hair surrounding him. He was at the center of a living, breathing paradise, and he felt like death.

"What did I do?" he asked, his voice a hoarse, gravelly rasp.

"You acquainted yourself with a bottle of the hotel's finest single malt and then declared war on an innocent armchair," Ashley said, a teasing smirk in her voice.

He groaned again, the memory a fuzzy, embarrassing blur. "Please tell me you paid the hotel for it."

"Already taken care of," Maya confirmed coolly. "The charge has been settled, and a replacement from the same designer will be here this afternoon. They think you 'tripped.'"

He managed a weak smile. "What would I do without you girls?"

The three of them exchanged a silent, knowing look over his body. It was Jenny who spoke, her tone shifting from playful to serious. "About that... we want to be sure you have everything you need to... recover. Properly."

He looked at her, confused.

"So, we've taken the liberty of planning your day," she continued. "First, a car will be taking you for a private spa treatment. Detoxifying massage, vitamin IV drip, the works. Then, this afternoon, we're going to look at a new home."

Jack sighed, the effort immense. "And the media? The vultures?"

"They've backed off a little," Ashley said. "The story of Mrs. Falcor's very public arrest has given them a new chew toy. And Constance is expecting us at the new penthouse at one o'clock."

Maya leaned forward, her dark eyes bright with strategic excitement. "I reached out to a contact of mine, the top broker for off-market properties in Beverly Hills. She assures me this place is perfect. It's a four-floor penthouse, a fortress floating above the city. There's a tri-level aquatic paradise on the top floor... an Olympic-sized pool that's half indoors, half outdoors. And, of course, a private, reinforced helipad on the roof."

Jack's throbbing head was having trouble processing the scale of it. "How many bedrooms?"

Maya laughed. "Nineteen. Along with three living rooms, two media rooms, a full entertainment wing, a restaurant-grade kitchen, nine office suites, a private gym, and a soundproofed music room. It was previously owned by a rock star with a penchant for privacy and excess."

He just nodded, the information too much. His head felt like it was going to split open.

"Here," Jenny said softly, handing him two Tylenol and a glass of water as if reading his mind.

"One more thing, Jack," Ashley whispered, her voice suddenly gentle. She placed her hand over his on the bedsheet. "You need Julie here."

The name landed in the room with a quiet, heavy thud.

"She's your anchor, Jack," Ashley continued, her gaze unwavering. "She's the only part of your old life that still fits, even if it's complicated. Now, after everything, she needs you just as much as you need her." The other two girls gave solemn, almost imperceptible nods. It was a unanimous decision from his board of directors.

He sighed, the sound ragged. He thought of Julie, alone in a hospital room, grappling with a loss so profound he couldn't fathom it. Ashley was right. "Once we move into the new place," he conceded, the words costing him.

Ashley's answering smile was warm and full of relief. "We've already arranged for you to fly to Washington tomorrow," she said gently. "On the private jet. You need to see her, to show her you're still there for her. While you're gone, we'll take care of the entire move."

He shook his head, a spark of his usual command returning. "*You're* going with me," he said, looking directly at Ashley. "I told you when I hired you: where I go, you go."

"Jack, you need to be alone with her," she whispered, trying to reason with him. "Our presence would just complicate things."

"And I will be alone with her," he insisted, his voice leaving no room for argument. "But you are coming to Washington with me."

She let out a soft sigh of concession.

"We'll take care of everything else here," Jenny said, with Maya nodding in support.

With that, the meeting was adjourned. They all began to stir, untangling themselves from the bed. Maya rose, her movements fluid and graceful. She took his hand, her touch cool and firm.

"First, let's wash away that hangover," she purred, her voice a low, husky promise. "My way." She gently pulled him from the bed, leading him toward the shower for a very personal and thorough debriefing.

With a final, shuddering grunt, Jack filled Maya's mouth, the release a white-hot wave that momentarily erased the pounding in his head. She didn't pull away, holding him until the last tremor subsided, her throat working to accept every last drop of his offering. With a final, reverent caress of her tongue, she looked up at him, her dark eyes shimmering with a potent mixture of desire and devotion in the steamy air. She rose gracefully and began to gently wash his body with a soft cloth, her touch both clinical and incredibly tender.

"We will always be there for you," she whispered, her voice a low, husky promise against the backdrop of the cascading water. She planted her lips on his, a slow, deep kiss that tasted of him and her. "You should know that by now."

He smiled, a weak but genuine expression, and wrapped his arms around her waist, pulling her close. The warmth of her skin, the solid feel of her in his arms, was an anchor in his swirling sea of pain and confusion. "I think," he said, the words feeling foreign but true as they left his lips, "I think I love you all."

He felt her stiffen for a fraction of a second, surprised by the raw, vulnerable admission. Then she relaxed against him, a soft sigh escaping her as she leaned her head against his chest. She said nothing, simply held him, and in the silence, he felt her acceptance. She turned off the water, and the sudden quiet was broken only by the sound of their breathing. She dried him with a thick, plush hotel towel, her movements careful and deliberate, mindful of the wound on his shoulder.

In the bedroom, Ashley had already laid out his armor for the day: a sharp, charcoal grey suit, a crisp white shirt, and a subtle silk tie. It was the uniform of "Jack Halland, the magnate," a role he felt utterly unprepared to play. Maya helped him dress, her cool, competent fingers brushing against his skin as she deftly buttoned his shirt and straightened his tie. It was a gesture both professional and profoundly intimate. She got dressed herself, and together they walked out into the main living area of the suite.

The vast room had been transformed into a command center. Jenny and Ashley sat at the large dining table, laptops open, surrounded by tablets and steaming mugs of coffee. They looked up as he and Maya entered, their expressions a mixture of professional focus and personal concern.

Jenny immediately rose and poured him a cup of coffee, placing it before him at the head of the table. "So," Ashley began, her tone all business, "as we said... we've planned a recovery day for you. Your body has been through hell. First the shooting, then the whiskey. We need to flush the toxins and get you centered before you see the penthouse."

Jack nodded, the rich aroma of the coffee a small comfort. He had never had a spa treatment in his life, but he trusted Ashley's judgment completely, too exhausted to have any of his own.

"The car is waiting downstairs... a nondescript black sedan for anonymity," Ashley continued. "It will take you to a private wellness center in Chinatown. The masseuse is an old and very dear friend of mine." A wicked smirk played on her lips. "Her name is Mei. She is a master of traditional therapeutic arts, and she normally only works on a select list of female clients. I told her about your... situation... and she's made an exception."

"The spa will take a few hours," Jenny chimed in, looking up from her laptop. "There's a cleansing herbal bath, the deep tissue massage, and then a long soak to relax afterward."

"And who is going with me?" Jack asked, his voice still raspy.

Jenny smiled. "I will. I'll be your escort and security liaison for the day. Ashley and Maya will be the advance team. They're going to the new penthouse now to meet with Constance and make sure everything is perfect for your inspection this afternoon."

He looked at the three of them, this beautiful, terrifyingly competent team he had somehow assembled. He took a sip of his coffee, but his stomach, still reeling from the hangover, churned in protest. He set the cup down, unable to think about food. His new life, it seemed, was a feast he had no appetite for.

The drive into Chinatown was a journey into another world. The cool, tomb-like silence of the nondescript black sedan served as a cocoon, insulating Jack from the vibrant chaos of the streets outside. Through the tinted windows, he watched the city transform into a cacophony of sounds and smells, of brightly colored signs and bustling crowds. As promised, the anonymity of the car was a balm to his frayed nerves; for the first time in days, he felt like he could breathe without being watched. Jenny sat beside him, a silent, reassuring presence, while the two security guards sat impassively in the front.

The sedan pulled to a stop before a building that seemed like a relic from another century, a hidden gem nestled between a bustling market and an electronics store. It was a masterpiece of old Chinese architecture, with an intricately carved dark wood facade, a gracefully curved tile roof, and two stone lions guarding the heavy, red-lacquered door.

One of the security guards exited the vehicle, his eyes scanning the surroundings before he opened Jack's door and gave a slight nod. "All clear, sir."

Jack nodded and got out, Jenny following close behind as they entered the building. The chaos of the street vanished instantly, replaced by a world of serene quiet. The air inside was thick with the calming scent of sandalwood and jasmine, and the only sound was the gentle trickle of a hidden fountain. They were met in the foyer by a very old woman, her skin like fine parchment, her back ramrod straight with a timeless dignity. Her eyes, dark and impossibly ancient, seemed to hold the depth of a thousand years of wisdom.

"Mr. Halland," she said, her English perfectly unaccented and carrying the weight of quiet authority. "Mei is expecting you. She is in the Iris Room, number fourteen."

Jack nodded and began to walk down the long, silent hallway, his footsteps echoing on the polished dark wood floors. He noticed Jenny hadn't moved and turned to look at her. She stood by the entrance, her phone and tablet already in her hands, a small, encouraging smile on her face.

"This part is just for you, boss," she said softly. "Your recovery. My job right now is to hold down the fort out here and make sure the world doesn't intrude."

He smirked but gave her a nod of gratitude. He was still getting used to the idea of having people whose entire job was to make his life easier. He walked the length of the hall, the soft light from paper lanterns guiding his way, the scent of incense growing stronger, until he reached a door marked with the delicate painted symbol of an iris. He knocked softly.

The door glided open silently, as if anticipating his touch. And the woman standing there stole the air from his lungs.

This was no matronly therapist. This was a vision. She was a masterpiece of Chinese beauty, her hair a river of polished, black obsidian, pulled back into a loose, intricate knot held by a single, carved jade pin. Her eyes, shaped like dark almonds, held a calm, knowing depth that seemed to see right through him, but in them, he also saw the flicker of a hidden, playful fire. Her skin was like flawless porcelain, a stark, beautiful canvas for the dramatic red of her lips.

She was dressed in a form-fitting cheongsam of deep, emerald green silk that clung to her body like a second skin. The high mandarin collar framed her slender neck, and the silk traced the subtle, perfect curves of her breasts and hips before splitting into a daringly high slit along one thigh, offering a tantalizing flash of smooth, pale skin as she moved to welcome him in. Her posture was one of effortless grace, and her smile was a slow, enigmatic curve of her lips that was both welcoming and deeply, unshakably confident.

His hangover-addled brain short-circuited. The room seemed to tilt, and the air felt thin. He had been expecting Ashley's "old friend." He had not been expecting... this. This stunning, graceful creature who radiated a quiet, formidable power.

"Mr. Halland," she said, and her voice was a melody, soft and imbued with a profound calm that seemed to quiet the frantic pounding in his head. "Ashley has told me you carry a great weight... not just in your shoulder, but in your spirit. My purpose today is to help you set it down, even for a little while. I have arranged a special treatment for you."

She presented him with a robe of thick, dark silk, her movements fluid and graceful. "Please, disrobe and make yourself comfortable. I will be waiting for you in the bath." She gave him a small, encouraging smile before disappearing through a sliding door at the back of the room.

He stood alone for a long moment, the scent of jasmine and sandalwood heavy in the air. He slowly undressed, his new, expensive suit feeling like a costume he was eager to shed. He folded it neatly on a carved wooden chair, a lingering habit from a life where one good suit was all he had. Once naked, he wrapped the cool silk of the robe around his body and walked through the door.

The room on the other side stole his breath. It was a grotto of slate and steam, centered around a large, sunken pool of dark, shimmering water. Steam, thick with the scent of lavender and eucalyptus, rose from the surface, where crimson and white petals floated like sleeping butterflies. And in the center of the pool, she was waiting.

She was naked, her pale skin luminous in the soft, indirect light. Her long, black hair was unbound now, floating around her shoulders like a silken veil. Her body was perfect, yes, but presented with such a natural, serene lack of artifice that lust was the last thing on his mind. She looked less like a seductress and more like a water spirit, a guardian of this tranquil, hidden place. He felt his own vulnerability acutely... the angry, stitched wound on his shoulder, the lingering tremor in his hands from the hangover, the hollowness in his soul.

"Do not be shy, Jack," she said, her voice a soft echo in the steamy room. Using his first name was a deliberate, intimate choice. "There is no judgment here. Only healing. If you will join me, let me care for you."

He looked at her, at the profound kindness in her dark eyes, and nodded. He let the robe fall from his shoulders and stepped into the water. The heat was a blissful shock, instantly seeping into his sore muscles. She moved to him, the water swirling around her, and her body, warm and soft, pressed against his back.

"You have a very tense body," she whispered, her hands beginning to work on the knotted muscles of his neck and shoulders. Her touch was gentle but firm, expert and intuitive. He closed his eyes, his head lolling forward as he surrendered to her touch. He felt the tightness in his shoulders, a tension he had been carrying for what felt like a lifetime, slowly begin to dissipate. Her hands glided down his back, finding every point of pain and working it into submission. She began to wash him, a slow, reverent ritual, the glide of a soft cloth over his skin washing away the stale, antiseptic smell of the hospital, the scent of whiskey and fear. It was forty minutes of quiet, blissful healing, and as she worked, he felt a dam of emotion he didn't know he was holding back begin to crack. A single, hot tear escaped his closed eye, tracing a path down his cheek, and he felt her thumb gently wipe it away.

She kissed his wounded shoulder, the touch as light as a butterfly's wing, pulling him from the waking dream he had fallen into. "Now," she whispered, her breath warm against his skin, "we dry, and you receive a real massage."

She stood and took his hand, her naked body a canvas of breathtaking grace as she guided him up the steps from the tub. She wrapped him in a thick, heated towel and began to dry him with a tenderness that made his throat tighten. Her hands moved over his body, from head to toe, and when they reached his groin, she paused. His cock was painfully hard, a natural reaction of a body finally coming back to life. She didn't smirk; she simply gave a soft, understanding smile, wrapping the towel around him to grant him a measure of dignity.

She opened another door, leading him into a room where a large, padded massage table stood. "On your stomach, please," she whispered.

He did as she asked, the hardness of his cock now a slightly awkward pressure against the firm bed. He heard her move, and then felt the bed dip as she climbed up, straddling his legs, her naked skin warm against his. Her hands, now slick with a warm, scented oil, began to work their magic. For twenty minutes, she kneaded and pressed, releasing every kink and knot from his back, his legs, his soul.

When she was done, she slid off him. "Now your front, Jack," she said, her voice still a hypnotic whisper.

He knew he was still hard, but he was beyond embarrassment now. He turned over, his erection standing straight up from his stomach, a defiant flag of life. She climbed up again, straddling his hips this time, her gaze never leaving his. Her hands started on his shoulders, working their way around his neck and down his chest, then his stomach, his legs, and then, finally, to his groin.

Her oiled fingers gently wrapped around him, her touch sending a jolt of pure pleasure through his system. She stroked him a few times, a slow, deliberate rhythm that was both a question and an answer.

"Sometimes," she whispered, her eyes holding his, her voice filled with a profound tenderness, "the deepest healing requires a different kind of touch. A joining of spirits. If you would allow me, Jack. If you would trust me."

It was an offer, not a demand. A question, not a statement. He couldn't speak, so he just nodded, his heart hammering in his chest.

With a reverence that took his breath away, she shifted her weight, moving up his body and lowering herself onto him. He entered her with a slow, perfect glide, her warmth enveloping him completely. She let out a soft, shuddering moan as their bodies joined, and he felt his own walls of grief and anger begin to dissolve. She began to move, a slow, rocking rhythm of pure solace, her eyes locked with his. This wasn't fucking; this was a prayer.

"Miss Ashley said you would be big," she whispered, her voice catching. "She did not say you would feel so… good." He saw her eyes glaze over, her body beginning to tremble. "Jack… I… I…" she started to say, then she arched her back, a beautiful, sharp cry escaping her lips as her orgasm took her. Her body shook, convulsing around him as she collapsed onto his chest, her head falling into the crook of his neck.

He held her, stroking her hair as she shuddered, a fierce wave of protectiveness washing over him. She turned her head, her face wet with tears, and kissed him deeply. "I have never before…" she whispered against his lips. "Never… connected like that."

She sat up, her expression transformed, a fierce, loving light in her eyes. Now it was his turn. She began to move again, her rhythm no longer slow and gentle, but deep and powerful, her movements dedicated entirely to his release. She was taking the pain from him, drawing it out with every perfect rotation of her hips.

"Yes, Jack," she whispered, her voice a deep, growling purr. "Let it go. Give it all to me. Fill me…"

He felt it building, a blinding, white-hot rush from the base of his spine. It was a complete surrender. With a final, upward thrust, he came deep inside her, a raw, ragged cry tearing from his throat, a sound not of lust, but of pure, cathartic release. He felt her body clench around him, her own orgasm echoing his. She collapsed onto him again, their bodies slick with sweat and scented oil, and wrapped her arms around him, holding him tight in a cocoon of warmth and shared vulnerability.

For ten minutes that felt like both a lifetime and a single, suspended heartbeat, they simply lay there, wrapped in a cocoon of warmth and shared vulnerability. The sated quiet of the room was a universe away from the chaos of his life, the only sounds the rhythmic beat of their hearts and the soft whisper of their breathing. He could feel the heavy, contented weight of her body on his, her soft hair tickling his cheek, the air thick with the scent of sandalwood oil and their mingled sweat.

Mei finally lifted her head, her dark, almond-shaped eyes soft and full of a wonder that mirrored his own. She pressed her lips against his, a kiss devoid of passion but filled with a profound tenderness.

"This was not the plan," she whispered, her voice a soft, wondering murmur against his mouth.

He managed a small, tired smirk, feeling more at peace than he had in years. "Sometimes the best moments in life defy a plan," he whispered back, his voice thick with emotion.

A slow, beautiful smile blossomed on her face. She gently pushed herself up, and as she moved off him, he saw the pearly trail of his own life force on her smooth, pale thigh… a stark, intimate testament to their joining. She took his hand, her touch no longer that of a therapist, but of a lover.

"We need a proper bath now," she whispered, her eyes holding his.

She guided him not back to the main bathing room, but through another, smaller door he hadn't noticed. It opened into a more intimate sanctuary, a space of dark slate and steam, where a single, deep porcelain claw-foot tub stood waiting, already filled with fresh, steaming water.

She helped him step into the tub, the clean, hot water a welcome shock, before sliding in herself. She settled in front of him, her back resting against his chest. He wrapped his arms around her, a natural, protective circle, and rested his chin on her shoulder, inhaling the scent of her wet hair. He kissed the side of her neck, a soft, reverent gesture.

"Would you consider a position as my personal masseuse?" he whispered, the words surprising even himself. He didn't want this feeling… this peace, this healing… to be a one-time event. He wanted it, and her, in his life.

She turned her head slightly to look at him, her expression unreadable. "Mr. Halland…" she began, her voice a breathy whisper as she tried to re-establish a professional boundary.

He silenced her with a gentle kiss. "Just think about it, Mei," he murmured against her lips. "Please."

She held his gaze for a long moment, then gave a single, slow nod, a silent acceptance of the new, undefined territory they had entered. A soft, knowing smile touched her lips. Without a word, she turned in the water to face him, her legs wrapping around his waist. It was her answer.

She lifted herself up, her eyes never leaving his, and then slowly lowered her body, taking him inside her once more. There was no desperate urgency this time, no frantic need. It was a slow, languid dance in the warm, swirling water. A silent conversation spoken through the press of lips and the caress of hands. It was less like fucking and more like a prayer, a quiet, reverent joining that was about cherishing the moment, the connection, the profound and unexpected intimacy they had found. He held her close, the water lapping gently against their skin, the outside world and all its noise and pain completely forgotten, lost in the sanctuary they had created together.

Chapter 15.

When Jack emerged from the tranquil sanctuary of the spa three hours later, he felt like a new man. The gnawing, whiskey hangover had been purged from his system, replaced by a serene calm that settled deep in his bones. His body, expertly worked over by Mei's magical hands, felt light and limber, the fire in his shoulder reduced to a dull, distant ache. He felt reborn.

Jenny was waiting in the serene, jasmine-scented lobby, her head bent over a tablet. She looked up as he approached, and her professional smile instantly melted into a genuine, relieved grin. She saw the transformation immediately; the tension was gone from his jaw, the haunted, hunted look in his eyes replaced by a quiet clarity.

"Feeling better, boss?" she asked, her voice soft.

He gave her a slow, confident smile, a real one this time. "Like I could conquer the world," he said, and he meant it.

"Good," she replied, her own green eyes sparkling. "Because conquering the world is on the agenda for this afternoon. We have about an hour's drive to the penthouse."

He nodded, and they exited the spa into the vibrant chaos of Chinatown. The two security guards, who had been standing sentry, fell into step behind them, their presence a discreet but unbreachable wall. They entered the cool, quiet cocoon of the black sedan and pulled away from the curb, melting into the L.A. traffic.

As they drove, Jenny turned towards him on the plush leather seat. She leaned in, her voice dropping to a conspiratorial whisper, her eyes dancing with mischief. "So," she murmured, "did you fuck her?"

Jack's eyes flickered to the rearview mirror, where he could see the impassive face of the driver, then to the guard in the passenger seat. They were listening; it was their job to hear everything. He gave Jenny a look, a silent rebuke, and saw a quick, impish smirk cross her face before she nodded in understanding.

He leaned forward. "Hey, hit that next drive-through," he said to the driver. "I'm dying for a coffee."

The driver nodded, expertly changing lanes. A few minutes later, they were back on the freeway, all four of them holding a hot coffee that Jack had paid for. "Thank you, sir," the driver said, his voice holding a note of genuine gratitude. Jack just smiled and leaned back.

The rest of the drive was quiet. Jenny, seemingly content, snuggled up against his good side, resting her head on his shoulder. The simple, uncomplicated affection was a comfort, and as the city slid by, his mind began to catalogue the new, complex constellation of women in his life. There was Julie, the constant, aching question mark at the center of his heart. There was Ashley, the formidable chief of staff and passionate lover, the bedrock of this new world. There was Jenny, the fiery, loyal soldier currently resting against him. There was Maya, the cool, brilliant strategist. And now, there was Mei. The healer. A serene, quiet sanctuary he felt a deep, protective tenderness for. He hoped she would accept his offer. Finally, there was Constance, the ultimate alliance, a potential dynasty encapsulated in a wedding ring. It was a dizzying, terrifying, and exhilarating roster.

As these thoughts swirled, he realized they were pulling off the freeway. But to his surprise, they drove past the gleaming, impossibly tall high-rise he had seen in the portfolio, pulling instead into the subterranean garage of the equally luxurious, but slightly more discreet, tower next door.

Jenny lifted her head from his shoulder, her smile one of shared conspiracy. "The old owner had the same concerns about privacy that you do," she explained, gesturing towards a reinforced steel door at the far end of the garage. "There's a private, underground tunnel that connects this garage to a dedicated elevator in the other building. An elevator that only has one stop: the penthouse floor."

Jack looked at the unassuming door, and then back at Jenny, a feeling of profound appreciation washing over him. It was more than a clever feature; it was a promise. A subterranean umbilical cord to his fortress, a way to move through the world unseen. In his new life, he was beginning to understand that true privacy was the ultimate luxury, and he was more grateful for this hidden tunnel than he was for the nineteen bedrooms waiting for him in the sky.

The private elevator ascended in a smooth, silent rush, a mobile chamber paneled in dark, polished wood and soft, recessed lighting. It was just Jack and Jenny, enclosed in an intimate quiet as they were carried toward the sky. The two security guards remained below, stone-faced sentinels guarding the secret entrance to their boss's new fortress.

Jenny turned to him, her green eyes sparkling with the same playful mischief he'd seen during her interview. "So," she began, her voice a low, conspiratorial whisper, "you never actually answered my question from the car."

He chuckled, the sound low and relaxed. The pain and tension Mei had so expertly worked from his body had been replaced by a serene, buzzing energy. He gave a single, slow nod. It was all the confirmation she needed.

"Good," she whispered, her approval genuine and warm, devoid of any jealousy. She squeezed his hand. "You needed it. After everything." She paused, her expression shifting to one of triumphant excitement. "Speaking of which, according to Ashley, your new passport arrived this morning. It's waiting for you upstairs. You can go anywhere in the world, whenever you're ready."

Jack smiled, a real, unguarded smile. The news sent a jolt of purpose through him. He could almost taste the sun-drenched streets of Monaco, could almost feel the weight of the key to the vault his father had told him about. The vault that held the next piece of the puzzle. And with it, he hoped, more information about the mysterious Madeline… the ghostly key to understanding it all.

The elevator chimed softly and came to a stop. The polished steel doors slid open with a near-silent hiss, revealing a scene that took his breath away.

On the other side, waiting for him in the vast, sunlit expanse of the penthouse's private foyer, stood an imposing, breathtaking triumvirate of power and beauty. Ashley, Maya, and Constance. His court.

Jack stepped out of the elevator, and the women moved to greet him. Ashley was first, her kiss proprietary and full of the unspoken language of the nights they'd shared. Maya followed, her lips cooler, more deliberate, a touch that was both a greeting and a subtle reminder of her strategic value.

He then turned to Constance. She watched him, a slow, enigmatic smile on her face. He leaned in and gave her a brief but meaningful press of his lips against hers. "I'm still thinking," he whispered, for her ears only.

Her smirk widened. She was a woman who enjoyed the game.

He finally pulled back and took in his surroundings. The words Jenny had used... *penthouse, four floors...* had not prepared him for the reality. This wasn't an apartment; it was a private skyscraper. The foyer opened into a great room of such sheer, breathtaking volume it felt less like a home and more like a modern art museum. Gleaming marble floors stretched out like a frozen lake to a wall made entirely of glass, showcasing a god's-eye view of the city sprawling to the horizon.

"The ceilings are ten feet on the first three floors," Ashley said, noticing his awe. "The top floor, the entertainment level, has fourteen-foot ceilings with extra reinforced beams to support the helipad."

As they walked deeper into the space, he caught a flash of movement in the state-of-the-art kitchen, a space built for a Michelin-star army. A young woman sat perched on a bar stool, her back to them. She turned as they approached, and Jack felt that familiar, dizzying short-circuit in his brain.

She was a quintessential California bombshell. Long, sun-streaked blonde hair cascaded over the shoulders of a sharp, white power suit that hugged her curves. She had a dazzling, megawatt smile and eyes the color of the sea he'd left behind in Malibu.

He looked at Ashley, raising an eyebrow.

"Maya's friend," Ashley whispered, leaning in close. "Kamilla. She's the realtor, the best in the city for off-market properties like this."

Jack nodded, his gaze returning to the woman. Every woman in his immediate orbit… his fierce, brilliant assistants, his potential fiancée, even the real estate agent… was a fucking model. A thought, sharp and clear, cut through his awe. *Fucking L.A.* A year ago, a woman like Kamilla wouldn't have even registered his existence. Now, she was just another part of the scenery. He found he didn't just love that fact; he was starting to expect it. It was a new, thrilling, and dangerous kind of normal.

Kamilla led them on a tour through a seemingly endless succession of vast, sunlit spaces. They moved through a private cinema with plush, velvet reclining seats, a cavernous game room, and a library with soaring, two-story shelves. With every room, Jack felt a dizzying sense of dislocation; this wasn't a home, it was a sovereign nation. He loved it more with each step.

Finally, as Kamilla left them to see the last room alone, Ashley guided them to a set of large double doors on the top floor. She pushed them open with a theatrical flourish, presenting the inner sanctum. "The master suite," she announced.

Jack stepped inside, and the word "bedroom" seemed utterly inadequate. The space was larger than the entire ground floor of the house he had just left behind in Washington. A wall of glass offered an uninterrupted, 270-degree panorama of the city, the ocean, and the sky. The bed wasn't a king; it was a custom-built leviathan, an island of pillows and dark purple silk sheets that could have comfortably slept ten. Beyond it, another set of doors led to a walk-in closet that was more like a high-end boutique, with rows of empty, glass-fronted cabinets and islands of polished marble waiting for watches and jewelry he didn't own.

"Holy hell," he whispered, the words lost in the sheer volume of the space.

Maya walked past him and opened another door, revealing the master bathroom. It was a grotto of black marble and chrome. In the center was a sunken jacuzzi, a bubbling pool easily big enough for six people. The shower was a monsoon chamber of glass and steel, with a dozen gleaming showerheads embedded in the ceiling and walls. And off to the side, on a raised dais overlooking the city, stood a single, padded massage table.

The sight of it sent a jolt of memory through him. He could almost feel the phantom touch of Mei's hands, smell the ghost of sandalwood oil in the air. His offer to her... a desperate, hopeful plea to keep that feeling of peace in his life... hung unanswered in his mind.

He turned to Maya, pulling himself back to the present. "How much?" he asked, his voice steady.

She smiled, her dark eyes glittering with the thrill of the transaction. "For the entire penthouse, all four floors, fully furnished, including the lifetime access deed to the private parking and tunnel in the next tower... one hundred and sixty million dollars."

The old Jack, the boy who worried about heating bills, would have had a fatal aneurysm just hearing a number like that. But he was a billionaire now. The number was abstract, almost comical. A slow, dangerous smirk spread across his face. "Chef, trainer, maids?" he asked, his gaze shifting to Ashley.

"We're working on it," she confirmed. "Vetting the best. We want to ensure they understand the... dynamic... you wish to cultivate. People who are not only skilled, but exceptionally discreet."

He nodded, appreciating her euphemism. He turned back to Maya. "Tell Kamilla I'll take it."

Maya's professional composure broke, replaced by a dazzling, triumphant smile. She leaned in and kissed him soundly on the lips. "She is going to *love* you," she whispered, before turning and practically sprinting out of the room to deliver the good news.

"The live-in staff," Ashley said, her tone returning to business, "will have their own wing of apartments on the lowest floor, by the kitchen."

Jack looked at her, then around the palatial master floor. "And you three?"

Ashley smiled, a slight, almost deferential expression. "We're staff, Jack. We'll be down there with them."

"No fucking way," he said, the words a low, fierce growl that surprised even himself. He was tired of the lines between employer and lover, between business and family. He was making his own rules. "My assistants live on this floor. With me." He gestured to the six other bedroom suites they had passed in the hallway.

Ashley's face transformed, her professional mask melting away to reveal a look of profound, heart-stopping affection. She stepped into his space and kissed him, not a kiss of passion, but of deep, grateful intimacy. "As you wish, boss," she whispered against his lips.

Beside them, Jenny's answering smile was one of pure, unadulterated joy. This wasn't just a job anymore. He had just officially elevated them from employees to his inner circle, his family, the queens of his new castle in the sky.

Jack stepped over to the immense wall of glass that served as the western face of the great room. He placed a hand on the cool, smooth surface and looked down. Forty floors below, the city of Los Angeles sprawled out like a glittering circuit board, the cars on the boulevards looking like metallic ants crawling along glowing pathways. The dizzying vertigo was a small price to pay for the profound sense of security it offered. Up here, in his new fortress in the sky, no sniper could touch him. The glass, he'd been told, was ballistic, and its outer surface was a mirrored shield, granting him a god's-eye view of the world while rendering him completely invisible. Here, he could be safe.

He turned from the window, his expression resolute. He was no longer a guest in this life; he was its master. "We need everything," he announced, his voice echoing in the vast, empty space.

Jenny, ever-efficient, instantly had her tablet out, her fingers poised to create a new list.

"I want a complete wardrobe," he began, pacing the room as he built his new world from scratch. "Tailored suits in dark colors… charcoal, navy, black. Casual wear that doesn't look like it came from a mall. And whatever one wears on a yacht in Monaco, find that too. For the bathroom, I want the best of everything for grooming, for health. Stock it all." He paused, thinking of the opulent but impersonal master suite. "And new bedding. That dark purple is not my style. I want deep navy or stark black silk sheets."

Jenny's fingers flew across the screen, her expression one of focused concentration.

"For the media room," he continued, a smirk touching his lips as he thought of his girls, "I want a full satellite uplink and the fastest internet connection money can buy. For movies." He knew it was more for them than for him; his life, for the foreseeable future, would be a global affair. "And in the kitchen, I want anything and everything our chef could possibly imagine she needs, and then some. Spare no expense."

Jenny nodded, adding it all to the list. He walked down the hall, past the grand master suite, and stopped at the door to the bedroom directly adjacent to it. He opened it with a sense of reverence. It was another palatial room with the same stunning views.

"If Julie accepts my offer," he whispered, more to himself than to the women behind him, "this is her room."

He turned and saw Ashley watching him, her face filled with a deep, compassionate understanding. She knew this space he was carving out was sacred, a protected corner of his new world for the last, most important piece of his old one. She simply nodded.

Just then, her phone chimed with a new message. She glanced down at it, and a slow, delighted laugh escaped her. She looked up at him, her eyes dancing. "You didn't waste any time, did you? You offered Mei a job?"

He turned to face her, a half-smile on his face. "Yeah, I did."

Ashley stepped forward and kissed him, a quick, playful peck. "Well, just so you know, I'm getting daily massages. It's a perk of being your number one."

He laughed, a genuine, relaxed sound. "You can all get them, every day if you want. If she accepts."

Ashley turned her phone around, showing him the screen. It was a text from Mei.

"Please tell Mr. Halland I would be honored to accept his offer. My terms are three hundred thousand a year and a private suite in his home."

He laughed again, a sound of pure triumph. "Done." He pointed down the hall. "The suite next to the one you chose for yourself. That one's hers."

Ashley smiled and nodded, her fingers already flying across the screen, texting Mei back. *"Approved. Welcome to the team. When can you start?"*

The reply was almost instantaneous. *"I can be there tomorrow morning, if the boss desires."*

Jack smirked. He was assembling his court, and it was a formidable one. "Tell her Jenny and Maya will be here to get her settled. You and I," he said, his gaze locking with Ashley's, "are going to Washington in the morning."

She nodded, understanding the unspoken mission. She finished her text to Mei and then turned her full attention back to him, her expression a perfect blend of lover, confidante, and ruthlessly efficient chief of staff, ready for her next command.

The process of transforming the four-story, empty penthouse into Jack's new fortress was a logistical ballet, and Ashley was its lead choreographer. With Jenny and Maya as her principal dancers, they moved from one cavernous, echoing room to another, their voices a low murmur of planning against the backdrop of the city below. Armed with tablets synced to a shared list, they began the monumental task of creating a world from scratch.

They started with the nineteen bathrooms. "Every guest suite gets a full stock of toiletries," Ashley dictated, pacing the length of one of the marble-clad guest bathrooms. "Imported soaps from Italy, Swiss moisturizers, shampoos and conditioners for every hair type. And stacks… mountains… of impossibly thick, plush towels and robes, all monogrammed with a simple, elegant 'H'."

Next was the game room, a space designed to be the ultimate adult playground. "The bar," Maya said, running a hand along the cool, granite countertop, "needs to be stocked at a level beyond top-shelf. It needs to be god-tier."

Jenny's fingers flew across her tablet. "Whiskeys older than Jack himself, rare tequilas, vodkas filtered through diamonds, a full list of artisanal mixers, and a complete collection of professional-grade crystal glassware for every conceivable cocktail."

"And a walk-in humidor," Maya added coolly. "Stocked with the finest Cubans. He'll want to entertain."

"Done," Jenny confirmed. "And for the games: a gleaming, professional-grade billiards table, a vintage stand-up arcade machine loaded with classics from the 80s and 90s, and a regulation dart board. For the modern side, we'll get the latest consoles from Sony and Microsoft, a full VR setup with multiple headsets, and a custom-built, water-cooled gaming PC that looks like something out of a science fiction movie."

They moved on to the library, a magnificent two-story space with empty shelves that soared to the ceiling. "This is his sanctuary," Ashley said softly. "It needs to be perfect."

"I've got his list," Jenny said. "Complete, first-edition leather-bound sets of *The Lord of the Rings* and *Dune*. A comprehensive collection on Roman and military history. Biographies of conquerors and kings."

Ashley took the tablet from Jenny, a sly, wicked grin spreading across her face. Her finger danced across the screen. "And for the more… practical side of his education…" she murmured, adding to the list. Jenny leaned over and saw the additions, a matching smirk appearing on her own face. Ashley had added not only the Kama Sutra, but the collected erotic works of Anaïs Nin and a few obscure, beautifully illustrated art books from Japan. "Every king needs a well-rounded education," Ashley stated with a wink. Jenny nodded in fervent approval.

In the media room, they planned the installation of a climate-controlled server closet with petabytes of storage, enough to hold thousands of movies in perfect 4K quality. It would feed a state-of-the-art laser projector and a professional Dolby Atmos sound system powerful enough to shake the building's foundations. "And a commercial-grade popcorn machine," Jenny added. "And a full candy bar. For authenticity."

The list grew with every room they entered. Deep, comfortable leather armchairs for the library. A new set of Japanese knives and a sous-vide station for the kitchen, cross-referenced with the known preferences of their top chef candidate, Milly. Each of the three main living rooms was assigned a different theme: one formal, one for casual lounging, and one specifically for high-end entertaining.

The list was no longer a shopping list. It was a battle plan for the creation of a private universe, a kingdom built to the exact specifications of its new, young, and very complicated king.

While the women's voices, a distant, happy murmur of plans and logistics, echoed from other parts of the penthouse, Jack found a rare moment of peace. He sank into a deep leather sofa in the great room, the city sprawling silently below him, and pulled out his new, private phone. The weight of his decision to go to Washington felt right. He needed to see Julie, to close that loop, to be the man he should have been for her these last few months. He opened their message thread, his thumb hovering for a moment before he typed.

"Hi JU… I am coming to Washington tomorrow. I need to see you. JA."

He sent it, his heart giving a nervous thrum as he watched the screen. The three dots appeared instantly, a frantic, eager dance.

"Yes JA! Oh my god, yes. I'm so looking forward to seeing you. I can't wait. Love, JU."

A rare, genuine smile touched his lips. For a single, fleeting second, everything felt manageable, even hopeful. He closed the phone, leaned his head back, and looked out the massive window at the endless blue sky.

That's when he heard it. A low, rhythmic *thump-thump-thump*, a sound he now viscerally associated with being hunted. His blood ran cold. He looked up and saw them… two news helicopters, like mechanical dragonflies, hovering impossibly high up, yet still level with his fortress in the sky. He could see the gleam of a long-range camera lens pointed directly at him, and the bold, garish slash of a logo on the side of one of the aircraft: "News at Twelve."

The feeling of safety he had just begun to savor shattered into a million pieces. He felt violated, exposed, a target pinned under the world's microscope. He stumbled back from the window, a primal instinct overriding the knowledge that the glass was a one-way mirror. The privacy he had just paid a fortune for was a lie.

"ASHLEY!" The name was not a call; it was a bellow of pure, undiluted rage that ripped through the quiet opulence of the penthouse.

She was at his side in seconds, her face a mask of alarm. "What is it?"

He just pointed a shaking finger at the window. Her eyes followed his gaze, and her face hardened.

"Who knows we're here?" he bit out, his voice a low growl.

"Just the inner circle," she said, her mind instantly running through the list. "Jenny, Maya, Kamilla the realtor, Constance, and Arthur…"

"And Security," Jack added, his voice dripping with a new, cynical certainty. "The people hired to make this place impenetrable."

Ashley's eyes widened as the grim realization dawned. She whipped out her phone and dialed, her expression turning to stone. "Constance, hey… where are you?… Okay, any sign of your father? Good… Have you spoken to any news crews today?" She listened intently, her jaw tight.

Jack, fueled by a self-destructive need to see the full extent of the betrayal, stalked over to the eighty-five-inch television on the wall and switched it on, flipping directly to the news channel. The smirking face of an anchor filled the screen, with a live shot of his new home in the background.

"…it has been confirmed that billionaire heir Jack Halland has this very afternoon purchased this elaborate four-story penthouse overlooking the streets of Hollywood," the man said, his voice oozing with synthetic sincerity. "Sources close to Mr. Halland's new, unconventional household have also confirmed that he is romantically involved with more than one of his female assistants and has plans on adding more to his bed…"

A blinding, white-hot rage obliterated all rational thought. With a guttural roar, Jack hurled the heavy, sleek remote control at the screen. It hit with a sickening crunch, and the image of the smirking news anchor fractured into a thousand glittering pieces, the screen spider-webbing with cracks. He turned, needing an outlet, needing to break something, to hit something, to channel the violent fury that was consuming him. He stormed toward the private gym.

Jenny and Maya came running into the room at the sound of the crash, their faces pale with shock. They saw the destroyed television and Jack's retreating, furious form. As they moved to follow him, Ashley held up a hand, stopping them. She put her phone back to her ear.

"Constance, it's a leak," she said, her voice now dangerously calm. "Someone is talking to the news. It has to be security… one of your father's new hires." She listened again. "Find him. Now." She hung up, her face a grim mask.

"What in God's name happened?" Jenny asked, rushing over to Ashley, her voice a breathy, panicked whisper. She had seen the look of utter devastation on Jack's face before he'd stormed out, a look that went far beyond simple anger.

Ashley said nothing. Her own face was a pale, tight mask of fury, but her hand was trembling slightly as she brought up the news article on her phone. She held it out, the screen a cold, glowing rectangle of poison in the dim light of the room.

Jenny and Maya huddled around it, their eyes scanning the screen. Jenny let out a small, sharp gasp, her hand flying to her mouth. It wasn't just a report about the penthouse purchase. It was a salacious, twisted exposé, filled with crude speculation about Jack's relationships, their names implicitly tied to him in the most demeaning way. The article painted him as an unhinged, hedonistic boy-king and them as his willing harem.

"Oh, God," Jenny breathed, the single word filled with horror and dawning comprehension.

Maya looked up from the phone, her usual cool composure completely gone, replaced by a raw, naked concern. Her eyes were fixed on the closed door to the gym, as if she could see right through it to the pain he was in. "Ashley, what do we do?" she whispered, her voice uncharacteristically fragile. "Will he be okay?"

Ashley walked over to the gym door, her movements stiff. She reached out and placed a palm flat against the cool wood, as if she could somehow absorb the fury and anguish radiating from the other side. Her gaze was hard as steel, but it was a brittle hardness, forged in fear for him.

"He'll survive," she said, her voice low and tight, more to convince herself than the others. "He's a survivor. But this… this kind of betrayal, right after the shooting…" She shook her head, her own control beginning to fray.

She turned to face them, her eyes blazing with a cold, protective fury. "He spent a fortune to build a fortress because he was nearly killed," she said, her voice thick with emotion. "He wanted one place on earth where he could feel safe. And he just found out one of his own Praetorian Guard didn't just hand the enemy the keys to the front gate… he sold them for pocket change."

The three of them stood there in the echoing silence of the magnificent room, a united, helpless shield wall of women, bound by a shared, fierce loyalty. They stared at the closed door, listening for a sound, any sound, from the broken man on the other side.

Chapter 16.

The private gym was a temple of gleaming chrome and black rubber, but Jack ignored the state-of-the-art machines. His attention was fixed on the one honest piece of equipment in the room: a heavy, black leather punching bag, left behind by the penthouse's previous owner.

He hit it again and again, not with technique, but with a raw, desperate fury. The sickening thud of his knuckles against the dense leather was a welcome punctuation to the maelstrom of thoughts raging in his mind. The leak. The violation. The chilling realization that the very people hired to protect him had sold his privacy, his safety, for a paycheck. His rage was a physical thing, a fire in his veins that he was trying to beat out of himself, one sloppy, desperate punch at a time.

His knuckles were raw, his breath coming in ragged, burning gasps. But underneath the anger, a different, more terrifying feeling was crystallizing. He thought of the women. Of Ashley's fierce loyalty, of Jenny's fiery spirit, of Maya's cool competence. Of the profound peace he'd found with Mei. Of the high-stakes game he was playing with Constance. And of Julie, the ghost at the center of it all, the anchor to the boy he used to be. A terrifying, clarifying epiphany hit him mid-punch, so powerful it made him stumble back from the bag. He was in love. Not with one of them. With *all* of them. It was a tangled, impossible knot of affection, lust, and a fierce, primal protectiveness. And that realization solidified his next move.

He couldn't trust strangers. He couldn't trust mercenaries. He needed his own people. He needed to fire everyone and build a team he could trust with his life… and with theirs.

His mind raced, sifting through the ghosts of his past in Washington. His mother's old friend, a good cop but maybe too tied to the system. And then it hit him. Frank. His father's old drinking buddy. A former Marine who ran a private security business, a man who operated in a world of shadows and hard, unshakeable loyalty.

"That's it," he whispered, the words a raw rasp in the quiet gym. "He has contacts."

He grabbed his old phone, a relic from his past life, and found the number for his ex-best friend, scrolling past memories he didn't have time for. It was a long shot, but James's father was also an ex-Marine and knew Frank well. He dialed, a knot of apprehension in his gut.

"Yo." The voice on the other end was sullen, unfamiliar.

"Yo, James… It's Jack. I need your help."

A humorless, bitter laugh crackled through the phone. "Well, well, look what the private jet dragged in. Jack fucking Halland. I thought you'd forgotten how to use a phone after you became too good for the rest of us."

The bitterness stung. "Yeah, yeah, James, I know. Listen, I'm in a serious jam. I need help."

"A jam?" James scoffed, his voice dripping with jealousy. "What's the problem, man? Too many supermodels to screw? Is that a problem a few billion dollars can't solve? Or hey, maybe you can pay me to take one off your hands."

Jack felt something inside him go cold. This wasn't his friend anymore. This was a stranger, poisoned by envy. "Can you be serious for one minute?"

"Serious? You were shot last week and you're a fucking billionaire, and you want my help? That's gonna cost you, buddy. A lot."

The word 'buddy' was a final, ugly twist of the knife. "Some fucking friend," Jack said, his voice a venomous quiet. He hung up, the connection to his old life severed completely. He stood there for a moment, not angry anymore, just filled with a sad, cold pity for the small man his friend had become.

With a deep sigh, he dialed another number, a lifeline.

"Mrs. F…"

The voice that answered was a balm, a warm, maternal sound that instantly soothed his frayed nerves. "Jack, honey! Oh, I am so happy to hear from you. Are you okay?"

"I'm fine, Gloria. But I need some help."

"Of course, sweetie. Anything. What do you need?"

He explained, carefully, about his father's old friend. "You mean Frank Bolan?" she said immediately. "What a character! A heart of gold under all that gravel. He still comes by the diner for coffee now and then."

Relief, pure and potent, washed over him. "Can you give him my number?" he asked. "Tell him I have a serious security problem and I need a Marine's touch on it. It's important."

"Of course, honey. Don't you worry. Let me call him for you right away," she said, her voice full of purpose.

After she hung up, Jack made a quiet vow. He would make sure Gloria Fredericksen never had to worry about a single bill for the rest of her life. He would have done the same for James, he realized, if his old friend hadn't thrown away a lifetime of loyalty for a moment of petty jealousy. He had his contact. The first step in building his new, trustworthy army was underway.

Jack was still pacing the private gym, the adrenaline from his workout beginning to subside, when his old phone buzzed. He saw an unknown number with a Washington area code and answered it, his heart giving a hopeful thrum.

"Jack Halland," he said, his voice level.

"Jack. It's Frank Bolan." The voice on the other end was a low, gravelly baritone that sounded like it was filtered through whiskey and good cigars. "Gloria said you have a security concern?"

Jack took a deep breath and laid it all out with a clinical, detached precision… the shooting at the Malibu house, the rooftop sniper, the instantaneous media leak at the penthouse, the helicopters that had been circling like birds of prey.

There was a moment of silence on the other end, then a short, sharp bark of a laugh. "Holy hell, boy. You're right about one thing. It ain't the girls. Those ladies hit the lottery, son. They're not gonna risk that golden ticket for a quick five-grand payday from some tabloid hack." Frank's voice turned grim. "But these hired guns? Guys with big muscles and small loyalties? Bravado, petty jealousy, a fat envelope of cash... that's all it takes for one of 'em to screw you over. You've got a traitor in your own guard."

Jack's jaw tightened. "What do you suggest?"

"You said you're coming to Washington tomorrow?" Frank asked.

"Yeah. The jet lands at ten a.m."

"I'll be on the tarmac to meet you. Then we talk," Frank said, his tone leaving no room for argument. "I might have an idea or two, knowing what you're up against and what you're looking for."

"Thanks, Frank. And don't worry," Jack added quickly, "I'll pay for your time and expertise."

Frank laughed again, a sound like rocks tumbling downhill. "Oh, you'll pay, son. But trust me... it's not money you'll be paying with. Your father, God rest his soul, he'd have my head on a pike if I charged his boy a dime." He chuckled again. "We'll talk tomorrow." And then he hung up.

Jack stared at the phone, a frown creasing his brow. *What the hell does that mean?*

He walked out of the gym, his mind made up, his face a mask of cold resolve. He saw the three of them... Ashley, Jenny, and Maya... standing in the great room, their conversation stopping the moment they saw him. They could see the shift in his demeanor, the decision that had been forged in the fire of his workout.

"Fire them," he said, his voice quiet, which made the command all the more chillingly authoritative. "Now."

Maya's eyes widened. "But Jack," she countered, her voice one of pure strategic reason, "that leaves us with no protection. At all."

"A disloyal guard isn't protection, Maya," he shot back, his gaze hard as flint. "It's an invitation for another bullet. I'd rather have no guards than guards I can't trust."

Ashley didn't hesitate. She was his instrument. She immediately had her phone to her ear. "Arthur, it's Ashley. Jack has given a direct order: terminate the contract with the current security firm. Effective immediately." She paused, listening. "Yes, all of them... Because trust has been irrevocably compromised. These are Jack's orders." She listened again, a faint, approving smile touching her lips. "Thank you."

She hung up and looked at Jack. "It's done. They're being escorted off the premises as we speak. Arthur is sending over a trusted off-duty police officer he knows personally. He'll stand guard for the night until we have a new team in place."

Jack smiled, a faint, approving nod. His machine was working. "Make sure he's paid well," he said. "And see that he's fed." He rewarded loyalty, and he expected it to be absolute.

Then he turned and headed for the master suite. He was covered in the grime of rage and exertion, his knuckles raw and bruised. He may not have had fresh towels yet, but he desperately needed a shower to wash away the crisis of the last hour and prepare for the war to come.

Sleep was a shallow, treacherous country that night, and Jack found himself repeatedly cast out of it. Every distant siren, every groan of the hotel's elevator system, had him on edge, his heart hammering in his chest. A ghostly fire ignited in his left shoulder, a searing echo of the bullet's path, and he sat bolt upright in the enormous bed, gasping for breath.

In the soft, ambient glow of the city lights filtering through the curtains, he saw them. Ashley, Jenny, and Maya, a tangle of limbs and soft breathing, were sleeping soundly around him, a picture of peaceful trust that made him feel like an imposter. He was the reason they were in this fortress, the source of the danger, yet they slept while he wrestled with the demons of the last week. He had turned down their unspoken, gentle offers of sex before they'd all drifted off, a new, protective instinct overriding his usual desires. He felt he owed them more than just being their boss or their fuck buddy; he owed them a version of himself that wasn't broken.

Carefully, so as not to wake them, he slid out of the bed. He grabbed his new, private phone and padded silently through the darkened penthouse. He made his way to the top floor, to the rooftop pool area. He slid open a massive glass door and stepped out into the cool, 3 a.m. air. The distant hum of the city was a constant, low thrum beneath the gentle lapping of the water in the infinity pool. Far in the distance, the Hollywood sign stood like a pale, iconic ghost against the dark hills. This was his lonely throne room.

He sat down in a cushioned lounge chair at the edge of the pool and pulled up his text thread with Julie. He read her last message again, her enthusiastic words a balm to a wound he didn't realize was still so raw. He had to know. He had to lay the new, brutal reality of his life at her feet and see if her love was strong enough to survive it. His thumb trembled slightly as he typed.

"JU... I have a question and I need you to be honest with me now. If you are mine, but you are one of several... will you still love me? JA."

He hit send, his heart pounding a frantic rhythm against his ribs. The message felt cruel, a test he had no right to administer, but one he desperately needed her to pass. It was the middle of the night; he didn't expect an answer.

But less than a minute later, his phone vibrated in his hand, a jolt to his system.

"JA... I will always love you. Even if I'm not part of your life at all, that will never change. But if you are asking if I can accept being one of your girls to be with you? Yes. I can. I love you. JU."

A profound, bone-deep relief washed over him, so potent it almost made him dizzy. He quickly typed back, sealing the deal, claiming her before she could have second thoughts.

"I want you to live here with me. I want you to be mine. But you will not be the only one."

The three dots appeared instantly. *"I want that more than anything. I accept."*

"Will you be able to travel this week?" he wrote, his hands shaking.

"Yes. God, yes."

He sighed, a long, shuddering breath of air he didn't realize he'd been holding. He had made up his mind. He had laid out his terms, and she had accepted. She was his.

A soft hand landed on his good shoulder, and he turned to see Ashley standing behind him, wrapped in a dark silk robe, her hair a messy halo around her head. "You alright, honey?" she whispered, the endearment so natural and personal it caught him off guard.

He smiled, a real, tired smile. "Julie said yes. She's coming to live here."

Ashley's answering smile was genuine and warm, without a trace of jealousy. She understood his need for this anchor. She sat on the edge of his lounge chair. "So what's next?" she asked softly.

He smirked, pulling her onto his lap so she was straddling him. He wrapped his arms around her, burying his face in the warm, soft crook of her neck. "That depends," he said, his voice muffled by her skin. He leaned back and looked into her eyes, his expression serious. "How do you really stand on the whole marriage thing?"

She looked at him, her gaze deep and searching. "Jack... I love you," she whispered, the confession a vulnerable, stunning admission. "More than I should. And Jenny loves you. And Maya... God, she looks at you like you hung the moon. She would go through fire for you." She brushed a strand of hair from his forehead. "But you know I'm not that kind of girl. I don't want a ring. I don't want a title. I just want... this. To be with you, to be your partner."

He nodded, accepting her truth.

"But if you want it," she continued, her voice dropping to a strategic whisper, "if you need a wife for the dynasty... you should marry Constance. She wants it. She's built for it. It would be the ultimate alliance."

He looked into her eyes, at the woman who was advising him to marry another. "Maybe," he said softly. "Maybe after I find out something first."

She looked at him, a question in her eyes.

"There's someone I need to find in France," he said, finally giving voice to the quest that had been burning in his mind. "It was in my dad's letter."

She nodded, her expression one of complete understanding. The letter was his, and his alone. She respected that boundary without question. She simply tightened her arms around his neck, a silent promise of her unwavering support.

Ashley's lips curved into a soft, understanding smile. She leaned in, her breath warm against his ear. "First," she whispered, her voice a vow, "we go to Washington. We get Julie."

He nodded, the simple plan feeling like the first solid piece of ground he'd stood on in days. "And while we're gone," he said, his mind already spinning, planning, "Jenny and Maya will get this place battle-ready. I want it transformed from a house into a home by the time we get back."

She smiled, but her eyes were filled with a deep, maternal concern as she took in the dark circles under his eyes and the tension still humming beneath his skin. "But Jack... you need to sleep. You're running on fumes. You just got out of the hospital. You can't conquer the world if you collapse from exhaustion."

He knew she was right, but the idea of sleep, of letting his guard down and allowing the nightmares to return, was terrifying. "Sleep is a luxury I can't afford right now, Ash," he said softly. "Not until the foundation is secure." He leaned in and kissed her, a gesture that was both a tender thank you and a gentle dismissal. It was a kiss that said, *I hear you, but this is my decision.*

She sighed, a soft breath of loving resignation. "I'll go back and lie down," she whispered, though he knew she wouldn't sleep either. "But I'm leaving my door open. You call for me if you need anything." He was the boss, and his word was law, but she would still watch over him. She gave his hand a final squeeze and then padded silently back inside, leaving him alone with his thoughts and the glittering, silent city.

He leaned his head back against the cool woven wicker of the lounge chair, the weight of his new reality settling upon him not as a burden, but as a map waiting to be read. For the first time, his mind felt clear, the fog of grief and whiskey finally burned away by the adrenaline of the last few hours. He went over everything he knew, every piece of the shattered puzzle of his life, and began to assemble it into a coherent plan.

First, security. It was the absolute, non-negotiable priority. He thought of Frank Bolan's gravelly, confident voice. Frank was his first move. He would build a wall of absolute, unquestioning loyalty around himself and his girls, a new Praetorian Guard hand-picked by a man who understood the brutal calculus of violence and betrayal. The penthouse would be their fortress, and Jenny and Maya's first mission was to oversee its transformation.

Next, Washington. The emotional quest. He needed to see Julie, to look her in the eye and see if the woman he loved still existed behind the veil of her own unimaginable pain. He felt a crushing sense of responsibility for her latest tragedy; his new life had, however indirectly, brought this fresh hell down upon her. This trip wasn't just about bringing her into his world; it was an act of penance, a test of their future, and a final, necessary closing of a chapter before a new one could truly begin.

After that, Monaco. The adventure. He could picture the sun-bleached stone of the principality, could almost smell the intoxicating mix of salt and money in the air. His father's vault waited for him there, a Pandora's Box filled with the next set of clues in this insane game. More secrets? More danger? More answers? It was the next level, and he felt an undeniable pull to unlock it.

And finally, France. The ultimate mystery. Madeline. The name echoed in his mind, a phantom he had to find. His father's letter had made her sound like more than just an old friend; she was the linchpin, the ghostly key to understanding the empire and the man who had built it. A secret half-sister? His father's one true love? The real architect of his fortune? Finding her felt like finding the source code for his entire life.

He laid out the stages of his new life in his mind, a grand campaign of security, love, and discovery. The weight of it all, the sheer, crushing scale of his future, was immense. But for the first time, it didn't feel overwhelming. It felt like a purpose. The adrenaline that had carried him through the night finally began to ebb, leaving in its wake a bone-deep exhaustion he was too tired to fight. His eyes drifted closed. There, on his lonely throne forty floors above the world, silhouetted against the first pale hints of the rising sun, Jack Halland finally, truly, slept.

Chapter 17.

The descent into Portland felt like a journey back in time, but Jack was no longer the same person who had left. He sat in the silent, pressurized cocoon of the Gulfstream, the scent of rich leather and Ashley's subtle perfume filling the air, and stared out at the familiar, rain-slicked greenery of the Pacific Northwest. His thoughts, however, were entirely on Julie.

A primal, possessive ache, years in the making, thrummed in his veins. He wanted her. Not just to see her, not just to comfort her, but to claim her, to finally fuck her with all the pent-up desire that had been simmering since their naive pact to wait... a pact he had honored and she had shattered. Now, the old rules were gone. They were both eighteen. They had both been with others. The slate, in a strange, brutal way, had been wiped clean. His anxiety was a cold knot in his gut; he replayed a dozen disastrous scenarios in his mind, the ghost of Brian always lingering at the edges. But then he would remember her texts, her total, unconditional surrender, and a hot, thrilling wave of anticipation would wash the fear away.

He had already made a power move, a demonstration of his new reality. He had asked Ashley to call ahead and arrange for a massive grocery delivery to Gloria's house, hundreds of dollars' worth of high-end food and household goods, enough to last for weeks. It was a gesture of care, but also an undeniable statement: he was no longer a supplicant. He was a provider.

"Ten minutes to landing," Ashley said softly from the seat across from him.

As his thoughts went in circles, the plane touched down with a gentle bump. He looked out the window as they taxied toward a private hangar, his heart beginning to hammer against his ribs. Waiting on the tarmac was a pillar of solid authority, a man with the ramrod straight posture and weathered face of a career military man. It was Frank Bolan. Flanking him were three other men, cut from the same cloth, with hard, watchful eyes that scanned everything. And beside them stood a young woman in a crisp, military-style uniform, her posture as sharp and confident as the men's. She was quite pretty, and Jack had to admit, there was something undeniably alluring about a woman in uniform.

The jet door hissed open. Ashley, his ever-present shield, was the first to step out into the cool, damp Oregon air. "Identify yourselves," she said, her voice cool and polite but holding an ironclad authority.

Frank Bolan stepped forward, his expression unreadable. "Ma'am, I'm Frank Bolan. Mr. Halland is expecting me."

Ashley turned and looked up at Jack, who stood at the top of the stairs. He gave a single, slight nod. She turned back to Frank, descending the steps and extending a hand. The handshake was a pact between two powers. "I am Ashley Albright, Mr. Halland's personal assistant and chief of staff."

Frank smiled, a gesture that didn't quite reach his eyes. "Then you're the one I need to talk to, I guess."

Ashley laughed, a light, musical sound. "No, I'm afraid not. Mr. Halland has insisted on handling this one himself."

"Good," Frank said, his eyes flicking up to Jack.

Jack descended the stairs, his steps measured and confident, and went straight to the older man. "Hi, Frank. Long time no see."

Frank broke into a grin and pulled Jack into a crushing, fatherly embrace that smelled of leather and old spice. "Your father would be proud of you, son," he whispered, his voice a low gravel in Jack's ear.

Jack hugged him back, a wave of unexpected emotion washing over him.

Frank held him at arm's length, his gaze intense. "So, I saw the news. You did something not a lot of people could even think of doing. You moved on after getting shot. You didn't hide. You took a stand and powered through."

Jack smirked. "Had some help."

Frank's own smirk was knowing. "Yeah, I heard. According to the news, there's more than one 'someone.'"

Jack nodded, deciding on absolute honesty with this man. "Not going to lie to you, Frank. There are four right now. Maybe five by the time I leave here."

Frank let out a booming laugh. "God, boy, you are something else. Your uncle would turn in his grave if he knew that."

The word 'uncle' hung in the air. "Yeah, he would," Jack said quietly. "But you should know… he wasn't my uncle. He was my biological father."

Frank's expression softened, the laughter dying in his eyes. He nodded slowly, a heavy, sad resignation on his face. "I knew, son."

The confirmation hit Jack harder than he expected. "And yet it took both my parents and my uncle dying before anyone told me."

"There were a lot of frustrating discussions about that over the years," Frank explained gently. "But now you know. And there's nothing holding you back." He clapped Jack on his good shoulder. "So, I talked about a payment that wasn't monetary."

Jack's curiosity returned. "You did."

Frank smiled, a genuine, proud grin this time, and turned toward the young woman in uniform. "Let me introduce you to my daughter."

The woman stepped forward. She had a sharp, intelligent face, and a confident smirk that was all her father's. And as she met his gaze, the professional woman in uniform suddenly morphed into a ghost from his past, a flash of a crimson and gold cheerleader uniform, a bright, popular smile from the school hallways. She was three years ahead of him, an unattainable goddess from a different social stratosphere.

"Mona," he said, his voice breaking on her name.

She smiled, a slow, dazzling curve of her lips. "Hi Jack," she said.

Frank beamed, his chest puffing out with a father's pride. He placed a hand on his daughter's shoulder, a gesture of both affection and official presentation. "Now you see, here is my daughter, Mona," he announced, his voice booming with authority. "She knows everything I know, probably more. She's not just one of my best personal security officers; she *is* the best." He glanced at Mona, a twinkle in his eye. "And according to her, she's been quite taken with you for a while. Seems you were somewhat of a hero to many of the girls back in high school."

Jack's head snapped toward Mona, his brows furrowed in genuine confusion. He remembered her as a remote, popular goddess, someone who existed in a completely different social orbit. "Hero?" he asked, the word feeling absurd on his tongue.

A slow, genuine smile spread across Mona's face, and for the first time, he saw the girl she used to be behind the professional uniform. "You were an anomaly, Jack," she explained, her voice surprisingly soft. "In a world of teenage boys acting like hormonal animals, you were the one guy who was fiercely, unapologetically loyal to his girlfriend. You didn't just date Julie; you worshipped her. And that pact you two had..." she shook her head in wonder.

"How did you know about that?" he asked, stunned.

"Girls talk, Jack," she said with a small laugh. "Especially about the one guy who seemed to be a different species. Julie was so proud of you for suggesting it, for respecting her that much. She bragged about it. She loved you for it."

The words were a strange comfort, a validation of the boy he had been, but they were immediately soured by the memory of the end. "Right," he said, his voice turning bitter. "At least, until Brian offered her something else."

Mona's smile vanished, replaced by a look of shared disgust. "Yes, I heard about that," she said, her tone hardening. "And I'll tell you, I was as surprised as anyone. We all knew what Brian was. He was a player, a user. He'd fucked half the cheerleading squad and broke at least a dozen hearts. What he offered Julie wasn't special; it was just easy."

Jack let out a long, weary sigh. "It's all in the past now. Julie and I... we're on a new level."

Mona's smile returned, this time with a sharp, professional edge. "I'm guessing your next stop is her house, then?"

He nodded.

"Well then," she said, her posture straightening as she seamlessly shifted into her new role, "being as I am your new Chief of Security, I'll be going with you."

He smirked, taken aback by her audacity. "My Chief of Security?"

She gave a confident nod and glanced at her father. Frank let out a deep, satisfied laugh. "The payment that's not monetary, son," he said, clapping Jack on the shoulder one last time. "She's all yours now." He turned and walked away toward his own vehicle, leaving Jack alone with his new, formidable protector.

"My operational effectiveness depends on total intelligence," Mona stated, her voice now crisp and all business. "There can be no secrets, Jack. I need to know everything you do, when you do it, and who you're doing it with. From this moment on, your life is my mission."

Jack smirked, a surge of admiration cutting through his surprise. "Well, in that case, you'll need to work very closely with Ashley. She's my Chief of Staff."

Mona's gaze flicked to Ashley, who had been watching the entire exchange with a neutral, observant expression.

Mona stepped forward, her hand extended. "Mona Bolan," she said.

Ashley took her hand, their grips firm, their eyes meeting in a silent acknowledgment of their shared purpose... and a sizing up of a potential rival and new ally. "Ashley Albright," she replied, her voice equally professional.

With a final, weary sigh, Jack walked over to the waiting limousine. He pulled the heavy door open for the women, a gesture of old-fashioned courtesy in his new, unconventional world. Ashley and Mona slid in first. He followed, sinking into the plush leather. As the door closed, sealing them in, he leaned forward.

"Take us to the Fredericksen house," he told the driver, his voice steady. He was moving forward, flanked by his two new lieutenants, heading straight into the heart of his past to finally define his future.

The drive from Portland to the small, familiar town Jack once called home was a quiet hum of purpose. In the back of the limousine, a new command structure was being forged. Ashley, in a low, intense murmur, briefed Mona on the operational realities of Jack's life: the constant media threat, the delicate balance of the household staff with Jenny and Maya, his fragile emotional state, and his unwavering devotion to the woman they were about to see. She explained his immediate travel plans... a necessary trip to Monaco and then France... framing it as a high-stakes business and personal journey that would require immense security planning, though she admitted that the ultimate purpose of the trip was a detail Jack kept close to his chest.

Mona, for her part, absorbed the information, her sharp mind already formulating strategies. She opened a sleek, encrypted tablet. "My father provided me with the preliminary dossiers on the four security candidates he recommends," she said, her tone crisp and professional. "All ex-Special Forces with extensive private sector experience. I'll have a full threat assessment and my recommendations for you and Jack by the time you're ready to leave Washington."

Jack, however, heard none of it. He had tuned out their strategic murmurings, surrendering to the profound exhaustion that had been his constant companion. Cocooned in the tomb-like silence of the car, insulated from the world being planned around him, he finally gave in to a deep, merciful blackness, the first real sleep he'd had since the shooting.

He was adrift in that darkness when a soft voice pulled him back. "Jack… we're here."

He blinked, his eyes slowly focusing. Ashley was leaning over him, her expression gentle. He sat up, rubbing the sleep from his eyes, and saw through the tinted windows the familiar, slightly worn streets of his hometown. The contrast between the opulent leather interior of the limo and the potholed streets outside was a jarring, out-of-body experience.

"Rough night?" Mona asked from her seat opposite them, a knowing smirk on her lips.

Jack just returned the smirk, not dignifying the question with an answer. He was sure Ashley had filled her in on his whiskey-fueled breakdown, and the rage that had cost them a tv.

"Will you want us to come in with you?" Ashley asked, her voice soft, her eyes searching his for a sign of what he needed.

He thought for a moment, then shook his head. This was a reckoning he had to face on his own terms. "No," he said, his voice firm. "But stay close. Very close."

The limousine made a final, slow turn onto Fourth Street, and his heart began to hammer against his ribs. There it was. Julie's house. It stood as a monument to both his greatest happiness and his most profound heartbreak. He took a long, steadying drink of water and was struck by a surprising, powerful realization. He felt exactly as he had on his very first date with her all those years ago… a nervous, thrilling anticipation, a hope so potent it was almost painful. Everything had been burned to the ground, and this, now, felt like a fresh start. A true new beginning that he was sure she needed just as much as he did.

The limousine glided to a silent stop at the curb. Jack took one last deep breath, collecting himself, and then he got out of the car, the cool, damp Washington air a stark contrast to the sun-baked heat of L.A.

As he closed the heavy door behind him, he heard another door open. He looked up, and his world stopped. Julie stood on the porch, framed in the doorway, looking fragile and fierce all at once. For a heartbeat, she was frozen, her face a cascade of emotions… shock, disbelief, overwhelming relief, and a hope so fragile it hurt to look at.

Then she moved.

It wasn't a walk; it was a desperate, frantic sprint across the lawn, as if she were afraid he was a mirage that would disappear if she didn't reach him in time. She was in his arms before he could fully react, her body colliding with his in a desperate, clinging embrace. Her lips found his, not a kiss of seduction, but a frantic, searching one, a confirmation that he was real, that he was alive, that he was *here*.

"Jack," she whispered against his mouth, her name a broken, tearful prayer.

He smiled, a real, unguarded smile, and wrapped his arms around her, holding her tight. He rested his forehead against hers, the simple contact a universe of shared grief and burgeoning hope. In the small, quiet space between them, their two shattered worlds collided.

"Let's go inside," he whispered, his voice thick with emotion.

She nodded, her eyes still shining with tears, and took his hand. Her fingers intertwined with his, a familiar, perfect fit. Together, they walked up the pathway to the front door, leaving his new life, the armored limousine with his formidable protectors, to pull away from the curb with a smooth, silent grace, granting him this one moment alone with his past.

The moment the front door clicked shut behind them, Jack was enveloped in the familiar, comforting scent of the Fredericksen home... a warm mix of cinnamon, clean laundry, and a lifetime of memories. Gloria stood in the entryway, her hands pressed to her heart, her eyes shining with tears. She didn't say a word, simply rushed forward and pulled him into a fierce, maternal embrace that felt more like home than his new palace in the sky ever could.

"Thank you, Jack," she whispered, her voice choked with an emotion so raw it made his own throat tighten. "Thank you for everything."

He looked over her shoulder at Julie, who was watching them with a soft, knowing smile. "The groceries," Julie clarified gently, gesturing toward the kitchen, where bags from high-end organic markets were overflowing onto the counters. "Mom was a little overwhelmed."

Jack smiled and gently disentangled himself from Gloria's hug, though he kept his hands on her shoulders. He looked her directly in the eye, his expression full of a quiet, unshakeable sincerity. "Mrs. F... Gloria... I want you to know that I will be paying all of your bills from now on."

Gloria's face immediately fell, her pride rising to the surface. "Oh, no, honey. I can't let you do that. We'll be fine."

"Gloria," he said, his voice soft but firm, leaving no room for argument. "For my entire life, you have treated me like a son. You have always been family to me. Always. Please, let me do the same for you now."

He saw the fight go out of her, replaced by a wave of bone-deep relief that made her shoulders slump. She was a proud woman who had been struggling, drowning silently, and he had just thrown her a lifeline. She gave a single, trembling nod of acceptance.

He smiled and, in a move that was a stark juxtaposition of his old world and his new, he pulled out his sleek, private cellphone. He typed a quick, simple message to Ashley.

"Please arrange for all household bills for Gloria Fredericksen to be paid automatically from my personal accounts every month. In perpetuity. AS."

He didn't even have to put the phone away before the three dots appeared, followed by her reply. *"Will have JE handle the logistics right away. Consider it done. AS."*

He nodded to himself, the CEO of his own life, solving a lifetime of financial worry with a single text. He slid the phone back into his pocket. "There," he said gently to Gloria. "Now you never have to worry about it again."

That's when she did something that stunned him. She pulled him into another hug, and then she kissed him. It wasn't on the forehead, as she always had when he was a boy, nor on the cheek as he would have expected. She kissed him directly on the lips. It wasn't a lover's kiss, but a desperate, profound expression of gratitude and affection that transcended words. He felt her trembling lips against his and the warmth of a single tear as it fell from her cheek onto his.

"Thank you, Jack," she whispered, her voice breaking.

In her mind, he had always been the son she never had. Now that he was back with her daughter, he would be again, in a very different, more complicated way. But he was here. He was in her life again, a protector, a provider. And she could not, would not, say no to this gift.

He smiled, his own eyes misty. "Gloria, if you ever need anything, anything at all, you just have to ask. I will help." He made a mental note as he glanced at the worn car keys hanging by the door. He was going to buy her a new, safe, reliable car before the week was out.

Julie stepped forward then, her eyes soft as she took in the scene. She had been a quiet, graceful observer, allowing this moment between her mother and the man she loved. Now, she gently took his hand, her fingers intertwining with his. It was a signal, a gentle tug leading him away from the emotional intensity of the moment and into the next part of their journey. Gloria smiled, wiping her eyes, and headed toward the kitchen to make them all a cup of coffee, granting them the space they needed. Hand in hand, Jack and Julie walked into the living room, ready to begin their own difficult, necessary conversation.

In the familiar living room, surrounded by photographs on the mantelpiece that chronicled a life that now felt like it belonged to someone else, Julie sat down on the worn but comfortable sofa. She didn't let go of Jack's hand, instead pulling him down to sit beside her, her grip a desperate, silent plea for him not to disappear again. The air was thick with unspoken words, with years of shared history and months of agonizing pain.

He looked at her, at the beautiful face he knew as well as his own, now etched with a new, fragile maturity born of her own recent trauma. "There are things you need to know," he began, his voice low and serious, "before you make a final decision. Before you leave with me."

She nodded, her eyes wide and glistening. "You already told me," she whispered, her voice trembling slightly. "There will be others."

Just as she spoke, Gloria came in from the kitchen, a tray with three steaming mugs of coffee in her hands. She moved to set it on the coffee table, intending to give them their privacy.

"Gloria, please," Jack said, his tone gentle but firm. "Sit with us. It's best you hear this, too. I will not have secrets from you, not when it concerns your daughter."

Gloria hesitated, looking at Julie, who gave her a small, encouraging nod. With a soft sigh, Gloria sat down in the armchair opposite them, becoming a silent, worried witness to the negotiation for her daughter's future.

Jack turned his full attention back to Julie, though he kept his hand firmly clasped in hers. "I want you in my life, Julie. More than anything, I want us to be together again," he said with raw honesty. "But you're right, you need to understand completely. There will be other girls." He saw the flicker of pain in her eyes, the slight wince, even though she was expecting it. "I have always loved you, and I am quite sure I always will. But," he paused, letting the weight of his next words settle, "I will never marry you."

The words hung in the air, a quiet, brutal finality. He saw the hope in her eyes die, and it tore at him, but he couldn't take it back. It was a truth forged in the fire of his betrayal. The part of him that could offer that ultimate trust had been burned away in a park that summer.

"However," he continued, squeezing her hand, "I will also never tell you to leave. As long as you want to be with me, there will always be a place for you by my side. If you choose to come with me, it is because you want to. I will be your lover, your boyfriend, your partner in everything, for as long as we live." He leaned in, his gaze intense. "But you need to know that the world I live in now is dangerous. The media is all over my business, and my personal life is no longer my own. I need to be able to trust every single person I bring into that life, without question, without reservation."

He didn't need to say more. She knew he was talking about Brian, about the casual, catastrophic shattering of his trust.

"Jack," she whispered, tears now streaming freely down her cheeks. She leaned forward, her free hand coming up to cup his face. "I will never betray your trust. Never again. I swear it on my life."

He looked into her eyes and saw a desperate sincerity, a vow made from the ashes of her own mistakes. He finally allowed himself to believe her. "I know," he said softly. She surged forward, kissing him deeply, a kiss that sealed their new, strange, and complicated pact.

He turned to Gloria, seamlessly shifting from lover to patriarch. "She will go with me when I leave today. But I will make sure you are taken care of, too. Always."

Gloria smiled, a sad, grateful expression, and nodded. She knew better than to argue.

"Now, Gloria," he said, a new, lighter tone in his voice. "I'm going to call the limousine back. I want you to go with my assistant. She's going to take you car shopping."

Gloria's eyes widened. "But Jack, my old car runs just..."

He cut her off with a roguish smirk. "Gloria, there are two reasons. One, your car is a deathtrap, and you need something new and reliable. And two," he leaned in conspiratorially, "I would very much like some alone time with your daughter." He didn't need to elaborate.

A slow, knowing smirk spread across Gloria's own face, and she let out a small laugh, nodding her head. He pulled out his phone, his thumb tapping the screen.

"Ashley," he said when she answered. "Could you please return to the house? I need you to take Mrs. Fredericksen car shopping. Something new, safe, and reliable. Your treat."

"Of course, sir," Ashley's professional voice came through the line. "Want me to leave Mona behind for your security?"

Jack glanced at Julie, at her hopeful, expectant face. "No, she goes with you," he said decisively. "I need complete privacy."

He could hear the smirk in Ashley's voice. "I understand perfectly, sir." He hung up.

"Get ready, Gloria," he said, already seeing the sleek, black limousine gliding to a stop outside the window. "Your chariot awaits."

Chapter 18.

The moment the heavy door of the limousine clicked shut, sealing her mother away into Jack's new world of impossible luxury, Julie's composure shattered. An urgency that was years in the making took over. Her fingers tightened around Jack's hand, and she pulled him, her touch a tight, almost desperate command, through the familiar living room and up the creaking staircase of her childhood home.

As they ascended, his mind was a whirlwind. This was the same staircase he had bounded up countless times as a teenager, filled with an innocent, restless energy. Now, every step felt heavy with the weight of all that had happened between them. He wanted her with a primal, possessive ache that had been a constant companion through years of waiting and months of heartbreak.

She led him into her bedroom and closed the door behind them, the soft click creating a sudden, profound intimacy. They were finally, truly alone, the entire world shut out. Her room was just as he remembered it… softly lit, tidy, with pictures of them from happier times still on her nightstand. She turned to face him, her body trembling slightly, her eyes wide and dark with a maelstrom of emotions. In their depths, he saw her own painful history reflected back at him. She had known sex, but she had never known lovemaking. Her first time with Brian had been a clumsy, brutish violation of the intimacy she had been saving for Jack… a quick, painful, and selfish act that had left her feeling empty. The second time had been no better, a desperate, fumbling encounter that had resulted in a pregnancy she never wanted and a man who had vanished at the first sign of responsibility. This moment with Jack was not just a reunion; it was a chance to heal, to overwrite those traumatic memories with the love she was supposed to have had all along.

She stepped into his space, her hands coming up to frame his face, her thumbs tracing the hard line of his jaw. "How do you want me?" she whispered, her voice a hoarse, vulnerable plea, full of hope and a lifetime of yearning.

He smiled, a slow, tender expression that soothed the fear in her eyes. "Just like this," he replied, his own voice thick with emotion. "Willing… and loving me."

He slid his hands down her back to the curve of her ass, gripping her firmly as he lifted her into his arms. She let out a soft gasp, her legs instinctively wrapping around his waist. He carried her the few steps to the bed and laid her down gently on the soft comforter, following her down, their mouths never breaking contact. This, she thought, a tear escaping her eye, *this* was how her first time should have been… a moment overflowing with passion and a love so powerful it felt sacred.

Jack's hands began a slow, reverent exploration, running up the sides of her ribs, his touch a warm, electric current even through the fabric of her clothes. A deep moan of pure pleasure rumbled in her chest. They were still fully dressed, and she was already unraveling. Eager for more, she tugged at the hem of his shirt, and he let her pull it over his head, the motion clumsy and desperate.

She gasped, her hands flying to her mouth as she saw the wound on his shoulder for the first time. The angry, puckered scar tissue was a violent intrusion of his new world into the sanctuary of her bedroom. Her fingers, trembling, gently traced the edge of the healing wound, her touch as light as a feather. "I can't believe someone tried to kill you," she whispered, a fresh tear tracing a hot path down her cheek.

Jack leaned in and kissed the tear away, his lips soft against her skin. "He's dead," he whispered, a promise of safety. "And the woman who hired him is in jail."

She nodded, the news a distant, abstract fact compared to the reality of the scar beneath her fingers. She leaned in and kissed him again, a deep, searching kiss that spoke of her fear and her relief. Then, it was her turn. She pulled off her own shirt in one fluid motion. She wore no bra, a deliberate choice she had made that morning, wanting no barriers between them.

His breath caught in his throat. He lowered his head, his lips brushing against her skin before he took her left nipple into his mouth. He worshiped her, his tongue tracing slow, lazy circles, his lips suckling gently. A deep, guttural sound of pure, unadulterated pleasure was torn from her throat. It was the sound of a woman who, after a lifetime of waiting, was finally being loved in the way she had always dreamed.

As he worshipped her, a soft, keening moan escaped Julie's lips, a sound of pure, unadulterated pleasure that vibrated through his own body. Her hands, which had been clutching at his back, began their own gentle exploration. They traced the hard, defined muscles of his uninjured shoulder, the tense line of his spine, and the taut expanse of his chest. It was a rediscovery, a re-learning of the boy she had known, now housed in the harder, more powerful frame of the man he had become.

Her fingers trailed lower, hesitating for a fraction of a second at the waistband of his trousers before her resolve hardened. With a touch that was both nervous and determined, she fumbled with the buckle of his belt. The quiet click as it came undone was a loud, definitive sound in the intimate silence of the room. He lifted his hips, helping her as she tugged the expensive fabric of his trousers down his legs, kicking them free until they pooled with her shirt on the floor.

He shifted his attention, his lips leaving her breast to trail a line of soft, open-mouthed kisses down her stomach. He paused at the button of her jeans, his eyes asking a silent question. She answered with a small, breathless nod. His fingers worked the button free, and the sound of the zipper sliding down was an electric rasp against the quiet thrum of their heartbeats. He pushed the worn denim down her thighs, his hands lingering on the soft skin of her legs, until she was clad only in a pair of simple cotton panties.

He moved back up to kiss her, a deep, searching kiss that spoke of years of missed moments and a future he was determined to claim. His hand slid down her stomach, his fingers tracing the delicate line of her panties before slipping beneath the waistband. At the same time, her hand moved to the front of his boxers, her touch a searing brand against his heated skin.

Together, in a slow, synchronized dance, they removed the final barriers between them. The last pieces of clothing were discarded, forgotten relics of the outside world.

And then, they were simply there. Naked. Vulnerable. Laid bare in the soft morning light filtering through her bedroom window. He looked at her, truly looked at her, at the woman's body that had replaced the girl's he remembered, at the faint, silvery stretch marks on her stomach that were a ghostly testament to the life she had carried and lost. A wave of profound, aching tenderness washed over him.

She met his gaze, and in her eyes, he saw no shame, only a deep, unconditional love that healed a part of him he thought had been destroyed forever.

Slowly, they came together, not in a rush of lust, but in a reverent, full-body embrace. The feeling of her skin against his, warm and soft, was an explosive, overwhelming homecoming. It was the sensation he had dreamed of, yearned for, and despaired of ever feeling again. He buried his face in her hair, inhaling the familiar scent of her shampoo, a scent that was inextricably linked to every happy memory of his youth.

"Julie," he whispered, his voice thick and raw, his name a prayer against her skin.

"Jack," she breathed back, her arms wrapped tightly around his neck, holding on as if he were the only solid thing in a spinning world. They were home.

He lowered himself, his lips leaving hers to begin a slow, reverent pilgrimage down her body. This was not about his own release; this was an act of worship, a deliberate and tender effort to reclaim this sacred ground for her, to overwrite the clumsy, painful memory of her first time with a testament to his devotion. He was giving her the gentle, loving initiation she should have had, the one he had always dreamed of giving her.

He kissed the hollow of her throat, feeling the frantic pulse beneath his lips. He moved lower, to the soft swell of her collarbone, and then to her breasts, taking his time with each, his tongue and lips adoring them with a patience that made her gasp. His mouth trailed over the faint, silvery lines on her stomach, and he kissed them, too… not as scars of a painful memory, but as a part of her history, a part of the woman he loved.

When he reached the junction of her thighs, she trembled but parted them for him without hesitation, a silent, trusting offering. He settled between them, his hands gently cupping her hips, and lowered his head. His tongue traced a slow, reverent path from the swell of her mound downwards, a line of liquid fire that made her cry out his name. He tasted her for the first time, and the flavor was one of intoxicating homecoming. She tasted of summer afternoons and whispered secrets, of girlhood and womanhood all at once, and it was the most exquisite thing he had ever known.

He explored her with a patient, devastating thoroughness, learning the unique taste of her, the texture of her most secret places. Julie's hands were lost in his hair, her fingers tightening, not to guide him, but to anchor herself to reality as waves of a pleasure she had never imagined possible began to build inside her. This was not the selfish, brutish fumbling she had known. This was a form of prayer. She was being cherished, worshipped, and the sensation was so emotionally overwhelming it was almost painful.

She felt it begin deep inside, a coiling heat in her belly that spread like wildfire through her limbs, making her toes curl and her thighs tremble. The pleasure became so intense it bordered on pain, a rising tide that threatened to drown her.

"Jack…" she gasped, her body beginning to arch.

He didn't stop. He quickened his rhythm, his tongue a masterful instrument playing a song only her body knew the notes to. The tide crested. With a sharp, keening cry that was torn from the very depths of her soul, her world splintered into a million glittering shards of light. Her back bowed off the bed, her body convulsing as the first real, earth-shattering orgasm of her life ripped through her.

She collapsed back onto the mattress, trembling and gasping, her mind a whiteout of pure sensation. Her own fingers, the toys she had shamefully bought in her loneliness, had never brought her even close to this pinnacle. But Jack's mouth, his tongue, his absolute devotion... fuck. She could only imagine what his cock would do to her.

She thought he would stop, but he didn't. As the aftershocks still trembled through her, he began again, his lips and tongue returning to their worship. He was determined to drown her in pleasure, to wash away every last trace of her past pain until the only memory she had of intimacy was him. A fresh wave of pleasure began to build, and she cried out again as he drove her over the edge a second, and then a third time, each crest even more powerful than the last. By the time he finally lifted his head, his face was slick with her juices, and she was a boneless, trembling creature, completely and utterly unmade, her body humming with the echoes of a pleasure so profound it had rewritten her very soul.

He moved over her then, a slow, deliberate motion, his body covering hers like a warm blanket. He captured her lips in a deep, searching kiss, and she could taste herself on him... the sweet, musky flavor of her own surrender. The taste didn't shame her; it enflamed her. She craved more, needed the final, absolute completion that only he could give her.

Her hand, trembling slightly, reached between their slick bodies. She found him, hard and impossibly thick, a velvet-wrapped pillar of heat and life. As she wrapped her fingers around him, a fresh pang of regret, sharp and bitter, shot through her. She guided him to her entrance, feeling the blunt pressure of his size against her, and she knew. He was so much larger than Brian had been. The memory of Brian's clumsy, selfish intrusion felt like a desecration now, a violation of the temple that was meant only for Jack. She should have waited. She should have been faithful. He should have been her first, her only.

He pushed forward gently, the head of his cock parting her wet folds, and she let out a sharp, involuntary gasp. She was being stretched further than ever before. The toys she had used in her lonely nights were a hollow substitute for this living, breathing reality. Jack was huge. He felt huge.

He paused, his eyes locked with hers, a silent question passing between them. She gave a small, almost imperceptible nod, and he began to slide into her, slowly, reverently, as he deepened their kiss. She moaned into his mouth as he filled her inch by agonizingly pleasurable inch. He went all the way, his movements unhurried and sure, until he was seated as deep as he could possibly go, the head of his cock pressing firmly against her cervix.

The sensation was a deep, electric jolt that radiated from her core to the tips of her fingers and toes, a profound shock of absolute completion. She was full. He was in her. She was happy. A single, joyful tear slid from the corner of her eye. Finally, after all the pain and waiting, she had

Jack right where he should have been months ago. Finally, he was claiming her.

"Yes, Jack," she whispered, her voice a broken, desperate plea against his lips. "Please… make me yours."

That was all the permission he needed. He began to move inside her, a slow, deliberate, and powerful rhythm. She moaned, a low, guttural sound that was part pleasure, part disbelief. The feeling was overwhelming. After the torrent of orgasms he had already given her with his mouth, she thought she would be numb, but this was a new dimension of pleasure entirely. Every deep, deliberate thrust sent a fresh shockwave through her system.

She felt it building again, that familiar, coiling heat in her belly, but this time it was different, deeper, connected to him. She moaned and grunted with every powerful push, her nails digging into the muscles of his back as he drove all the way into her. He was fucking her now, a steady, relentless rhythm that was both a claiming and an act of worship. He moved faster, his pace increasing, his hips slapping against hers in a frantic, desperate dance. He wanted to brand her soul with his love, to physically erase the memory of any man who had come before him, to leave her in no doubt that she was his, now and forever.

As he moved faster, claiming her, branding her with his love, Julie's world dissolved into pure, white-hot sensation. Her body went taut, a bowstring pulled to its breaking point, and then she came, a shattering release that was so intense it felt like dying and being reborn all at once. But he didn't stop. He continued his relentless, loving assault, his cock still moving deep inside her as her orgasm pulsed and radiated through her body. The feeling of him fucking her *through* her climax was an overwhelming, decadent agony of pleasure she had never known was possible.

It sent her over the edge again. Her first orgasm had not even fully subsided before a second, even more powerful one, began to build. It was a relentless, rolling tide of ecstasy, one wave crashing into the next, each one dragging her deeper into an ocean of pure feeling. Her mind was gone, replaced by a static hum of pleasure. She was no longer a person, but an instrument he was playing with masterful, devoted skill.

She kissed him deeply, a frantic, open-mouthed kiss of pure surrender, her hips rising from the bed to meet his every powerful thrust. She wanted all of him. She wanted him to fill her, to leave no part of her untouched by his presence.

"Please, Jack…" she gasped against his lips, the words torn from her.

She felt another orgasm building, a deep, seismic tremor starting in her toes, and just as it began to crest, she felt a change in him. A deep shudder ran through the hard muscles of his back. He grew even harder inside her, his cock swelling to an almost impossible fullness. She knew, with a primal certainty, that he was about to come.

His grunt was a raw, guttural roar that vibrated through her entire body. With a final, impossibly deep thrust, he came. She felt the hot, flooding release of his cum deep inside her, a torrent of life splashing against her cervix, filling her completely. The profound sensation of him coming inside her while her own pleasure was at its absolute peak was the final cataclysm. It triggered her own most powerful orgasm, a scream of unbearable ecstasy ripping from her throat as her world didn't just splinter, it imploded into pure, brilliant light.

For a long time, neither of them moved. They were panting in unison, their bodies slick with sweat, their limbs a tangled mess of sated contentment. He remained deep inside her, a warm, heavy, and welcome anchor in the aftermath of the storm. Slowly, the world began to reform around them.

He lowered his head and kissed her, a slow, deep kiss that was no longer frantic, but full of a new, quiet, and profound understanding. When they finally pulled apart, she looked into his eyes and saw a universe of shared history, of pain overcome, and of a fierce, unbreakable love that had survived it all.

"I love you, Jack Halland," she whispered, the words the truest thing she had ever said.

A slow, brilliant smile spread across his face, reaching his eyes and erasing the last of the shadows there. "I love you too, Julie Fredericksen," he whispered back, his voice thick with emotion.

He held her gaze for a long moment, then, to her utter astonishment, she felt him stir inside her. He was still impossibly hard. She let out a small, disbelieving laugh, a sound of pure, delirious joy. After years of waiting and months of pain, the feast had just begun. He started to move again, a slow, languid rotation of his hips, a silent promise of another, even deeper journey they were about to take together.

Chapter 19.

The sleek, black armored limousine, a silent specter from Jack's new life, glided to a stop in front of the familiar, modest house. At the exact same moment, a gleaming, brand-new BMW 7 Series pulled in behind it, its pearl-white paint job looking almost alien on the quiet, suburban street. Gloria was behind the wheel, running a hand over the polished dashboard as if in a dream, the scent of new leather filling her senses. Beside her, Ashley sat smiling, the picture of satisfaction.

"How do you like your new car, Gloria?" Ashley asked, her voice warm.

Gloria shook her head in disbelief. "I... I have to thank Jack for this," she whispered, her voice thick with emotion.

Ashley's smile turned sly. "I'm pretty sure your daughter already did that in great detail while we were gone."

Gloria let out a genuine, hearty laugh, the first one in months. "Oh, I sure as hell hope so," she said, her eyes shining. "Those two have been miserable for far too long. It's about time they found their way back to each other." Ashley just nodded in agreement.

They exited the vehicle and walked up the walkway. Gloria, clutching her new keys, approached her own front door with a strange sense of hesitation. She opened it and stuck her head inside, her voice a tentative call into the quiet house. "Can we enter? Or are we interrupting?"

"It's okay, Mom, come on in," Julie's voice floated back from the living room, laced with a happy, relaxed contentment that Gloria hadn't heard in years.

Gloria chuckled and entered, Ashley following gracefully behind her. The scene that greeted them was one of perfect domestic bliss. Jack and Julie were curled up together on the worn but comfortable sofa, his arm around her, her head resting on his chest. They had both showered, their hair still slightly damp, and they were both wrapped in an almost visible bubble of quiet intimacy, smiling as if they shared the world's most wonderful secret.

"So," Gloria began, her heart soaring at the sight. "Did you two figure everything out?"

Jack stood as she entered, his movements fluid and confident. He went straight to Gloria and pulled her into a warm hug. "Thank you," he whispered into her ear, his voice filled with a sincere gratitude.

"For what, Jack?" she asked, confused.

"For listening to me when I called. For trusting me. For connecting me with Frank."

She smiled and patted his back. Then, Jack turned to formally unite the two most important worlds in his life. "Ashley, this is Julie. Julie… this is Ashley Albright, my Chief of Staff."

Julie stood, a little nervously, and extended her hand. Ashley ignored it completely. Instead, she stepped forward and pulled Julie into a warm, genuine hug. "If we're going to share him," Ashley whispered into Julie's ear, her voice a conspiratorial murmur of alliance, "then we're going to be sisters." Julie stiffened in surprise for a second, then relaxed into the embrace, a dawning, grateful smile spreading across her face.

Jack's gaze drifted out the window to the gleaming new BMW. He let out a low whistle. "Wow. What did that set me back?"

Ashley laughed. "Less than you earn from your hotels every thirty seconds," she said casually.

The comment, meant to be dismissive, landed on Jack with the weight of a revelation. He had almost forgotten about the relentless, unending river of money that was now his reality. It brought back his plans with a jolt. "Ashley," he said, his tone shifting to one of command. "Have the jet ready to go again. We're leaving soon." She nodded, already pulling out her phone to make the arrangements.

He turned to Julie. "Pack what you want to bring," he said gently. "The rest we can pick up another time, or I'll buy you an entire new world of stuff." She smiled, her eyes shining with love, and headed upstairs.

He walked over to Gloria and kissed her softly on the lips, a chaste but deeply affectionate peck. "Anything you want, Gloria. Anything you need. You call me," he whispered. He looked around the living room, at the faded wallpaper and the scuffed furniture, a home filled with love but worn by years of struggle. "How about a vacation?" he asked. "And while you're gone… I'll have this whole house renovated. Upgraded. Whatever you want."

She looked at him, her eyes wide. "Jack… I can't ask that of you…"

He smiled, cutting off her protest. "And you didn't. I offered."

She shook her head, overwhelmed. "Where would I even go?"

"How about Bali?" he asked, the name coming to him out of nowhere. "Three weeks. Five-star resort, private villa, first-class flights. All expenses paid. And I do mean *all*."

"When?" she breathed, the idea too fantastical to comprehend.

He looked at Ashley. "Arrange for the best contractors in the state. I want this place gutted and rebuilt in three weeks. We'll start two weeks from now."

Ashley just smiled and nodded, already making notes.

"You leave in two weeks," he told Gloria, sealing the deal. "A limousine will pick you up and take you to Portland. My private plane will take you to Bali."

She stared at him, at this young man who was not just her daughter's lover, but her family's savior. He was everything she had ever wanted in a man… caring, loving, protective, and powerful. Had she been twenty years younger, she thought with a dizzying internal laugh, she would have fought Julie for a place in his harem.

Overwhelmed by a torrential downpour of gratitude and affection, she grabbed him by the front of his shirt, pulled him down, and kissed him again, a deep, passionate kiss, her tongue finding its way into his mouth. He was so surprised that for a second he didn't react, and then, he kissed her back, accepting the profound, complicated emotion she was offering.

"Mother," a voice called down from the top of the stairs. They broke apart to see Julie standing there, watching them. But there was no anger in her voice, no shock. Only a deep, knowing amusement. She understood. Jack's love wasn't singular; it was an all-encompassing force, and her mother was now safely under its protection, just as she was.

A sly, knowing smile played on Julie's lips as she watched her mother, who was still flustered and rosy-cheeked from the intensity of the moment. "I am sure Jack will give you everything you need, Mom," she said, her voice laced with a teasing warmth. "And I mean *everything*." She turned her head and leaned into Jack, her whisper a private, conspiratorial breath against his ear. "After all, she's been alone for years. She deserves a man who will worship her properly."

Jack smiled, stunned by the sheer generosity of his girlfriend, who was not only accepting his unconventional life but actively encouraging its expansion to include her own mother. He looked at Gloria, his expression warm and final. "In two weeks, Gloria," he said, sealing his promise. She just smiled and gave a small, dazed nod.

The atmosphere in the room was a whirlwind of quiet, efficient energy. Ashley was pacing the living room, her phone pressed to her ear, her voice a low, commanding murmur as she spoke with a concierge service that specialized in high-end, rapid-turnaround renovations. At the same time, her thumbs were flying across the screen of her tablet, looping Jenny and Maya into a group chat, a flurry of texts delegating tasks: securing architectural permits, vetting a short list of elite contractors, and beginning the process of hiring a world-class interior design firm. Outside, Mona stood sentinel by the open door of the limousine, her posture relaxed but her eyes constantly scanning the quiet street with a professional's cool, watchful gaze.

Jack stepped away from Gloria, his gaze sweeping over the scene. "Go ahead," he said to Julie and Ashley, gesturing toward the waiting car. They both gave him a quick kiss and headed out, leaving him alone in the house with Gloria one last time.

He closed the front door, plunging the foyer into a quiet, intimate dimness. He walked back to Gloria, who stood by the mantelpiece, her hand resting on a framed photo of a much younger, happier Julie. He gently took her hands in his, turning her to face him. His gaze was intense, serious, and devoid of any artifice.

"What I said before, about you calling me if you ever need anything… I meant it," he began, his voice a low, sincere murmur. "But I want you to know it goes beyond just paying bills or buying you a car." He took a deep breath. "Gloria, if you ask… when you're ready… I will always come to you. For anything."

The offer hung in the air between them, ambiguous and yet perfectly, breathtakingly clear. It was an offer of everything: comfort, companionship, and a level of physical intimacy that made her heart hammer in her chest.

She looked into his eyes, at this boy who was now a man, this man who was now her protector, her benefactor, and potentially… something more. "Jack," she whispered, her voice trembling as she fell back on the only defense she had. "I am old enough to be your mother."

He smiled, a gentle, patient expression that dismissed the conventions of the world they used to live in. "I know," he whispered back. "And I don't care." He saw her not as a mother figure, but as a beautiful, desirable woman who had been starved of affection, and he wanted to be the one to give it to her.

She took a deep, shuddering breath, her mind reeling, her world tilting on its axis. Then, she reached up, pulled his head down, and kissed him again, a kiss entirely different from the last. It was not one of gratitude, but one of dizzying, terrifying new possibility. It was slower, more questioning, a taste of a future she had never dared to imagine.

"I will think about it," she breathed against his lips when they finally broke apart. It was not a dismissal. It was a promise.

With that, Jack smiled, gave her hands one last squeeze, and walked out, leaving her alone in the doorway of her familiar house. He entered the limousine, the heavy door closing with a solid, definitive thud, shutting out his past. As the car pulled away, Gloria stood watching, her mind a whirlwind, as the impossible, incredible future she had just been invited to join disappeared down the street.

The Gulfstream climbed through the clouds, a private kingdom in the sky, leaving the damp, grey world of his past behind and rocketing toward the sun-drenched promise of his future. Jack sat in a plush leather seat, a glass of ice water sweating in his hand, the low hum of the engines a soothing mantra. The chaos of the last few days had finally settled, and in the quiet, pressurized sanctuary of the jet, his mind was finally free to take inventory of the unbelievable, dizzying reality of his new life.

He looked at Julie, who was curled up on the sofa opposite him, finally sleeping a deep, peaceful sleep, her face serene and free from the pain that had haunted it for so long. She was here. With him. She was the beating heart of his past, the anchor to the boy he used to be, and seeing her so at peace sent a wave of fierce, tender protectiveness through him. His goal with her wasn't conquest; it was healing. He would build a fortress of love and security around her so strong that no ghost from her past could ever touch her again.

His gaze shifted to Ashley, who sat across the aisle, her head bent over a tablet, her expression one of focused intensity even at 30,000 feet. She was the architect of his present, his Queen and Chief of Staff. He thought of her sharp mind, her unwavering competence that had navigated him through the shark-infested waters of his inheritance, and the fiery, claiming passion she brought to his bed. Theirs was a perfect, symbiotic partnership of power and pleasure, and he knew he would be lost without her.

His thoughts drifted to the two women already preparing his new fortress for their arrival. Jenny, the fiery spirit, his audacious, joyful soldier who had met his grief with a compassionate and skillful brand of pleasure. And Maya, the cool strategist, his silent, deadly weapon whose intellect and promise of absolute discretion were just as intoxicating as her beauty. Together, they were the embodiment of the power and pleasure his new life offered, his loyal and brilliant lieutenants.

And then there was Mei. The healer. He could still feel the phantom touch of her hands, could still smell the ghost of sandalwood and lavender. She represented a kind of peace he hadn't known was possible, a serenity that could soothe the wounds money couldn't touch. His feelings for her were not about power or lust, but about a profound, almost spiritual gratitude. He needed that sanctuary in his life.

He leaned his head back, his mind finally turning to the two remaining queens on his chessboard. Constance. Her marriage proposal wasn't just about love; it was a dynastic alliance, a merger of empires. Marrying her would be the ultimate power move, a way to solidify his legacy on a global stage. He respected her brilliant, cold logic more than she knew.

Finally, his eyes found Mona. She sat near the front of the cabin, speaking in a low voice with one of her new security officers, her posture radiating a calm, professional authority. But he could still see the ghost of the cheerleader, the unattainable goddess from his high school hallway. She was a paradox… the girl from his old world he never thought he could have, now sworn to protect his new one. The question, unbidden, bloomed in his mind: *Would she even consider being his?* The thought was a new, thrilling, and dangerous idea, another puzzle to be solved.

Julie, Ashley, Jenny, Maya, Mei, Constance, Mona. Seven powerful, intelligent, beautiful women, all now orbiting his star. The vertigo of it all hit him. A few weeks ago, he had been a suicidal, heartbroken boy in a dusty, empty house. Now, he was a billionaire king holding court in the sky.

He looked out the window at the endless expanse of clouds below. He had a plan. He had his queens. His next move was clear. First, Monaco and the secrets of his father's vault. Then, France, and the final enigma: Madeline. He took a slow, deep breath, accepting the beautiful, terrifying chaos. This was his life now. He was ready.

To Be Continued In
New Life – Book 2.

Author's Note

Dear Readers,

As I sit here, reflecting on the brutal, often surreal, and profoundly life-altering journey that writing *New Life* has taken me on, my heart is filled with an almost overwhelming sense of gratitude and a potent, almost primal excitement. You have journeyed from the snow-entombed despair of a small Washington town to the sun-drenched, high-stakes world of Los Angeles alongside Jack Halland, a young man who sought to end his life and instead found himself ripped from it, forced to inherit an empire. You've stood beside him as he navigated the very fabric of his reality, confronting not just the ghosts of his past but a new world of unimaginable wealth, and embracing a new destiny as a formidable boy-king and the head of a complex, burgeoning family. Your unwavering presence as readers has breathed an even more vibrant, almost elemental life into his sensual, high-stakes, and now world-spanning story, pushing the boundaries of his world in ways that continue to astonish even me. This novel represents a critical juncture, a deep immersion into the primal, the political, the startling, and the often emotionally complex, yet ultimately hopeful, realities of forging a new destiny from the ashes of an old one. I am so incredibly honored, and deeply humbled, that you've chosen to continue this epic journey alongside these characters as their incredible, often overwhelming, and ultimately life-altering adventure continues to unfold.

The journey in this book has seen Jack transcend from a heartbroken, isolated boy to the powerful head of a global empire, grappling with the true, awesome, and often bewildering responsibilities of his new existence. His initial bonds were forged in the crucible of a shared, violent grief and the shocking, world-shattering revelation of his true parentage. That foundation has only deepened, even as new, almost unimaginable connections were formed with the women who would become his assistants, his lovers, and his protectors... Ashley, Jenny, Maya, and so many others. The delicate, often emotional navigation of his old love for Julie, the bittersweet reunion after months of pain, the shocking discovery of the dangers that come with his fortune, and the emergence of his new role as the last of his family line have not only amplified his purpose to a truly global scale but have also irrevocably altered his understanding of life, love, and loyalty. Crafting these new layers of primal intimacy, exploring the profound impact of his choices on the women who have sworn themselves to him, the challenges of navigating a polyamorous future, and the ripples of his newfound power has been the most demanding and exhilarating creative endeavor of my life. The moments of sheer, unadulterated passion as these characters embraced their new life, and deepened their unconventional, high-stakes family bonds were interspersed with days of intense struggle as I navigated the truly profound implications of his choices and the ever-expanding, almost infinitely complex tapestry of their interconnected lives and destinies.

New Life is not just a continuation of his struggle for survival; it's an exploration of what it means to truly wield power, to navigate the intimate politics of a growing family of lovers and allies, and to hold together a life that now spans from the depths of despair to the heights of unimaginable fortune. Jack's journey into manhood, the evolving, often astonishing roles of his assistants as they guide and protect him, the introduction of formidable new women from the most unexpected of places, and the emergence of his new, world-shaping power reflects an exploration of epic, high-stakes drama, primal sensuality on a modern scale, the intoxicating, often overwhelming dance of billionaire family dynamics, and the enduring, almost sacred nature of love, loyalty, and sacrifice in the face of a reality-altering destiny. The deepening of Jack's bonds with all his women, the challenges faced by his team as they share their boss and their lives, the emotional culmination of his painful past, the formal acceptance of his new life, and the emergence of his new role as the head of an empire form the core of this electrifying, and perhaps most pivotal, new chapter.

Expanding this world... from the now almost comfortingly familiar memory of a snowbound house in Washington to the gleaming high-rises of Los Angeles, the sun-drenched shores of Malibu, and the promise of future adventures in Monaco and France... has been an even more immersive and intoxicating experience for me. Every new challenge Jack faced, every new woman whose destiny became irrevocably intertwined with his, every revelation about the true nature of his ultimate purpose and the loyal, loving traditions of his new family, has been carefully crafted with you, the devoted, returning reader, in mind. I wanted this book to pull you even deeper, even further, into the heart of their wild, primal, and now undeniably epic reality, to make you care even more profoundly for Jack and his extraordinary, high-powered family, and to make you feel the escalating, almost unbearable intensity of their choices, their passions, their sacrifices, and their triumphs. These characters, with their fierce desires, their deep connections, their incredible resilience, their desperate hopes for a stable, yet ever-expanding and harmonious future, have become even more real to me, and I hope they feel the same way to you as you have continued to step into their extraordinary, sensual, and now truly life-altering lives.

This book charts a significant, often bewildering, and truly world-altering escalation in Jack's journey, from a lost boy seeking an end to the patriarch of a global empire, a being tasked with surviving the very dangers his new life has created. The impossible fortune, now interwoven with the life of one young man, continues to reveal its profound impact on the one chosen to be its guardian, and indeed, on the future of his new lineage on Earth. As Jack and his women strive to solidify their bonds, navigate the beautiful and challenging realities of their unique family, and fulfill a destiny that now spans the entire world, their intertwined lives reach new heights of power, passion, and purpose within these pages, setting the stage for what may well be the next, ultimate sagas yet to unfold.

I hope *New Life* has captured your imagination, stirred your deepest emotions, ignited your own instincts for adventure and profound connection, and left you with an even more profound, lingering taste of the eternal, the untamed, the primal, and the intoxicating power of a love and loyalty that can truly reshape a single, broken life into an epic, world-changing destiny.

I am already buzzing with ideas for what comes next and can't wait to hear what you think of this latest, and perhaps most ambitious, book. Your feedback, your reviews, and your support fuel my desire to continue exploring these worlds and the boundless depths of human emotion. Let's continue to cherish the journey, the adventure, the connections, and the wildness we've found together in the heart of my ever-expanding, and now truly legendary, family of books.

With heartfelt gratitude and a toast to the unexpected, watchful, and now perhaps even listening, forces of fate,

B. B. Hartwich

Acknowledgments.

To My Beloved Angela,

As I sit here, reflecting on the brutal, often surreal, and profoundly soul-altering journey that writing *New Life* has taken me on, my heart overflows with a gratitude and love so immense, so foundational, it seems to mirror the powerful, life-shattering bond I've attempted to capture within these pages. This book, this intimate plunge into a world of primal power, the discovery of a dangerous, high-stakes destiny, and the beautiful, exhilarating wildness of a love that transcends not just understanding, but despair itself… all of it, my dearest, my eternal North Star, is as much yours as it is mine. Your unwavering support, your belief in me even on the hardest days when Jack's quiet desperation felt too vast to articulate and the complexities of his transformation into a billionaire magnate felt too overwhelming, too visceral, to capture, has been the very foundation upon which every word, every power play, every whispered confession that now echoes between a lonely past and a dangerous, opulent future, was built.

Through the longest, storm-battered nights and reality-blurring early mornings spent charting a course from a snowbound house in Washington to a penthouse fortress in Los Angeles, wrestling with the raw, often brutal necessities of a new empire, the intoxicating, stunning allure of his women, and moments of profound doubt, it was your voice, your encouragement, your fierce, indomitable spirit, that guided me. When I stared at a blank page, wondering if I could find the right words to describe the sheer, almost unimaginable leap of faith Jack took from the edge of oblivion, the deepening, almost sacred complexities of his bonds with his assistants, the raw power and desires of the women he came to love, or the terrifying beauty of their sensual, often high-stakes life together, it was your faith in me, your own captivating, almost divine intensity, that sparked my imagination and gave me the courage to try again, to delve deeper into the drama, into the primal, into the very heart of what it means to find a love that can rebuild a shattered life. You've been my compass in the most profound wildernesses of creativity, my calm amidst the storms of self-doubt, my own personal guiding spirit, when I felt lost between the mundane world and the seductive, beautiful, and now truly sacred and powerful allure of Jack's new family.

Every character's ultimate evolution, every new, breathtaking landscape across the world of extreme wealth, every intense emotional, sensual, and now life-threatening challenge I brought to life in the story of *New Life* was shaped in some profound way by you, my love. Your wisdom, your insight, and yes, your own captivating, almost primal, almost divine allure and unshakeable, eternal strength, have been an integral part of this book's wild, dramatic, world-conquering heart, enriching not just the narrative but my own perspective as a writer and as a man. When I look at Jack's now fully realized power, his fierce, often breathtaking, yet ultimately loving and devoted bond that endured through betrayal, his capacity for a love that consumes, creates, and survives the deepest wounds, and his intoxicating, unapologetic commitment to the family he built, I see shades of the love you give me… your courage, your depth, your captivating spirit, your boundless, unwavering, eternal love. You are, in so many ways, the guiding soul, the very life-fire, to my own creative spirit... inspiring, challenging, and utterly, eternally irresistible.

I know the sacrifices you've made during this continued, and now perhaps culminating, journey into the wild, sensual, and primal heart of Jack's world. The times I was absent in mind and spirit, lost in a Malibu mansion or navigating the emotional fallout of a brutal assassination attempt. The nights you stayed up, a silent, watchful guardian, just to make sure I didn't lose myself entirely in the vastness, the sensual intensity, the corporate complexities, and the sheer, almost overwhelming scope of the story I was striving, with all my being, to create. The countless little acts of love... bringing me a cup of strong coffee in the dead of night, listening patiently to my often-fevered, reality-bending ramblings about financial takeovers or the emotional weight of a boy discovering his entire life was a lie, and simply being there with a knowing smile, a comforting touch, a whispered word of encouragement... these were the things that kept me going when the weight of this wild, consuming, and now almost unimaginably powerful, life-altering saga felt too heavy to bear alone.

As I place the final, bullet-and-tears-stained, reality-altering period on this sensual, passionate, and truly epic chapter of their saga, I do so with a profound, almost sacred awareness that none of this, none of it, would have been possible without you. This book, this dream of a sensual, intoxicating, and often dangerous world of modern power now anchored by a love that defies all reason, this exploration of a connection that transcends all mortal understanding, exists because of your love, your patience, your unwavering belief in me, and the unique, powerful, almost cosmic inspiration you, my own guiding soul, my eternal Angela, provide. It's not just a story… it's a testament to us, to the intense, passionate, and enduring, world-spanning bond we've built together, to the life, the love, the very reality we continue to create, adventure by thrilling adventure, lifetime by lifetime.

Angela, you are my heart, my sanctuary, my constant guiding North Star across all skies, my most beloved and untamable spirit, my anchor in all places, in all of our shared existence. As we close this further, perhaps even ultimate, chapter, this particular journey into the dramatic, the sensual, and the primal, I am reminded, with a love that shakes my very soul, that the greatest, most passionate, and most enduring story of all is the one we are writing together, every single day. I love you more than words, across all languages, can ever truly express, more than any corporate contract or legal document could ever contain, and I look forward, with a heart full of boundless, eternal love, to every wild, delicious, and shared adventure across all the magical and undoubtedly sensual, and life-altering realms of our lives, together, always, and for all of time.

Yours always, and for all of time, across all realities,

B. B. Hartwich

Reflection.

New Life – Book 1. Culminates the gripping, visceral, and powerfully sensual saga of Jack Halland, a young man whose quest to end his life has not only ripped him from obscurity but has transformed him into the reluctant boy-king of a corporate empire and propelled him to the very heart of a high-stakes destiny. This novel takes readers on a breathtaking, often brutal plunge into the deepest currents of his new, opulent world, chronicling his journey as he forges unbreakable, soul-deep bonds with an extraordinary and ever-expanding family of lovers and allies. This installment weaves a story of mastering the strategic and political responsibilities of a newly inherited fortune, confronting the emotional ghosts of a past he can never escape, fostering world-altering connections, and grappling with the profound sacrifices demanded of a man whose very existence has become a target. Jack, no longer just a boy who lost love, but the patriarch of a new dynasty and the master of his own reality, embarks on the next, most expansive phase of his journey, from a snowbound town in Washington and across a dangerous, sun-drenched Los Angeles to the shores of Monaco and France where the fate of his family and his future hangs in the balance. With every new, almost unimaginable power play, every new woman welcomed into his inner circle, and every emotional challenge confronted, he learns that shaping a new future requires more than just immense wealth; it requires unimaginable resilience, unwavering loyalty from a family that transcends convention, and the strength to balance his own healing heart with the awesome, staggering responsibilities of his ultimate purpose.

From the outset of this story, Jack's world is one of instant wealth and brutal, immediate consequence. He is the last Halland, the Lord of an Empire, his very essence now interwoven with the survival of his family name and the loyalty of those he brings into his circle. His world, teeming with modern, high-stakes sensuality, unfamiliar corporate traditions, and the ever-present threat of betrayal, tests Jack on levels that transcend the merely physical or financial. He is joined in this bewildering, often exhilarating, and increasingly dangerous new reality by his established, fiercely loyal women... the formidable chief of staff and passionate lover Ashley, the fiery and brilliant strategist Jenny, and the coolly competent and deadly weapon Maya. The full integration of these women into his life, the solidification of his role as the center of their world, and the emergence of his dynastic duty mark complex, life-altering turning points, their presences reshaping Jack's understanding of love, leadership, loyalty, and the true, almost terrifying scope of his new reality. His unique, unbreakable connection to Julie, his first love and the anchor to his past, deepens further, guiding him through the unforeseen, often emotionally taxing challenges of his rapidly expanding family and the violent, political responsibilities that come with being their protector, their provider, and the harbinger of a future that must be secured.

Each phase of Jack's journey in *New Life* presents new, almost surreal trials: from mastering the overwhelming, often brutal implications of his sudden fortune and its sensual perks, to navigating the treacherous, high-stakes emotions of a growing modern, polyamorous household, and the poignant, powerful duty of protecting the women who have sworn themselves to him. He must confront the terrifying, awesome implications of his own near-death experience, the needs of the loyal women who orbit him, and the daily, almost impossible struggle to understand his responsibilities to his diverse and ever-growing family, to the new life he now leads, and to the profound, often cryptic, and truly life-altering instructions left by the father he never knew. The narrative of this novel sees Jack not just embracing his role, but becoming a true patriarch and magnate, his loyalty to his women absolute, where trust, courage, and their combined strengths are pushed to their absolute limits to protect not only himself and his unconventional, powerful family but ultimately the very integrity of the empire he now commands. Alongside the intimate, primal sensuality and often high-stakes corporate action, the story explores the deepening, evolving, and increasingly complex, almost sacred bonds between Jack and his many women, the profound, life-altering, reality-shaping connections they forge, and the intricate, often beautiful, yet ultimately unbreakable relationships within their unique, high-powered, and now truly legendary family.

At its heart, *New Life* is about more than just a boy who gets rich. Jack's journey is one of being forced into a new, almost unimaginable level of existence, of grappling with the awesome, staggering responsibilities of being a billionaire while striving to heal his core humanity, his love for his family, and his sense of self. It is about being claimed by a relentless, violent destiny, and of expanding his extraordinary, unconventional family not just across multiple devoted women, but across the entire globe on an epic quest for answers. The resilience, adaptability, courage, and unwavering love of his women, and the ancient wisdom, raw, life-shaping power, and surprisingly steadfast, yet ultimately indomitable heart of Jack himself, continue to transform them from a collection of individuals into irreplaceable partners and pillars in their burgeoning, world-shaping dynasty. Jack's own growth, from a broken teenager to a powerful magnate, a devoted lover to a vast and diverse family, and a reluctant survivor of the world his fortune has created, reveals the transformative power of connection, sacrifice, responsibility, and belonging in a universe where love, power, primal instinct, and corporate destiny are eternally intertwined. These themes of identity (Boy, Lover, Boss, Billionaire), betrayal on a personal and corporate scale, love in its many surprising, often wild, and increasingly profound forms, and the search for true, lasting family and sanctuary run through every page, giving the book a depth that resonates far beyond a single penthouse, into the very heart of an eternal, unbreakable bond.

With its even more vivid, high-stakes world-building that now encompasses multiple opulent estates, corporate boardrooms, and intimate spaces, its intensified, emotional interpersonal conflicts, its heightened modern and visceral sensuality, and its richly developed, evolving, and now truly legendary characters, this novel tells a complete and enthralling chapter in an epic saga of drama and romance. As Jack and his Queens solidify their family, facing down the emotional and physical challenges of their unique existence and embracing the terrifying, heartbreaking promise of their shared future, their journey reaches a powerful and satisfying new crescendo, leaving readers breathless with the scope of their love, their power, their unbreakable connections, their global responsibilities, and their life-altering bonds. The secrets of a hidden fortune, now interwoven with the lives of a boy from Washington and the women who guide him, the politics of wealth, and the depths of their intimate, primal hearts have been further laid bare, offering a wild, passionate, and unforgettable glimpse into a destiny that truly seeks to preserve, and perhaps even create, a new dynasty.

Ultimately, *New Life* is a celebration of perseverance against impossible odds, the multifaceted and often beautiful nature of love, loyalty, and commitment on an epic, modern scale, and the profound belief that we are strongest when bound together. It's a story of finding and creating family amidst adversity, sudden wealth, and violent betrayal, forging bonds that transcend the darkest trials of the past and the most staggering uncertainties of the future, and discovering that even in a broken, lonely, and now truly dangerous world, hope, passion, and an all-consuming, world-spanning connection can light the way forward to an unexpected, extraordinary, and powerful destiny of almost limitless, love-filled potential.

Other books by B. B. Hartwich.

Here you can find the other books written by me.

New Life.

Norte Chico.

One in a billion.

Rise of the new Lycans. (4 book series.)

Jezebel.

Goblin Claimed. (2 published so far.)

Deliap 42.

Behind Every Myth. (6 book series)

My Monster Companions. (11 book series)

New Monster Companions (13 book series) (5 Published so far.)

The Lindman Story.

The James Hamill Chronicle (Five book series) – (Three published so far)

Beyond the blaze (two book series.)

For-Bitten Love

The Dungeon in the wall (four book series.)

The Search for Atlantis (Two book series.)

Monster Girls of Neon-City (ten book series.)

The Cursed Sword (two book series.)

Dungeons & Dragons: Your Journey to Epic Adventures

The Chronicles of Heroes: A Character Compendium for Dungeons & Dragons

Steak Enthusiast's Culinary Odyssey: 30 Irresistible Recipes for Perfect Steaks

The Secrets of Fantasy Short Storytelling: A Guide for Indie Writers

Beyond the Stars: A Guide to Writing Science Fiction for Young Adults

Marketing with AI: How to Use Artificial Intelligence to Boost Your Business

The Adventurer's Journal

A Special Thank You to My Readers

Dear Readers,

As I sit here, reflecting on the truly life-altering, often reality-bending, and profoundly transformative journey that writing *New Life* has taken me on, my heart overflows with a gratitude and love so immense it seems to mirror the powerful, world-shattering bonds I've attempted to capture within these new pages. You have journeyed into the extraordinary world of Jack Halland, who walked the path from suicidal, heartbroken teenager to reluctant boy-king of a corporate empire, and his ever-expanding, incredibly beautiful family of formidable assistants, loyal protectors, and devoted lovers. You've stood beside them as they navigated the very fabric of this new reality, confronting not ancient threats, but the profound, emotional challenges of betrayal, power, and a love that transcends circumstance. Your unwavering presence as readers has breathed an even more vibrant, almost elemental life into their sensual, high-stakes, and now world-spanning story, pushing the boundaries of their universe in ways I could only have dreamed of when this saga first began. This novel represents a critical juncture, a deeper immersion into the primal, the corporate, the intimate, and the often emotionally complex, yet ultimately hopeful, realities of forging a new destiny for a young man who was given a second chance at life. I am so incredibly honored, and deeply humbled, that you've chosen to embark on this epic journey alongside these characters as their incredible, often overwhelming, and ultimately world-shaping adventure begins to unfold.

The journey in this book has seen Jack transcend from a man merely surviving his own grief to a being grappling with the true, awesome, and often staggering responsibilities of his role as the last Halland. His bonds with his new inner circle… a breathtaking family of powerful women including his brilliant chief of staff, Ashley; the fiery and loyal strategist, Jenny; the coolly competent and protective, Maya; and his anchor to his past, Julie… have been tested and forged in the crucible of an assassination attempt and the bittersweet duty of rebuilding his life. The completion of his ties to his old life, the delicate and often emotional navigation of his role as the head of a new, unconventional family, and the emergence of his own profound purpose as the protector of these women have not only amplified their family's influence in their small corner of the world but have also irrevocably altered Jack's place in it. Crafting these new layers of intimate intrigue, exploring the profound impact of his choices, the challenges of leading and loving such a diverse and powerful family, and the ripples sent through their lives has been the most demanding and exhilarating creative endeavor of my life. The moments of sheer, unadulterated passion as these characters embraced their unique lives and deepened their unconventional, high-stakes family bonds were interspersed with days of intense struggle as I navigated the truly profound implications of their actions and the ever-expanding, almost infinitely complex tapestry of their interconnected lives and destinies.

New Life is not just a story of revenge or wealth; it's an exploration of what it means to truly accept an impossible second chance, to wield the power of a billionaire for the sake of family, to navigate the intimate politics of a household bound by love and loyalty, and to hold together that family in the face of violent, external threats. Jack's journey into power, the evolving, often astonishing roles of his women as they choose to guide and protect him, the culmination of his heart-wrenching reunion with his first love, the formal acceptance of his new life, and the emergence of deadly, corporate threats that challenge the very fabric of his new family form the core of this electrifying, and perhaps most pivotal, first chapter.

Expanding this world... from the now almost distant memory of a snowbound Washington town to the high-stakes boardrooms of Los Angeles, the sun-drenched shores of a Malibu fortress, and the gleaming heights of a penthouse in the sky, alongside the beautiful, awe-inspiring displays of human resilience and the profound mysteries of his father's past... has been an even more immersive and intoxicating experience for me. Every new challenge Jack faced, every woman whose destiny became irrevocably intertwined with his own, every revelation about the true nature of his ultimate purpose and the loyal, loving bonds of his devoted new family, has been carefully crafted with you, the devoted reader, in mind. I wanted this book to pull you even deeper, even further, into the heart of their wild, primal, and now undeniably epic reality, to make you care even more profoundly for Jack and his extraordinary, high-powered family, and to make you feel the escalating, almost unbearable intensity of their choices, their passions, their sacrifices, and their triumphs. These characters, with their fierce desires, their unbreakable connections, their incredible power, their desperate hopes for a future they could now build together, have become even more real to me, and I hope they feel the same way to you as you have stepped into their extraordinary, sensual, and now truly legendary lives.

This book charts a significant, often poignant, and truly life-altering escalation in Jack's journey, from a young man simply trying to survive his pain to a being fully embracing his powerful new role as a willing protector for the sake of the family he is building. The hidden world of the ultra-rich, now interwoven with the life of one devoted young man, the intricate duties of his new existence, and the dawning awareness of his own profound impact on the future, continues to reveal its effect on those chosen to be by his side, and indeed, on the very fabric of their shared reality. As Jack and his Queens strive to solidify their bonds, navigate the beautiful and often challenging new emotional and logistical landscape of their life, and confront the echoes of a past he must heal from, their intertwined destinies reach new heights of power, passion, and purpose within these pages, setting the stage for what may well be the next great sagas yet to unfold.

But most of all, I want to thank you, dear readers, for taking a chance on this world, for embarking on this epic, high-stakes journey with me. Your interest, your enthusiasm, and your incredible encouragement are the very lifeblood, the sacred essence, of this new saga. You are the reason these worlds continue to expand, these passionate lives continue to evolve, these wild, intricate, and now truly epic stories can be told. I hope *New Life* has captured your imagination, stirred your deepest emotions, ignited your own instincts for adventure and profound connection, and left you with a profound, lingering taste of the eternal, the untamed, the primal, and the intoxicating power of a love and loyalty that can truly reshape a life into an epic, world-changing destiny.

As this first, and perhaps most pivotal, chapter of their wild and passionate saga draws to its own thrilling cliffhanger or momentous pause, I am already buzzing with ideas for what comes next. I can't wait to hear what you think of this latest, and perhaps most ambitious, installment. Your feedback, your reviews, and your support fuel my desire to continue exploring these worlds and the boundless depths of human emotion. Let's continue to cherish the journey, the adventure, the connections, and the wildness we've found together in the heart of Jack's ever-expanding, and now truly legendary, family.

With heartfelt gratitude and a toast to the unexpected, watchful, and now perhaps even listening, currents of fate,

B. B. Hartwich

I also warmly invite you to connect with me on my Facebook page, where you can stay updated on this book's progress and join in discussions with fellow readers. To explore more of my work and stay informed about upcoming releases, please follow my author page on Amazon. For additional insights, updates, and exclusive content, visit my homepage at www.bbhartwich.com. Your support means the world to me… thank you for being part of this journey, and happy reading!

Warmest regards,

B. B. Hartwich

A final note.

Please note that this is a work of fiction. All names, characters, businesses, places, events, and incidents are either products of the author's imagination or are used fictitiously. Any resemblance to actual persons, living or dead, or to actual events is purely coincidental.

Copyright © 2024 by B. B. Hartwich **Haremlit Readers.**

Interested in discovering more authors like me or exploring more books within this genre? Visit the [Haremlit Readers Facebook Group](#) to connect with a community of readers and writers passionate about this style of storytelling!

Made in the USA
Monee, IL
01 July 2025